TOUCHED BY EVIL

NICOLE LECLERCQ

ACKNOWLEDGEMENTS

As always, I'd like to thank Claire Chilton and Jennifer Ellis for all their help.

In addition, I'd like to thank Bernadette Fiefe for checking and correcting my Haitian Creole.

TOUCHED BY EVIL

NICOLE LECLERCQ

www.ragz-books.com

ONE

Erin Holland didn't hear the master vampire of Hope Acres enter her bedroom, but her body could sense his seductive presence. In an instant response, her breath quickened as her pulse began to race. Her skin tingled with anticipation of what was to come, of what had come every night for the past week.

Dane Lynch was on a mission. He had picked a more realistic setting for his seduction than he had the previous nights. Maybe he thought that the moving boxes surrounding her would make her let down her guard, give her a false sense of security and fool her into giving in.

She refused to turn around, although she knew ignoring him wouldn't make him go away. He was too determined. She kept her gaze aimed at the quiet street outside, impressed with all the details of her dream. The lanterns cast shadows along the Spanish moss hanging from the oaks lining the sidewalk. She spotted her fat cat, Willow, as she dashed through her new neighborhood at a remarkable high rate of speed.

When Dane moved behind Erin, she saw the look of determination on his face in the reflection of *the window.*

Is it tonight that he is going to enforce his claim? Could I resist it? Do I want to?

In the next heartbeat, he had her pinned against the glass as his stronger, taller body pressed against her back, trapping her face-first against the cold glass.

She desperately wanted to turn around. She wished she could pull at him, touch him as he was touching her now. She swallowed tightly while feeling the hard muscle of his naked chest and thighs pressed against her, holding her in place. The hair on his legs prickled against the back of her thighs while his hot breath fanned the sensitive spot below her ear. How could a dream awaken all her senses? She breathed in the masculine scent of him and lost focus. Something hard nudged her back. Luckily, she was resolved not to give in. She was terrified that if he succeeded in convincing her to surrender to him in her sleep, she would remain his after she woke up. Completely. Forever.

She tried to move, but Dane kept her trapped between him and the window. He scraped his fangs along the side of her neck, causing goosebumps to rise on her skin. Her head fell backward in surrender, and her golden curls cascaded over his shoulder. Her fingers curled into fists against the window. She noticed his hands were glued against the cool glass too, his fingers stronger and bigger. Her hands looked pale beside his darker skin.

"Stop messing with my dreams," she whispered.

"How do you know it's not you messing with

my dreams?" he teased. "I'm the one not wearing any clothes. Now, if I were in charge of this dream, you wouldn't be wearing this ugly excuse for a nightgown."

He removed his left hand from the window, but before she could take advantage of that newly-found freedom, he slid it under her oversized t-shirt. He let his hand drift over the soft curve of her stomach, toward her swollen breast. Before his hand could reach its goal, his fingers found the thick scar beside her heart. It was the mark of where her father's sword had entered her body during his twisted ritual. Seconds passed, and Dane's hand fisted. He rubbed the knuckles against her chest. She swallowed, wondering if her coarse skin was such a mood killer that it would end Dane's seduction.

Please don't stop.

She wondered if she had said it aloud as Dane's hand continued its journey upward. He raked his thumb over her nipple, coaxing it to a pebble-hard peak. Her lungs constricted, and it was difficult to suck in air. He nibbled at her ear, the touch firing a jolt straight to the heat between her thighs, and she gasped.

His hand released her breast and slid down her skin. Anticipation fluttered deep in her belly, but he barely brushed the soft curls between her legs, gliding further down until his hand stopped between her thighs, mere inches away from where she needed it most. She wanted to grab his hand, guide it to the core of her agonizing need. No. She had to be strong. Memories flashed through her mind of Dane sucking her blood while she had been passed out. He can't be trusted.

"*I thought you weren't going to hold that against me anymore, Goldilocks,*" he murmured.

"*Get out of my head,*" she demanded.

"*How can I, when you were the one to invite me in? Or are you going to deny that now?*" *The amusement in his voice was a challenge.*

She couldn't deny it. Last week, she asked Dane to help her break her blood bond with Jonathan Stratton by allowing her to enter into a blood bond with him instead. Of course, the only reason she had got the blood bond with Stratton had been to undo the blood exchange Dane had forced on her previously. She just hadn't realized what a nightmare it would be to be tied to a monster like Stratton. In exchange for Dane's help, she had promised him she wouldn't complain about being linked to him again. But that was before he had started to invade her dreams...

She had been expecting Dane to demand they meet in person, but the manipulative bastard wanted her full surrender, and he was using dreams to wear her down. He is succeeding. *Resentment warred with desire—right after she had found out about the blood exchange he had forced upon her, he hadn't apologized. He had given her flimsy excuses about doing it for her own protection. Worse, he had claimed he loved her. But when she had asked him for help with breaking the bond with Stratton, he hadn't acted very loving. He had made her beg. She took a deep breath and tried to shake off the humiliation.*

His raspy tongue licked her neck. She whimpered, exerting herself to keep her wall up, but no matter how much her mind protested, her body refused to listen to what common sense dictated. Need was pulling at her with heated demand, and she fell back onto Dane Lynch's chest. He caught her effortlessly, gripping her with one arm around her waist while his other hand slid up her thigh, moving slowly toward the moist flesh between her legs. With a gentle push, he spread them wide, and she arched to feel his touch on the most sensitive part of her body.

"Dane!" His name, a husky, anguished plea burst from her lips before she could stop it as his fingers caressed the saturated flesh of her folds. He rubbed her at an excruciatingly slow pace, easing his fingers up the slit, coaxing the lips apart. She jerked in reaction when he touched her clit, and his arm tightened around her. He stroked her with slow, calculated movements, taking his time while keeping her a prisoner in his tight hold. She tried to twist her hips, hoping to make each light thrust firmer, go deeper, but Dane wouldn't ease up on his hold. His wicked fingers continued to tease while drawing torturous circles around the folds of her sex.

"Please!" she cried out as she struggled to find a release that stayed out of reach.

"What is it, Erin?" he asked.

I mustn't say it.

She experienced every brush of his finger, sliding with slow, conscious movements and short caressing thrusts until he finally buried the digit completely inside her.

But his fingers weren't enough. She needed him fully inside her. She needed to experience the release she knew she could only find inside his *embrace, and she needed him to lose control with her.*

Let's see if I can make him beg too. It's only a dream. It doesn't mean anything, *she told herself as she moved her hand behind her back. She brushed the inside of his thigh.*

Erin awoke to a loud buzzing sound. She forced open her eyes and glared at her cell phone, which was vibrating on top of one of the boxes that was marked 'magic'. She considered not picking up. It was probably Dane playing games. But then it struck her that him calling her made no sense. He wouldn't be able to break into her dreams and call her at the same time. She grabbed the phone, frowning at the lit-up screen when she recognized the number.

"Margot?" she asked after accepting the call. She heard someone breathing. "Margot is that you? Please say something. I've been worried sick."

"Since when are you so concerned with my well-being?" Margot Sloane snapped. Erin couldn't blame the woman's irritation. Margot had a hard life as the secretary to the particularly sadistic vampire Jonathan Stratton.

Erin's fingers tightened around her cell phone. "Of course I'm concerned. I'm sorry. Stratton attacked me. He tried to strangle me and threatened to kill not only us, but our friends too. I tried to call you to explain, but I couldn't reach you."

"I don't need your pathetic excuses. Of course, he threatened to kill your friends! How did you think he would react after we tried to blackmail him with his sick trophies? Did you think he'd give you a bunch of flowers?"

"I'm sorry," Erin said again.

"Stop apologizing." Margot's voice raised in anger. "I'm not calling you at five o'clock in the morning to discuss your failure."

"Five in the morning?" Erin checked out the time on the radio alarm, and a chill of apprehension shot down her spine. "Why *are* you calling me now?"

"Mr. Stratton wanted me to call you before he went to sleep, so I can inform him of your response before he goes to bed."

"My response to what?"

"Your new job. He told you that I would give you a call about it during your little chat last week."

"It wasn't a little chat, Margot. He attacked me. I did try to fight him."

"I don't care." But Stratton's secretary sounded as if she did care. Erin's failure to defeat Stratton must have had consequences for her.

"What did he do to you?" Erin asked softly.

"Do you really want to know how he punished me after you told him about my betrayal? Do you know what he did when he heard that I had applied for a job elsewhere?"

Regret squeezed a lump into Erin's throat. When she had been in Stratton's mind, she had gotten a glimpse of someone so evil, it was impossible to forget. "I know."

"I blame you. I could have continued working for him before, but you gave me hope. You would get me out. You promised you would fight him if I gave you the evidence." Margot's voice was hoarse to the point of being unrecognizable.

Erin opened her mouth, only to shut it again. There was nothing she could say to make it up to her.

"But let's not discuss my punishment. Let's talk about yours," Margot said with obvious glee. "Stratton wants you to come to Las Vegas this afternoon on the three o'clock flight from New Orleans."

"This afternoon?" she echoed faintly.

"Stratton can't pay you for doing nothing," Margot snapped.

"I liked being a security guard at the hospital. I miss working with Frank. Stratton could have continued to let me work there," Erin countered.

"The taxi will pick you up at twelve thirty," Margot continued as if she hadn't spoken. "You should bring a suitcase too. You'll need to pack clothes to last you about a week. Summer clothes this time."

Erin swallowed. "Do you know what the job entails?"

"Yes."

After a lengthy silence, Erin realized that Margot wasn't going to enlighten her. "You can tell him I will be there. Margot, I wish…" Erin's voice shook.

"Yeah, me too. I'll see you soon." Margot disconnected the call.

With guilt assailing her, Erin put the phone back on the box.

"Erin, is everything okay?" Pauline asked after she opened her bedroom door.

Erin rubbed her eyes before glaring at the light in the hallway. "Sorry. I just got a call. Did I wake you?" She took in her roommate's appearance.

"You're already dressed?"

"Yes." Pauline avoided her gaze. "I couldn't sleep. I wanted to get up early and continue unpacking."

Erin sat up. "Just leave it. We can continue to unpack tomorrow."

"Uh, okay," Pauline said softly, her tone uneasy. "So, what was the phone call about? Was it Dane?"

She grimaced and shook her head. "It was Margot Sloane."

"So, she finally called you back. Good to know that her boss didn't kill her."

Erin sighed. "There are worse things than death. Margot sounded so empty. Like he crushed her. She said she blames me, and she's right. I fucked up."

"Easy for her to say when she let you face him alone!" Pauline burst out indignantly.

"What could she do? She's only human, and he's a powerful vampire. I have all these powers, and I let him intimidate me too. I should have tried to kill him." Her voice shook.

Pauline walked up to her and sat down on the bed. She leaned forward and covered Erin's hand with hers. "You're not a cold-blooded killer."

Erin lifted her lashes. "You know I have killed. Twice."

Pauline shrugged. "It was self-defense. Besides, you had transformed into a wild beast, a leopard then. That psychiatrist tortured you. The leopard had to protect you. And that werewolf you killed was out to kill you too."

"I should have transformed into a leopard when I went to see Jonathan Stratton. I should never have threatened him with the police. He was right. Juries and cops can be bought, and he's loaded." She withdrew her hand from Pauline's. "He's a threat to you too now."

"Don't worry about me," Pauline murmured. "I have magic to protect me."

Fear welled up inside her. "As have I. It's not enough. I'm about to find out what Stratton has planned for me," she rasped. "I have to fly to Las Vegas this afternoon. Margot told me to pack clothes for a week."

"Oh no! To do what?"

"Margot wouldn't tell me. She's still mad that I couldn't convince Stratton to let us go. She talked about this being my punishment."

"Can't you ask Dane to help you?" Pauline asked.

Erin hesitated and glanced at her phone. "Maybe. I know Dane's waiting for me to contact him, but not for this." When her roommate raised her eyebrows, Erin explained, "He expects us to rekindle our relationship. The worst thing is, I want that too. I keep dreaming about him."

Pauline blushed. "Well, er, I don't know much about relationships, but if you both want to, maybe you should forgive him?"

"For tricking me into making me his blood slave? I don't know. I tell myself that my feelings for Dane are a side effect of the blood exchange, but it doesn't make the feelings go away. I want to please him so badly that I'll probably forgive him soon, but the rational side of me wants him to hurt. He made me beg for help!"

"He's a jerk. I can curse him for you if you like."

Erin's belly knotted at the thought. "No. Please don't!" She forced a smile. "See? I am conflicted."

"I can do it without telling you," Pauline suggested. "Then you have nothing to feel conflicted about."

Erin shook her head. "Never mind. I should probably ask him for help. He hates Stratton too, and he has a lot of power. But if you can find a curse for Jonathan Stratton, I'd owe you one."

"I'll see what I can do. Do you have anything that used to belong to him?"

"No. I can try to snatch something at his place when I go to Las Vegas."

"Just be careful, Erin."

Erin nodded at the radio alarm. "Shouldn't you catch a bit more sleep? Doesn't Mrs. Beauchamps expect you at eight? You'll be exhausted."

"Never mind me. If I were you, I'd call Dane. Let him work a little before you give in. It sounds like you will give in to him anyway. Good night." Pauline shut the door behind her.

"Sleep tight. Don't let the bed bugs bite." Reluctant to fall asleep again and continue to dream, Erin turned on the light by her bed.

"*Bed bugs biting you doesn't sound very nice. But how do you feel about vampires biting you?*" Dane's deep voice echoed in her mind.

Erin sighed. She hated it when Dane used telepathy to reach her. She already had to share her mind with the ghosts of the four creatures that Oliver Merenda, her voodoo-priest father, had killed during a ritual where he had also tried to kill her.

Thoughts of her father made her feel helpless. She had been seven years old when he'd tried to kill her. Erin had survived the ritual, but her mother and sister hadn't. Afterward, her father had mysteriously disappeared while Erin had ended up with the powers he had intended to steal and the spirits who had died that night. She had only recently accepted that they would always be a part of her life, but she doubted she could get used to hearing Dane in addition.

"Shut up, Dane," she murmured. "You got my promise not to complain about the blood exchange, but you have to stop harassing me."

Long moments of silence passed before Dane said, "*You're the only one who talks to me like that.*"

"That's because everyone is afraid of you," she blurted out.

"*And you? Aren't you afraid?*"

She wavered, contemplating whether she should tell him about Stratton.

"*What's wrong?*"

Erin took a deep breath and let it out. "I just got a call from Stratton's secretary. He's ordering me to go to Las Vegas tomorrow or is it today?"

The phone buzzed again. Erin saw Dane's name on the screen. She picked up the phone. "No more telepathy?"

"I wanted to make sure that there's no misunderstanding. You can't go." Dane bit out the words.

"I wish, but he threatened Pauline and Frank. He threatened you too."

"I can protect myself, and I will protect you."

"I can't risk it, and maybe what he wants me to

12

do isn't so bad."

He snorted. "You're kidding yourself. He feeds off other people's misery."

"I remember." She spent some time inside Stratton's sadistic mind, and she was not likely to forget his cruelty. "He's not gonna kill me. He needs me to do this job. Let me find out what it is first. It will buy us time while we think of ways to fight him."

"*I* will fight him. I don't want you anywhere near him."

"Don't make me regret telling you this."

"Move in with me. You can even bring your friends while I solve our little problem."

"Thank you. That's very generous of you," Erin said. "But he also threatened Margot Sloane, and she's in Las Vegas. I'm not saying no to your help. But for now, I need to see what he wants."

Dane was silent.

"Please. I can't let Margot Sloane down again. I caused her enough problems before."

"Okay. I'll let you go, but you'll keep me informed all the way," he ordered.

"Fine... And I'm not afraid of you."

"Liar. You're terrified. Good night, Goldilocks. Pleasant dreams."

She didn't answer. He was right. She was terrified—terrified how much she liked him despite his controlling behavior.

"*So Dane is trying to seduce you again?*" Leila asked.

Erin rubbed her temple, feeling a headache come up. "You're not trying to push me into Dane's arms again, are you?" A previous wereleopard, the ghost of her half-sister used to suffer from constant hormonal cycles where she was in heat. Now she was living vicariously through Erin.

"Oh Erin, you're such a bore."

"Stop it, Leila." Erin's mother always rushed to her defense. Even in death, her mother continued to watch over her, or maybe she didn't want her daughter to end up with a vampire boyfriend. *"Let her sleep. She needs all her strength if she has to confront Jonathan Stratton again."*

"She really should have a little fun. We could all use a little fun," Leila whined.

"Shut up, Leila," Altman said. *"Erin's better off without Dane Lynch."* Altman would know. Before he died, the vampire had been Dane's second-in-command. He probably knew all about his previous master's nasty traits. *"Although he might be of use against Stratton."*

"Can we please all shut up! Some of us would like to get some sleep!" Gideon called out.

Great, now everyone had made an appearance. Her head felt like rush hour central.

"You've all had a say, and guess what? I agree with the warlock! Will wonders never cease? Good night."

She closed her eyes, hoping she wouldn't get nightmares about Stratton or Dane. Before she had discovered Dane's deception, she had changed herself just to please him—buying dresses, trying on make-up and letting down her curly blond hair instead of tying it in a knot. She cringed at the memories, but she needed to remember them if she wanted to keep her distance from him. Intellectually, she knew she should resist his attempts at seduction, but she feared that because he had conquered her heart during his dishonesty, it was too late to take it back. Her heart already belonged to him. She just hoped that Dane wasn't aware of his conquest.

A combination of masculine satisfaction and alarm surged through Dane after he hung up the phone. He knew he hadn't imagined her hand on his thigh just before Erin woke up, but he hated the danger constantly surrounding her. The irony was that Dane had tried to get rid of Stratton the previous month, but that she had been the one insisting that he could not kill the boss of her company—not that she had been able to convince him. His attempt to set Stratton on fire had not been successful due to the large crowd of men protecting him. It was a nightmare to get him alone. Stratton had many enemies, and he did not go anywhere without bodyguards. He doubted Stratton would allow him to get close to him again. Dane didn't like the idea of outsourcing, but he realized that a hit man might be the only solution. He had contacts, but his acquaintances were the same as Stratton's. Dane needed to find someone outside their circle. He pushed his hand through his hair, and his mouth tightened. He couldn't lose her—he wouldn't. He was so close to showing her how much she needed him. They needed each other.

Yesterday, he would have said she would put up

a hell of a fight if he demanded they meet, but now he could tell that the dreams were getting to her. They were weakening her resolve to keep him out of her life.

She was someone who could be made to see things differently. Her relationship with Pauline was a good example of that. Erin hadn't wanted the witch as a roommate at first, she had only offered her a temporary place to stay, but today they had moved to a bigger apartment together. It had become clear to him that if he inserted himself deeply enough in Erin's life, he would benefit from the same degree of affection she gave Pauline. The whole tactic of his pursuit of Erin was founded on that observation.

As usual, thinking of Erin made him hungry, and he left his apartment in the basement to get some food. When he entered the kitchen, Sandy put down the romance novel she was reading. She eagerly jumped up, and her short brown curls charmingly bounced above her shoulders.

"Hello sir. Can I offer you something to drink?" Sandy showed him her neck, while stroking it with her index finger.

He narrowed his eyes. "No, and stop asking me."

Her lips thinned, and she lowered her gaze. "Yes, sir."

Annoyed, Dane opened the large fridge and took out a bag of blood. Sandy picked up her book and left the room while he drank from the bag. He tried to ignore her as she put the back of her hand against her mouth and sobbed. Brock passed her on his way in and shook his head. "Couldn't you at least take one sip from her? Or does Merenda's daughter have you wrapped around her little finger so much that you can't even drink from another woman?"

Dane sighed. "Why should I care about hurting the feelings of our blood donors? If she can't handle this, she should find another profession. And I'm not going to justify my actions to you either."

"Do you think you're going to get Erin back if you don't drink from other women?"

Dane clenched his jaw at the thought of having his behavior analyzed by his second-in-command. Brock was only partially right. Dane had a feeling that Erin wouldn't appreciate him drinking from life donors, and he didn't want to give her any excuse to reject him. Another part of him found the thought of sinking his teeth in any neck other than Erin's repulsive. This weakness wasn't something he wished to share with Brock. "What part of 'not justify my actions to you' didn't you understand?"

"Fine. There's something else we need to discuss. Eve and Maura are both sick. We should investigate if another vampire wishes to join us. We're vulnerable now."

Dane blinked in shock. Never in all his two hundred forty-three years as a vampire had he heard of vampires getting sick. "Sick? Impossible! What are their symptoms?"

Brock shrugged. "They seem to have the flu. Fever, throwing up blood, fatigue... Maybe it's a lesbian thing."

"Don't be ridiculous! It sounds like witchcraft to me."

"Witchcraft..." Suspicion appeared on Brock's face. "Hey, Erin is part witch, right? And her roommate is a witch too. You're not just saying this so that you have an excuse to talk to Erin again, are you?"

When Dane cast him a glare, Brock raised his hands in surrender. "Hey, it was only a question. Never mind. But now that Maura is sick, she can't perform any of her duties. Vincenzo's watching our security monitors, but we haven't got anyone to replace her for the meeting with city hall about those building regulations. You know that I'm no good with legal stuff."

"Don't worry about it. I will check out her notes and go instead. I look forward to it." It would be a good distraction from his obsession with Erin. He was fighting his instincts that told him to forget his plan to slowly break down her defenses and to go to her apartment that instant and claim her as his.

After a hesitation, Brock asked, "Dane, do you think those witches who had kidnapped Vincenzo could be responsible? In revenge for us killing their head witch?"

"I doubt it. They ran like cowards when we attacked them. The only person stupid enough to launch an attack against us is Stratton."

Brock swallowed nervously as sweat beaded on his bald black head. "Stratton has an army. If he launched an attack, he would win. There are only five of us. Please consider getting more vampires."

Dane raised his eyebrows. "Don't worry, Brock. Stratton would never launch a full-on attack. He prefers acting in a sneaky way. If people don't know what he's doing, and he doesn't succeed, he won't lose face."

Brock frowned as he walked up to the door. "You say it like that's a good thing."

"In this case, it is. Just keep an eye on Maura and Eve, and let me know if their health deteriorates."

"You don't want to have more vampires join us, do you?" Brock left the kitchen before Dane could respond.

Dane wasn't interested in ruling more vampires. He liked not having to answer to another vampire, and after he had killed the sadistic Gregorio, he had automatically gotten his position as Hope Acres' master vampire. He was in charge of the vampires Gregorio had left behind, but he would have been happy not to have that responsibility. He didn't wish to have more vampires move into his large home.

He was however, determined to have Erin join him.

And she will join me, no matter what it takes, he vowed.

TWO

After a restless night, Erin found herself watching her roommate pace up and down their tiny kitchen while she waited for the taxi to arrive.

"I wish they hadn't made you give back your gun when you handed in your security guard outfit. It would have been nice to blow Stratton's brains out." Pauline turned to face her.

"He's a vampire," Erin said. "You don't kill them with bullets. Besides, Dane once took hold of my mind and made me put my gun against my head. Stratton would do the same."

Pauline gasped. "Dane did *what*?"

"It was in the early stages of our relationship." Erin sighed. "Please have a seat, Pauline. You're making me nervous."

Pauline glanced warily at her. "How can you sit there so relaxed?"

Erin hid a smile and tapped the package in her front pocket. "I have the gris gris you created in my coat for protection, and I have the tuna sandwich you made me, so I don't need to worry about starving on the plane either. I'm probably flying commercial this time."

"No private jet?" Pauline asked.

"It's okay. I would rather not get any special treatment from Jonathan Stratton anyway. I don't want him to think I'm indebted to him."

"Can you call me after you talk to him?"

"Of course." Erin studied the witch, feeling a moment of gratitude to have such a protective friend. "I'm so glad that you're my roommate."

Pauline snorted. "Right. That's because I'm the only roommate you ever had."

"No, I've had roommates before, and you're still the best. Listen, I'd better wait outside. I might end up having to pay the taxi myself, and I'd rather not have him charge me while he's killing time."

"I'll help you with the doors."

As they left the building, Erin heard a masculine voice behind her say, "I'll get that." She instantly froze as a feeling of recognition and dread swept over her. She turned to find Billy Blair, the werewolf who had bit her several months ago, holding open the door to the entrance.

Billy narrowed his eyes at her. "Erin Holland?"

Panic surged through her. "What are you doing here?" *Is he watching me?*

"I live here." He shrugged. "Well, not anymore since I have to live with the pack now, but my family still lives here."

Pauline regarded him suspiciously. "Who are you?"

Large teeth flashed when he grinned. "I'm Billy Blair. Pleased to meet you." He held out his hand. Pauline watched it as if he was holding a snake.

Pauline gasped. "Billy… Billy the intern?"

He lowered his stretched-out hand and winked.

TOUCHED BY EVIL

"It's Billy the werewolf now. The hospital won't take me back after I had attacked one of the security guards."

"You mean Erin," she lashed out. "You attacked my friend." Pauline moved to stand in front of Erin. Erin was touched that she cared enough to put herself in harm's way, especially with Billy's current appearance. His transformation from skinny, sweaty, bald hospital intern to muscular, clean—still bald—werewolf was nothing short of miraculous.

His jaw flexed. "But I didn't bite your friend. Or are you telling me I did?"

"No!" Pauline said immediately. "But you could have."

"Good." Billy's gaze shot to Erin's. "Very good. Otherwise we'd both be in trouble."

Erin tilted her head in silent acknowledgement.

"I thought that the werewolves didn't allow you to leave their pack." Pauline frowned at him.

Billy's predatory stare turned to fixate on Pauline. "And who are you that you are so well informed?"

Pauline's blue eyes defiantly flashed at him, and Erin couldn't help but admire her roommate's spirit.

"My name is Pauline Collins, and don't think you can intimidate me, Mr. Werewolf. I'm not without some power of my own."

"Pauline!" Erin snapped. She did not want Billy to find out about their affinity with magic. They had used a spell to successfully hide the werewolf in Erin after he had bit her. If the werewolves found out about their deceit, Erin would be forced to live with them and their misogynistic rules.

She stifled a sigh of relief when the taxi stopped in front of them. "Gotta go. Thank God," she muttered.

"Where are you going to?" Billy asked.

"None of your business!" Pauline said.

Anger tightened Billy's features, and he growled, "I'll be seeing you around."

"Not if I see you first," Pauline said to his retreating back.

"Well, I've got to run." Erin kissed Pauline on her cheek. "Now, don't go poking sticks at large dogs while I'm away."

"I don't like that we're running into him."

Erin opened the trunk of the taxi and dropped her bag into it slamming it shut. "Me neither, but I'm sure it's a coincidence."

"I don't believe in coincidences."

"He defended me against Victor when he could have told the other werewolves the truth," Erin said.

Pauline shook her head. "No, don't make him sound all noble. He lied because he would have gotten in trouble if the other werewolves found out that he had bit you. What if they're still watching you?"

Erin opened the front door of the taxi. "Maybe you can check how long Billy's family has been living here. We haven't even unpacked yet, so I doubt that they moved in immediately after we did."

"I'll let you know." Pauline looked over her shoulder and glared at the taxi driver. "Shouldn't you have gotten out of the car to take her suitcase?"

The unshaven man merely smiled baring his rotten teeth.

"Eew!" Pauline called out. "Don't give him any tips."

Erin's nose wrinkled in disgust as she climbed into the passenger seat beside the driver. The scent of decaying flesh made her gag, and she opened the window to let in some fresh air. She waved at Pauline.

"Let me know what Stratton wants!" Pauline said.

"I'll call you," Erin promised.

They drove away, the driver glancing her way, instead of watching the road. She turned in her seat, displaying her back to him while she gazed out the window at the trees flashing by.

"So, you're going to the airport?" the taxi driver asked.

Erin hummed her agreement without making eye contact, hoping that he didn't expect her to talk to him all the way.

"Do you know which terminal?" he asked.

She let out a deep sigh. "I don't know, but it's not a very big airport. Just drop me off at the first terminal."

"Where are you off to?"

She turned her head to watch the man sitting beside her, and a tiny shiver went through her as he shot her a brief predatory grin.

"Las Vegas?" she murmured.

"You're not sure?"

She shifted uneasily beneath his stare. "No, I mean, yes. Yes, I'm sure."

"Business or pleasure?"

"I'm sorry, I had a really bad night, and I could

use some shut-eye before we get there. I hope that's okay," she said before turning her head and closing her eyes.

"That's very polite of you," Leila's voice echoed in her mind.

"Be quiet, Leila," Altman said. *"Erin will need to be sharp for the confrontation with Stratton."*

"No."

Erin assumed it was one of the voices inside her head, so she ignored it.

The engine roared, and the car trembled as it gained speed. She opened her eyes, examined the speedometer on the dashboard and gasped in horror. "Are you mad? You're going seventy miles per hour in an area where you probably shouldn't go faster than forty!"

"I said 'no'. I don't like being ignored." The taxi driver's black teeth flashed again in a smile that held more menace than humor.

"So, you're trying to get us killed?"

He hit the brakes, abruptly stopping the car. The seatbelt cut her in her skin, and she cursed.

The driver leaned toward her. His eyes glittered, filled with evil intent. "Come on Erin Holland. Don't you feel more alive when you're closer to death?"

She went very still. "W-what?"

He grinned and settled back. He hit the gas and drove at a more leisurely pace. Erin did have a plane to catch, but she kept quiet.

"Oh no," Gideon said. *"I think I know who that is."*

"Don't worry, Erin Holland. You still have plenty of time."

She tasted fear in her mouth. "Why do you keep repeating my name like that?"

"Names have power. Surely Gideon must have taught you that?"

"That's for summoning demons, and that's what he is," Gideon said. *"Ramin Sceledorse. Remember him?"*

Unfortunately, she did remember. Could this day get any worse? "Argh!" She curled her fingers into fists. Last month, Gideon had suggested she call on his demon friend during a hellish team building event organized by Jonathan Stratton to help her perform some black magic. It had been a matter of life or death, or she never would have considered it. The second time, the demon had helped her get rid of the evidence that she had killed a werewolf before his werewolf friends had found the body. In his spell, Gideon had stated to Ramin Sceledorse that the murder had been a sacrifice in its name. Afterward, Gideon had claimed the demon wouldn't mind that the death had been an accident instead of a real sacrifice. "He's not that popular anymore," Gideon had said. "He'll take what he can get."

Wouldn't mind, my ass. If Gideon weren't a ghost, I'd kill him. She studied the possessed taxi driver next to her. "I thought using names only worked on demons."

"Ah, but I can compel humans with their names too. Especially humans who owe me something."

She fixed him with a brief glare. "I don't owe you anything," she snapped.

Rage burned across his face, making her shudder. "Yes, you do! I helped you get rid of the evidence that you had killed that werewolf, thinking you had killed him to feed my power, but honoring me was only an afterthought. You had killed him in self-defense. You used me Erin Holland. I understand using people. I use them all the time."

"*Thanks Gideon, for getting us into this mess with your black magic,*" Leila said. "*What was it that you had said when you called on this guy? 'Don't worry. He's not that popular anymore?' Well, it looks like we should worry after all!*"

Her stomach rebelled. She pressed her lips together, swallowing back her nausea. "What makes you think I used you?"

"I was in your head, remember? Such an interesting place your little head was. You can learn so much about people when you're in their heads. Would you like to know what I learned while I was in your head, Erin Holland?" He snarled the question at her.

"Um. Not particularly," she mumbled.

"Let me tell you," he began in a gentle tone that she thought sounded too friendly for someone who enjoyed having people bleed for him. "I experienced your power, so much power in a female form. I didn't know a simple human could contain the powers of a vampire, leopard, warlock and werewolf without bursting apart with all the energy. It was very educational."

He forgot the magic she had inherited from her mother, but she thought it wise not to educate him further. She expected him to have plans for those powers. Like Jonathan Stratton had plans for her too. Tired of everybody wanting to use her, anger tightened her throat, but she feared expressing it would cost her dearly. Fortunately, they had just passed a sign for the exit to the Louis Armstrong New Orleans International Airport.

"But then you're no simple human being." A dark little smile played around his lips. "You have powerful blood coursing through your veins. I ran into your father a couple of times. Now, *him* I would have liked to have work for me. We could have gone far together, but I'll lower my standards and make you my pupil instead. Under my tutelage, you'll become so powerful people will worship you as a goddess. All I want in exchange is the occasional sacrifice. In my name, of course."

"Of course. Well, um. Thank you for the honor, but I'm afraid I'll have to pass," she quipped. "My dancing card is full enough as it is."

His victorious grin ebbed. "I wouldn't be so quick to reject me Erin Holland. While I was in your head, I also saw some images about the people in your life and how you felt about them." He pulled up at the departure terminal and stopped the car. Then he pressed a button, locking them in. "Your friend Gideon might think I'm not so popular anymore, but I have a lot of followers who are keen to do whatever it takes to make me happy. But I don't need to rely on anyone else when I have the power to possess all those who have asked me for help at one point."

She glared at him. "Why don't you just possess me then if you're so powerful?" As soon as she said the words, she wished she could recant.

"Oh Erin. Don't you know that you should never taunt the evil demon?" Gideon sighed.

"What was it that you told Pauline before you left? Oh right. Something about not poking sticks at large dogs," Leila added helpfully.

Ramin Sceledorse's features darkened with anger. "Careful, Erin Holland. I could lose my temper, and you wouldn't want that to happen. Someone might get hurt—someone like that witchy friend of yours." He nodded at a man in uniform as he walked past the taxi. "Or maybe I could possess that pilot and crash your plane."

He unlocked the doors, and she struggled out of her seatbelt. He stuck out his hand. "That's eighty dollars. Don't forget the tip."

"Yes, tip the nice demon," Leila agreed.

Erin gave him an extra five dollars. "You didn't even help me with my luggage," she muttered. She jumped out of the car and slammed the door shut. This time he followed her out and lifted the suitcase out of the trunk. He cast her a malicious smirk. "Have a nice flight, Erin Holland."

Erin shivered as she watched him get back in the driver's seat and leave. "Listen guys, not that I'm not grateful, but why isn't he just trying to possess me again?"

"He is only able to possess someone right after that person invoked him," Gideon explained.

Relief sailed through her so strong that she sat down on one of the benches in front of the entrance hall. "So, unless the pilot flying my plane has just called on him, I should be safe, right?"

"Right. As I said before, he's just not that popular anymore," Gideon joked. *"The chances of him possessing a pilot would be slim. Just a random*

taxi driver however... I mean, he could drive back to your address right now and wait for Pauline to leave the building and run her over."

Undiluted panic flooded her. "Oh shit, and I just taunted the guy! I need to call Pauline straight away!"

"Calm down. He still needs to drive back to Hope Acres. You'll have plenty of time to warn her. I think you should check in first," Altman said. *"You don't want to miss that plane."*

Erin was about to respond when she noticed a group of people watching her with suspicion in their eyes. *Oh right, I'm talking to myself.*

After she had dropped off her luggage, Erin used the cell phone Dane had given her to call Pauline. She answered on the first ring. "I'm so tired of everyone threatening us," Erin said after having explained the situation to her roommate.

"I'm pretty sure I can create a spell to warn us when the demon is close to us," Pauline said. "Like a necklace or ring that heats up when he's there."

Pauline's calm response reassured her, her confidence in her witchcraft was proving contagious. "That's a great idea. Thanks! I'm so sorry that your friendship with me keeps putting you in danger."

"Hey, without you, Selena and the other witches would have sacrificed me months ago."

"My pleasure."

"Good luck. And don't worry about the flight," Pauline said before she disconnected.

As Erin put the phone away she realized that with all the things for her to worry about, her biggest fear was her confrontation with Stratton. The last time she had seen him he had been squeezing her neck, his nails cutting her skin open, and he had threatened her, Pauline, Dane, Frank and his poor secretary who had helped her, and whom she had let down.

But I'll make it up to her, she told herself. *As soon as this knot of dread in my chest lessens.*

THREE

"Anderson, Jones, Brown… Where, oh where, are you?" Pauline mumbled. After reading the names of the other tenants in her building on the mailboxes in the entrance in silence, she tried reading them aloud, hoping she had somehow overlooked the werewolf's last name. But no. She couldn't find anyone named Blair. With both Jonathan Stratton and some mysterious demon threatening them, Erin couldn't afford having the werewolves spy on her as well. On the other hand, she would be better off knowing this sooner rather than when it was too late.

"Damn." *Erin had been so sure that she had convinced them she wasn't one of them.*

"Are you looking for someone?" a female voice asked.

Pauline turned to find a brown-haired woman, who appeared to be in her early fifties, cocking her head and inquisitively studying her. The woman was carrying a bag filled with groceries. She put it down to open a mailbox with the name Miles. "Nothing," the stranger said with a smile as she closed the mailbox. "That's a good thing. The only mail I get are bills!"

Pauline returned her smile. "Same here. Or advertising."

The woman stuck out her hand. "Hi. I'm Sophie Miles. I don't believe I've seen you here before?"

Pauline nodded, shaking her hand. "I'm Pauline Collins. I just moved into an apartment on the third floor."

"No nametag yet on the mailbox I see. You'll need to ask the landlord to arrange that. It could take several months if you don't."

Pauline hesitated. "Actually, I wasn't looking for my name. I um, I met someone who said he lives here."

"Oh, and is this someone a handsome young man?"

Pauline felt her cheeks heat with a blush. She wanted to contradict Sophie, but she quickly realized the misunderstanding gave her an excellent excuse to investigate, so she nodded.

"Ah, to be in love again. So, what's his name?"

"Eh, Billy Blair. Do you know him?"

Sophie narrowed her brown eyes. "And he told you he lives here?"

"That's right." Pauline's heart sank. She was going to have to tell Erin that Billy had lied to them.

Something flickered in Sophie's eyes. "When did he tell you that?"

An uneasy sensation crawled across her skin. "Um. This morning?"

"You don't know?"

Pauline thrust her chin upward. "Yes, I do. I talked to him this morning."

Sophie's eyebrows drew together in confusion.

"Really? Strange that my son told you he lives here when he moved out several months ago."

Embarrassment suffused Pauline. "I um, I must have misunderstood."

"Of course you did. You're one of those reporters, aren't you?"

"No! Not at all."

"My son is not a story!" Sophie snapped.

"Why would he be a story? Oh, you mean because of the werewolf thingy?"

Sophie raised her finger. "A-ha! I knew you were lying. He would never have told you that. Well, I'm not telling you anything! I'm warning my son about you."

Pauline cringed. "Please don't." But the woman walked away without sparing her another glance.

Pauline waited until she heard the door slam shut before she returned to her apartment upstairs. *Miles instead of Blair? Of course. She's probably divorced.*

She hoped Billy wouldn't be angry because she had been checking up on him. She sighed worrying that while Billy hadn't been watching them before he sure as hell would be watching them now.

"Sorry, Erin," she whispered

The gates to Jonathan Stratton's house opened, and the taxi drove up the driveway, which was lined with palm trees on both sides. Erin watched the winter sun set as it cast a pale-yellow light over the Nevada desert surrounding the villa. She thought back to the last time she had visited the house.

Stratton had sent his darkened limousine to pick her up at the airport. This time there was no such pretense—not that there had been any pretense at the end of her last visit.

She felt sick, and her stomach knotted with apprehension as the car stopped in front of the entrance.

"Thank you," she said to the taxi driver, grateful that Ramin Sceledorse had not made a reappearance.

"*I guess not all taxi drivers call on your evil friend, Gideon,*" Leila taunted.

"*As I said before, he's not that popular anymore,*" Gideon said.

"Come on guys," Erin muttered. "Please be quiet. I need to focus."

"What?" the taxi driver asked as he clicked on the button that opened the trunk.

Erin's cheeks burned with embarrassment. "Nothing."

She paid him a ten-dollar tip. As soon as she opened her door and slid out, a gust of cool wind slapped her in the face. It was ten steps to the villa, but she still zipped up her black winter jacket. She was glad she had decided to wear her jeans too.

"I won't let him intimidate me," Erin muttered. The words were a silent mantra.

"*Don't worry,*" Leila said. "*He won't kill you. He wants something from you.*"

The driver handed over her suitcase from the trunk. She spotted Margot Sloane waiting for her at the entrance of the modern villa. Erin's hand moved to her pocket, wondering when she would have the opportunity to call Dane and Pauline. While a part of her recognized that she needed help fighting Stratton, another part of her resented that she couldn't do it alone. Since when had she given up her independence and turned into a needy damsel in distress? She detected Margot's blank-eyed expression, and she knew she owed it to Stratton's secretary to swallow her pride and ask for help, even if Dane made her beg again.

She couldn't wait for this night to be over, but she was also worried about the task she would be given. After taking a deep breath, she forced herself to walk up to Margot while steeling herself for the condemnation she expected to see on the woman's face.

"Hi," Erin said. She had trouble meeting Margot's eyes.

When Margot didn't respond, Erin gazed up at her from beneath her lashes. Suddenly she noticed the cane in Margot's left hand.

"Oh, no! Did you fall?"

Margot shook her head and turned around. "You can leave your suitcase in the hallway." Erin followed her and frowned when she saw Margot walking with a marked limp. The brunette was somewhere in her forties and too young to be needing a walking aid.

She touched Margot's arm, halting her. "What happened?"

Margot nodded to the office ahead, saying, "Now is not the time."

"Is it the butler's night off?" Erin whispered.

"I thought it would be nice if I let Ms. Sloane welcome you so the two of you would have a chance to catch up," Jonathan Stratton said as he exited his room. As always, he was wearing a suit and tie, ready for a business meeting.

I suppose we do have some business to discuss. The Las Vegas master vampire regarded her with a cynical half-smile. "Why do you look so surprised? I'm very considerate. You mentioned her the last time you were here, didn't you? I thought the two of you were best buddies. Hmm?" He pointed at the cane. "Or maybe not anymore."

Erin watched Margot nervously, but she seemed to have a lot of experience of not allowing any of her emotions to show to her boss.

"Or perhaps you are surprised I could overhear your little conversation with Ms. Sloane?" Stratton continued. "Did you forget that vampires have super hearing?"

"I forgot nothing," Erin stated.

"Good. Then I suppose I won't need to repeat the last conversation we had here," he said as he entered his office.

She gritted her teeth and moved behind him.

"Do you need me, sir?" Margot asked.

"Not right now," Stratton replied. "But Ms. Sloane?"

"Yes sir?"

"Don't wander off too far. I don't want to worry about you." He made it sound like a threat.

"No sir," Margot said in a brisk tone before leaving the room. She didn't close the door, and Erin had to suppress her instinct to follow her out of the office. She watched Stratton sit down and point to the chair in front of his desk. She decided not to antagonize him and accepted his instructions. *For now.*

"Ms. Holland, you're probably curious about your new job."

She expected that he was going to keep her waiting, so she deliberately shrugged. *I won't let him intimidate me.*

His features turned sly as he leaned forward. "I know I just told you that I wouldn't repeat the last conversation we had here, but it might be useful to give you a little bit of background information to explain why I want you to do this job before I send you off."

Thinking about Margot's blank expression, Erin chose to emulate her.

He narrowed his eyes. "As I told you before, twenty years ago your dear daddy invited me to his lovely ritual where he promised me amazing powers. Fortunately, I couldn't make it, but I got very annoyed when I discovered afterward that your daddy had performed the ritual with another vampire that he then killed. Worse was that your dad had disappeared without any trace. I wanted to punish him so bad, but he wasn't there, so I've been taking it out on you—an innocent."

She blinked in surprise. He appeared almost apologetic.

"I realize that what I did to you wasn't fair. It's not your fault that your dad tried to kill me. You were just a child, and your daddy had tried to kill you too, so it's not as if you were an accomplice. Don't you think you've suffered enough?" He spoke soothingly.

Friendliness didn't suit his face, and it put her on high alert when he smiled. She felt a spike of alarm.

She had been in his head before, and she didn't trust his sudden kindness. The man didn't have an empathetic bone in his tall corpse. She refused to betray any of her confusion and remained quiet.

Swift anger crossed his face. "Maybe you think you haven't suffered enough. Maybe you like the suffering? Some people do, you know? Maybe Ms. Sloane does too."

I won't let him intimidate me.

He chuckled. "Do you know what I did to Ms. Sloane? Would you like me to tell you?"

"I'm sure you'll tell me whether I want to hear it or not." She hated that she sounded as if she had shards of glass in her mouth.

He cast her a cruel smirk. "I had her big toe removed."

She sucked in her breath. "You sick fuck!"

"Finally, some response! It's just no fun if people don't react. And there's no point in trying to hide your feelings. It doesn't work. It only makes me want to work harder at finding ways to get to them. I remember when I made Dane Lynch break down at our party. Such a proud man. Some people are so hard to break."

He studied her intensely, and her breath stilled in her lungs.

"Ms. Sloane is tough too. She has tried to leave me twice now, but I don't like it when people walk away from me. I guess I have abandonment issues." He snickered. "I thought I had convinced her how precious she was to me before, but then you told me that I had to let her go…"

She winced, experiencing a flare of remorse.

"Well, it dawned on me that maybe she keeps trying to walk away because it's easy for her to do so. Now it's not so easy."

"You're insane," she said, her voice hoarse.

He smiled humorlessly. "It's only a toe. But if it's still not clear to her how important she is to me, I'll have to make it even harder for her to walk away... What do you think? A whole foot? A leg?"

"Stop it."

"Ah, you're probably right. I can stop now. Well, stop talking about Ms. Sloane. I still need to address your job. Sorry, I got sidetracked there." He opened a drawer and pulled out a gray file that he dropped on the desk in front of her. Then he leaned back, watching her. There was only one word on the cover. It said Merenda.

Her heart skipped a beat.

"Yes, your sweet daddy," Stratton said. "Well, not quite. He's still gone without a trace, but there may be someone who might know where he is. It's your grandfather, Emanuel Merenda."

"*Oh no*," Erin heard someone mumble in her mind. *Mom?*

"Ah, I hear one of your ghostly companions," he said. "Your mother? Sister? Maybe they know Emanuel Merenda."

"Are you sure? I don't remember ever meeting my grandfather. I didn't even know I had one."

"It doesn't matter. You'll meet him now. I arranged a flight to Haiti." Stratton grabbed the file and opened it. "No pictures, I'm afraid, but I do have his address. He resides in a church at Petit Espoir."

"If he's there, why didn't you go before?"

"Are you questioning me?" he asked, his expression grim. "I didn't say your father was there, your grandfather is. Your grandfather's church is a fortress, very heavily guarded, and he is known for being a powerful bokor too. Nobody gets in unless you're one of his zombies. If I were to visit him, I would stand out like a sore white thumb, but I'm sure he'll be happy to meet his granddaughter. You have his son's golden eyes. Maybe he'll recognize them."

He got up, closed the file and threw it at her. Automatically, she caught the file, holding it against her chest. "What if my dad is not there?"

"If he's not there, your grandfather will lead you to him."

Bile rose, nearly choking her. "My dad tried to kill me once. He may try again."

"Then blow him up. I've already thought about that. Ms. Sloane!" he called out. "Could you please come in here?"

Margot entered the room, leaning heavily on her cane. Erin's gut churned as she stared at the woman's foot. Margot ignored her and focused her attention on Stratton. "Finally," he said. "Do you have the explosives?"

"They are in the other room," Margot answered.

"Good. Nobody can survive an explosion, Erin. Not even your powerful daddy." He sighed. "I'd rather kill him myself, but if I can't get to him, I might as well have his daughter blow him up instead."

She found herself trembling and could barely breathe. *I can't kill my dad!* She pushed air through her lungs. "What about collateral damage? I don't know anything about bombs. A lot of innocent people could get hurt. Or I could end up in jail."

He made a noise of derision. "They're not innocent if they hang out with him. Also, people don't care if you kill a bokor there. It was only a couple of years ago that many voodoo priests were lynched for spreading cholera."

"I don't want to blow up anyone," she pleaded.

Stratton turned around, facing the indoor swimming pool. He obviously didn't consider her to be a threat. She felt her leopard pushing under her skin and considered shifting and launching herself at him.

"I thought I wouldn't need to repeat the last conversation we had." He sighed. "Do you think you're strong enough to fight me now, Erin? You'd better be sure, because if you fail, your friends will be the ones getting hurt. I won't be cutting off any toes then." She saw that he was watching her in the reflection of the large window. Their gazes met. Reluctantly, she shook her head. "Ms. Sloane will get you the explosives," he said. "I'm surprised you don't see what a great opportunity this is."

When she snorted, he explained, "Justice. Don't you want justice for your mom and your sister and those other two creatures you have in your head? Don't you want justice for the loss of your family and your childhood?"

"Justice by blowing him up?" she asked.

"Justice or revenge. Does it matter?" She didn't respond. After a moment of silence, she noticed Margot signaling her.

Without saying goodbye, Erin left the room.

They passed a room where she spotted a group of men in tuxedos that made her think of wise guys. She hovered, wondering if she recognized some from the night Dane had tried to set Stratton on fire. "Hey," someone said when he caught her staring. She saw that Margot had moved on and hurried along to find her. She found Margot in a second office where she was busy unlocking a cabinet. The secretary pulled out what appeared to be a gym bag.

"You really shouldn't bother, Margot. I have no idea how to work with explosives. With my luck I'll probably blow myself up," Erin quipped.

"*I didn't want to distract you in there, but I think Stratton has a point,*" Gideon said. "*It always pissed me off that your father got away with it. Nobody punished him for getting us to kill ourselves.*"

"*Er, maybe someone did punish him,*" Leila said. "*Maybe that's why he disappeared.*"

"*We can discuss this later,*" Erin's mom said.

"Mom?" Erin murmured.

"What?" Margot asked when she removed one of the packages from the bag and gave it to her. It was wrapped in a black garbage bag. "Oh, you're acting schizo again. It must be a nightmare having voices in your head."

She smiled shyly at Margot—grateful that she was talking to her and showing some understanding. "Try having a romantic relationship when your mother and sister are watching your every move."

"*Hey! That's not fair,*" Leila said.

It seemed like Margot was about to return her smile when she lost her balance. Leaning heavily on her cane, she sat down before switching back to talking business. "There's some explanation in the plastic bag on how to use the explosives. It's pretty straightforward. It's just a question of setting the timer, but be aware that if you set it too soon, then you could end up blowing yourself up. Whereas if you set it too late, he may have moved, or other people may be too close to the device."

"Uh, okay. Does it also say how big the explosion would be with this?"

Margot pointed at the content of the gym bag. "I suppose one brick should be enough to blow up a car or a desk. I think they gave me enough, so you could blow up his entire church. There are three additional packages in here, but I doubt you need all of them. Do you want them?"

It suddenly struck Erin how strange it was to be talking about explosives with Margot Sloane. The woman was dressed like a secretary from a sixties show with a green tweed two-piece skirt suit and her hair in a tight bun. She looked more like someone who would worry about the turkey being undercooked for her husband's dinner party than someone teaching people how to blow up voodoo priests.

"What? Do you want them or not?" Margot repeated.

"I just thought about how badass you looked holding those explosives," Erin said.

Margot stiffened and threw her a stern expression. "I'm happy that I can provide you with something to laugh about. I guess I'll keep these then. You'll probably mess it up anyway."

Erin's smile faded. She turned her head, but she

couldn't see or hear anyone nearby within hearing distance. She then leaned forward. "Again, I'm really sorry," she whispered. "I know that's easy for me to say with all my toes intact, but I want you to know that I haven't given up."

Alarm flared in Margot's eyes. "Don't say anything. Just drop it."

Erin realized that the office was probably bugged, or Margot really didn't want to discuss it. "Okay, I won't talk about it anymore."

"Good, and don't worry about transporting the bomb. You'll get to use Mr. Stratton's private jet on the way to Haiti, so there'll be no issues with customs. Of course, the jet won't stay, so you'll have to take a regular flight to New Orleans afterward when you're done with the assignment. Here is some information about the hotel you'll be staying at." Margot smirked as she gave Erin a thick envelope. "It's called Hotel Fantastique, but don't get your hopes up. It was chosen because of the location, not the facilities. In here you'll also find the address of the church where your grandfather is supposed to live."

"Fine," Erin said, her mouth suddenly dry thinking about the upcoming search for her father. She turned to leave the room, when Margot said, "Wait! We're not done." She picked up the phone and said, "We're ready."

"Ready for what?" Erin asked.

"Ready for me," a black man said with a big grin. He wore a white coat and carried a brown suitcase. He put it on the desk. She frowned at the man, who was obviously a doctor. She heard the familiar clicking sound of hook-and-loop openings. She remembered a sadistic psychiatrist carrying a similar bag with syringes, and she winced.

"Could you please take off your coat, so I can give you your shots?"

She glared at Margot. "You never mentioned anything about shots."

Margot shrugged. "You're flying to Haiti. What did you expect?"

The doctor tapped Erin's left arm. "Don't be alarmed. I've given shots a million times. I'll be gentle. Do you know if you're up-to-date on the routine vaccinations?" When she didn't respond, he said, "Measles, mumps, tetanus, chickenpox, polio?"

"She stayed in a medical facility until last year," Margot answered for her. "I'm sure they didn't want to risk their patients infecting each other with diseases that could easily have been prevented."

Erin gritted her teeth. "I suppose. I got so many shots there, who knows what was in them."

The doctor eyed her in speculation, but she refused to let it bother her. "All righty then," he said. "If you think you already had the routine ones, I will only do the vaccines for hepatitis and typhoid."

"Isn't it a little late to be giving me these shots?" Erin asked. Reluctantly, she removed her coat and rolled up the sleeves on her left arm.

"Well, yes, it would have been better getting vaccinated at least four weeks before your trip, but late protection is still better than no protection at all. Especially if you end up staying in Haiti for months and run the risk of contamination. Just try to avoid drinking dirty water, and don't eat undercooked food." He tore off the plastic tip from the needle and grabbed a vial. After he filled up the syringe and cleaned her arm, he stuck the needle in a muscle of her upper arm. "And that is one."

She flinched. "How many do I need?"

The doctor glanced at Margot, but she didn't respond. "Three," he said while taking out another vial. Something was off. *Why would he look at her for that question?* She felt the sting of the second vaccination. A burn.

Her eyebrows shot up. "One for hepatitis, but what are the other two for?"

The doctor stared at her arm while he arranged the final shot. "You need hepatitis vaccinations, namely against hepatitis A and B, and the other is to prevent typhoid."

"Thank you, Doctor Miller," Margot said. "We appreciate that you're willing to make a house call at night."

He laughed. "My pleasure. The remuneration is more than adequate. I'd best be going now. Young lady," he said to Erin. "If in the unlikely event you end up feeling feverish or dizzy within the next couple of hours, then you should see a doctor as soon as you arrive. There could be side effects."

She tilted her chin at Margot. "Great! So, I could possibly confront my dad while I'm weak?"

Margot sighed. "I'm sure you can spend the first night at the hotel before you go out on your assignment. Come on, I'll see you both out."

"If you like, I can drop you off at the airport," Doctor Miller kindly offered as they walked through the hallway.

"That won't be necessary," Margot said. "She can take the limo this time."

Erin waited for the doctor to drive away before she confronted Margot. "Why didn't you want us to drive together?"

"He's too curious. I saw the way he was watching you, and I thought with your history with doctors you'd prefer not to spend too much time alone with one."

"Oh, that's nice. And thanks also, I guess, for the vaccinations."

Margot waved away the gratitude. "You're welcome, but it wasn't my idea. Stratton demanded it."

"Stratton?" A chill shot down her spine. "Really? I would have thought that he didn't care whether I lived or died."

Margot signaled the driver of the elegant black limousine. "Oh, I suppose he wanted to make sure that you won't get sick while you're there. Healthy enough at least to kill his enemy."

"His enemy." She moistened her dry lips. "My father."

"You'll be fine," Margot said as she opened the rear left-side door to the limousine. Erin climbed into the passenger seat and pulled the door closed. She tried choking down the terrifying apprehension that she might soon come face to face with the man who had sought to kill her when she was a little girl. For a second, she considered calling Dane for help. He could arrange a flight to New Orleans instead of Haiti for her, and perhaps he'd allow Pauline, Frank and herself to hide at his mansion while he thought of a way to get rid of Stratton.

She froze when her eyes met the limo driver's in the rearview mirror. He was watching her with an unnatural intensity. Attempting to remain calm on the outside, regardless of her racing pulse, she deliberately stared outside, pretending not to notice. Her hand entered her pocket and touched the cell phone. She wanted to call Pauline and Dane, but she didn't feel comfortable calling them while the limo driver could be listening in. After noticing some buttons on a panel on the door, she realized she could put up a screen between them.

Idiot! I should have thought of that before. I've been in this car before, and the screen was up then.

"Do you know how to put up the screen?" she asked while attempting to smile apologetically. "I need to make some phone calls."

"Oh, I don't mind," he said, but he put up the screen anyway. She wondered if he would still be listening in, but she decided not to let that stop her. Stratton expected her to kill her father—the father she hadn't seen for twenty years. *Could I really kill him? Maybe he's changed now. It's been so long. People do change.*

"Before I reach out to Dane and Pauline, I need some info from you guys," Erin whispered. "Leila, you mentioned something about our father—that someone may have already punished him. Is that wishful thinking, or is that something that really happened?"

"*I'm not sure,*" Leila said. "*But I had talked to our grandfather previously, and he'd told me that he intended to take our dad back to Haiti.*"

"Take him back to punish him or to protect him?" Erin asked.

"*Or maybe to steal your father's powers so he could use them for himself,*" Erin's mom said.

"*Could be,*" Leila admitted. "*Like our father, he can absorb power from others. Dad did say that he should have taught me about voodoo, like his father had taught him.*"

"Did you like our grandfather?"

"*I only met him once. He made me feel nervous, but he warned me not to go to the Devereaux Church that Halloween.*"

"Why did he make you feel nervous?" Erin asked.

"*I felt sort of intimidated. I thought he was very intense. I called him before to see if he could help us, but he acted quite aggressively. When I told him who I was, his tone changed completely—really friendly. It just didn't seem real, so I hung up,*" Leila explained. "*But then he ended up tracking me down. When I finally met him, it felt as if he was interrogating me. He didn't really act like the grandfathers you see in movies, but I suppose our father doesn't act like the fathers you see in movies either.*"

"No," Erin agreed. "He doesn't."

She didn't remember much about her father. She couldn't picture him reading bedtime stories to her or picking her up at school. Her father had antagonized many people, and now she was forced to kill him—if he was still alive.

Stratton's enemy. Her father.

My enemy.

FOUR

T here was a knock at the door, and Pauline looked up from her tablet in alarm. Willow, who had been sleeping on Pauline's lap, opened her eyes wide and hissed with flattened ears. She meowed up at Pauline before jumping off her lap and running off to the bedroom.

Pauline wasn't expecting anyone. She didn't know many people, and the people she did know, she did not want to have knocking at her door. Maybe if she didn't move, the person would assume nobody was home and go away. A second knock caused her to stiffen. She was doing research on the demon that Erin had warned her about and worried that she had somehow summoned him. *What if he's performing black magic in the hallway?* Of course, if it was that Ramin Sceledorse character, she may not be able to recognize him unless he used the body of that disgusting taxi driver again. She told herself that she had to find out who it was as she slowly put down her cup of chamomile tea. Silently, she rose and crossed the room, trying to make as little noise as possible. She stood on tiptoe to peer through the peephole. A jolt went through her when she recognized the ripped, bearded man with brown eyes looking straight into the spy-hole. Billy Blair. She quickly covered her mouth to keep quiet and moved away from the door.

Can you see people when you're gazing into a peephole from the outside?

"Pauline Collins? There's no need to hide. I know you're in there," Billy said. "It's Billy. You know, Billy the werewolf, who has supernatural senses, like heightened hearing and smell. Please, don't tell me you're afraid of werewolves?" She heard amusement in his deep voice.

Nervous, she wondered what Erin would do. *She wouldn't hide, that's for sure. Would she use her powers?* The only powers Pauline had were her magic spells, but she hadn't prepared anything, and if she were to recite a spell, Mr. Supernatural-Senses would know.

"Come on. Open the door. I promise I won't bite."

Too bad. Oh shit, where did that thought come from?

She had always been drawn to muscular men with shaved heads and beards, and she remembered that he had looked very handsome in his black, leather jacket and tight blue jeans the other day.

"My mom told me you were asking questions about me. If you're so interested in me, why won't you open the door?" Billy asked.

Shit. What if he realizes that he bit Erin after all? Come on. Stop being a chicken, she told herself as she walked up to the door again. *You can do this.*

Channeling Erin, Pauline exhaled a slow breath while trying to find a sense of calm before she unlocked the door and opened it.

She immediately wished she had kept the door shut. Billy's domineering presence hit her so hard, she worried he could hear her heart hammering with his super hearing.

"Yes?" she asked. She managed a smile but doubted it was convincing.

Billy grinned, and Pauline shivered at the sight of his big white teeth. *All the easier to devour me with.*

"I thought you said I couldn't intimidate you." He leaned in the doorway, towering over her with a wicked grin on his face.

She lifted her chin before stepping forward. "I didn't answer the door because I was busy."

He peered inside, taking in the tablet lying on the table next to the cup of tea. His eyebrows rose in a sardonic query.

"I spent several days unpacking boxes. I needed a little break."

Without asking for permission, he entered her apartment. "Good, I could use a little break too."

"Hey! I didn't tell you that you were allowed to come in!"

"Well, we have some things to discuss. If you prefer, I can go back out in the hallway, but I didn't think you'd want your new neighbors to know your business. Just like I don't want my neighbors knowing my business either."

Pauline's face warmed as she recalled her botched attempt at spying on him. She hesitated a second before finally closing the door.

"Besides, isn't it a good thing that I didn't wait for your permission? Otherwise, you'd be sitting here all alone."

She narrowed her eyes. "Maybe I'd rather be alone."

"Well, if you wanted to be left alone, then you shouldn't have been asking my mom questions about me. And about that… Why have you been asking my mom questions about me?"

To avoid his gaze, she walked over to the table and picked up her teacup. Her hands trembled slightly, making the cup rattle against the saucer. She was about to take it into the kitchen when he stepped in front of her, and she froze. "Uh, would you like a cup?"

"No, I would like an answer."

The rattling of the cup got louder, and she quickly stepped around him, so she could put the offending cup down on the kitchen counter.

After taking a deep breath, she turned around to face him. He must have been following her closely because she bumped into him and found herself about to speak to his broad chest. Having him stand so close was unnerving. Her throat closed, and she couldn't get the words out. She took a step back, but he took a step forward. She took another step backward, but her back hit the counter while he moved ahead once more, and his body trapped hers.

She watched him inhale deeply as if he could smell her, and she felt dizzy by his proximity. His eyes had really long lashes for a man. They were dark chocolate pools that she was entranced by. "Um, w-what?" she stammered.

"You were questioning my mom," he reminded her.

"Oh, right. Um, do you mind?" she asked as she

pushed at his chest. "I can't focus when you stand so close."

He chuckled but complied by taking a step back.

"Thank you." *I guess honesty is the best policy?* "Um, I was trying to find out if you were stalking my roommate."

"What? Why the hell would I do that?"

"Well, you attacked her before, and maybe you resented her when she got Victor kicked out of the pack."

He shook his head. "That's ridiculous! Victor's false allegation that Erin was a werewolf got him kicked out of the pack. That's not her fault, so there's nothing to resent her for, and I attacked her only once! It was the first time I shifted to a werewolf, and I apologized to Erin already. First shifts are hard, and I had no control over the werewolf. Thank God, I didn't bite her, so, she's not a werewolf. There's no need to accuse me of stalking her," he snapped.

She was sure a red flush was creeping over her cheeks. "I w-wasn't accusing you! I j-just wanted to see if you were angry."

"Angry? Why would I be angry?"

Because we lied to you. Because we tricked you when we hid her werewolf using magic. Fortunately, Pauline managed to stop herself before she blurted out that confession. "Um, I thought maybe you were on Victor's side. I thought it was too much of a coincidence that you were in the same building as us, just a month after Victor's expulsion."

"So now you know that my family lives here, and has been living here since before you moved in. Does that mean that you won't be asking my mom questions about me anymore?"

"I won't. I promise." She shot him a sincere glance.

"Oh, that's too bad," he said.

"What?" She frowned. *He wants me to ask his mother questions about him?*

"You figure it out." He winked at her with a confidence that she found sexy, and she scolded herself for melting a little under his intent gaze.

"No! There's nothing to figure out. I'm sorry. It's just a misunderstanding," she rushed to explain while her pulse rushed right along with her words.

He grinned, a wolfish smile as he leaned over her, his hot breath warming her cheek. "I don't think our attraction is a misunderstanding."

"I-I'm not attracted to you. Y-you arrogant—"

"You forget, Pauline, I am a werewolf." He made a show of sniffing the air. "With a werewolf's sense of smell."

She stamped her feet in frustration. They could not afford catching Billy's attention. Terrified that he would find out their lies she pointed at the door. "Get out!"

His lips were curved as he tilted his head in acknowledgement before he turned and walked to the exit. He turned the knob and opened the door. "I'll be seeing you around," he vowed without looking at her.

As he shut the door behind him, Pauline muttered, "Not if I see you first!"

Her words seemed to hang in the air. It suddenly hit her that the previous time she had spoken to Billy, they had exchanged the exact same words at the end of their conversation. This time there had been a threatening undertone to his voice. Suddenly, she had trouble standing, and she collapsed to the floor, overwhelmed by the risk they were running. If the werewolves found out that Pauline had helped Erin hide her inner werewolf from them, they would come after them. She knew she had to stop Billy from being interested in her. *Maybe a repulsion spell?*

Her phone buzzed, and for a second, she thought that would be him. *That's stupid, he doesn't even have my number.* She saw Erin's name on the screen and answered the call.

"Hi. I'm calling you from Stratton's limo," Erin said.

"I understand. So, there may be someone listening in on our conversation. Do you think they can hear me too?"

Pauline heard Erin exhale heavily. "I don't know. I guess not. I'm not sure I care. Should I?"

Pauline squeezed her hand around the phone. Erin sounded so dejected. "It doesn't matter. I'm so happy to hear your voice," Pauline said. "What did Stratton want? Can you share that? Are you okay?"

"He hasn't physically hurt me. He wants me to find my dad. He told me to go to Haiti and talk to my grandfather."

"Your dad? Why would he want you to seek out your father? Sorry, no offense, but shouldn't we say: 'Good riddance?'"

"None taken," Erin said. "I'm not exactly best friends with my dad. The last time I saw him, he tried to kill me. Maybe this time he will succeed." Her words were hoarse.

The hair on the back of Pauline's neck rose.

"Then don't go! We'll find a way to protect you from Stratton. Were you able to take something of his?"

"What?"

Pauline frowned. "For a curse. Please don't tell me that you forgot!"

"Shit! Sorry, it completely slipped my mind."

"It's okay." *It's not.* "Just fly home. We'll think of something else."

"That's sweet, but it's not just me."

There was a short silence. "You mean that it's not just you he threatened. And he didn't just threaten me, but you're also doing this to stop him from hurting Dane, Frank and his secretary?"

"His secretary. Oh God!" Erin's exclamation came out in a pained whimper.

"I take it that Margot is still angry at you?"

"As she should be. But no, it's— We'll talk later. Listen, it looks like we're already arriving at the airport. I just wanted to let you know where I'm going. I'll try to reach Dane before I leave too."

"But you wanted to call me first." Pauline smiled, feeling flattered. "I'll look for a spell that will send you some strength and see if I can do it tonight."

"Thanks. I don't know if white magic is stronger than my dad's black magic, but anything helps. I'll continue to carry your gris gris for protection."

"Do you think your grandfather will help you?"

"I don't know. I don't remember him. Leila told me that he's the one who taught voodoo to our father and that he could absorb powers from others. Stratton said something about him being some kind of a bokor. Maybe that's what they call a voodoo priest in Haiti. Apparently, my grandfather's house is like a fortress, and he has zombies."

"What! This sounds a lot worse than anything Jonathan Stratton might do," Pauline said. "Forget it. We'll risk it. Maybe he's just bluffing."

"It's not your decision to make, Pauline, but thanks for the offer. We just stopped the car. I really need to call Dane now. Talk to you later, okay?" Erin's voice was an unsteady combination of determination and fake light-heartedness.

"No! Not okay." But Erin had already disconnected the call. "Fuck!"

As soon as Pauline put the phone down, she realized that she forgot to mention Billy's visit. She decided it was probably for the best. Erin had enough on her plate, and Pauline didn't want to add to her worries. Pauline was the one who had caused the problem when she got caught during her investigation, so this challenge she would solve alone. She was going to show Billy that she was a force to be reckoned with. All she needed was a lock of his hair and a good spell.

But how to get a lock of his hair? His beard? She decided to wait for him to come to her. He said he would see her again, and she would make sure that when they did meet each other again, this time she would be ready for him.

The door of the limousine was opened for Erin, and she felt she had little choice but to get out. The chauffeur carried her bag, signaling her to follow him as he walked across the tarmac to the plane. With her ear against the phone she waited for Dane to pick up, but it was difficult to hear anything over the noise coming from the plane engines.

She was tempted to go back to the car and call Dane there. She expected he would not like to be presented with a fait accompli. Calling him from a plane, as it was about to depart to Haiti, meant that there was nothing he could do to stop her from leaving. Not that she expected that he would have had a solution for her problem if she had called him before.

"Are you coming Miss?" the limo driver asked as she hovered in front of the airstairs. He was at the top of the stairs, about to enter the plane. She nodded and hurried up the stairs. A woman in uniform greeted her, holding a tray with a glass of champagne. "Hello, Erin?" she heard Dane ask through her cell phone.

"Ah, inside the sound is much better. Thank you," she said to the flight attendant before accepting the drink. She decided the alcohol would help calm her nerves. "Sorry about that," Erin said to Dane. "We just arrived at some executive airport, and we're about to take off."

"Madam, could you please switch off your phone?" the flight attendant asked.

"One minute," Erin mouthed while holding up one finger in the air. The woman nodded as she closed the door, shutting them inside.

"So, what happened?" Dane asked. "What's this job Stratton wants you to do?"

"Well, Stratton told me to fly to Haiti. He uh, he wants me to meet my grandfather." She glared at the flight attendant who was tapping her watch to indicate that her time was up.

"No." Dane's refusal came out as more of a growl than a word.

"Stratton thinks that my grandfather can lead me to my dad. He—"

"No," he cut her off. "You said that Stratton needed you alive for this job, but this is a suicide mission. I'm not letting you get killed."

"Stratton doesn't want me dead. He even cares enough to get me vaccinated. Besides, I'll be visiting my grandfather. An old man."

"I can't believe you're so naïve! As if Stratton would bother with vaccinations! It was probably his secretary's idea. And thinking your grandfather is just an old man! After what your father tried to do? If you go off to Haiti, I won't be able to protect you."

"It's too late. Look, I need to disconnect. We're ready for take-off."

"Erin—"

"Goodbye, Dane." She cut off their conversation and set her cell phone to flight mode. The flight attendant nodded at her when she put on her seat belt. Erin took a large sip of champagne and glanced wistfully outside, wishing she could stay in the US. She could see the back of her suitcase that had been placed between the cockpit and the large seat where Margot Sloane had been working at her laptop the last time she had flown in the private plane. She wondered if the flight attendant would get upset if she got out the bomb and studied how to get it to work. She felt panic rising within her just thinking of having to try to find her father and blow him up. *I don't want to kill him.*

TOUCHED BY EVIL

The plane was lined up on the runway, and the whine of the engines increased as it gained speed. Her heart rate sped up too. She pressed her hand to her chest, convinced her heart was pounding so wildly that it was about to burst through.

"*Erin.*" She gripped the armrest with her left arm when she recognized Dane's voice reaching out to her telepathically. "*See, it's a good thing that we did the blood exchange. I didn't lie when I told you I needed to do this for your own protection. You have too many enemies.*"

"It must be my charming personality," she said aloud. The flight attendant shot a suspicious look in her direction, and Erin smiled, trying to portray innocence but knowing she failed when the woman frowned at her.

"*You don't need to speak for me to hear you. Just think it. You've done it before when you got stuck as a leopard, and you needed my help to shift back to your human form.*"

"*But then I didn't have a choice. I didn't have a voice as a leopard,*" she thought.

"*That's right,*" Dane's voice echoed through her mind.

Erin gave an inward sigh of relief when she realized it worked. She had the ghosts in her head supporting her, but Dane could physically help her if needed. The downside was that she was starting to rely too much on him, and she doubted that any help he provided would come without a price. If he ever discovered how she secretly fantasized about paying that price, she would be doomed.

"*Doomed? Sorry, Goldilocks you need to put in*

more effort when you're using telepathy. Are you doomed?"

Shocked that she had nearly revealed her vulnerability to him, she inhaled deeply, trying to focus. "*Sorry. I'm just worried about my trip.*"

"*Do you have a plan at least? If your father is still alive and hiding in Haiti, there may not be a friendly reunion. He may want to finish what he started all those years ago.*"

"*Let him try,*" she thought.

"*What!*"

Anger began to build up inside her. "*Yes. Let him try. I'm tired of being scared, and you know what, nobody's seen him since the ritual. If he were such a powerful voodoo priest as everyone is saying, he would have succeeded in killing me all those years ago. Also, if he were so terrifying, why would he have gone into hiding? Only people that are scared hide away.*"

"*Don't underestimate him.*" Dane sounded angry now too.

"*I'm not going completely unprepared.*" Erin eyed her bomb-filled suitcase. "*If my dad got away with killing my mom, my sister and all those other people, it would be good if someone went after him.*"

"*Yes, but it shouldn't be you!*" A hint of fear entered his deep voice.

"*Maybe it should. He's my father. He took away my family, and because of him, I'm... Because of him, I'm now different. I should hold him accountable for that.*"

"*I thought that you'd accepted that you're different.*"

"Yes, you're right. Not only have I accepted that I hear the voices of those who died during my dad's ritual, I love them. Well, maybe not Gideon, but the others are important to me. And they've saved my life a couple of times too."

Dane let out an annoyed growl. *"By taking over your body."*

"Yes, sometimes, but they also saved my life by teaching me how to use their powers. Although I'm aware that I probably wouldn't have to save my life all the time if it weren't for the fact that my powers attract unwanted attention."

"Not all attention it drew was unwanted," he teased.

"Yes, that's true," she admitted. Even though Dane had terrified her at first, she had evolved from appreciating his attention to craving it.

"The ritual made you strong. Do you still want to be human?"

Erin chuckled. *"Don't sound so disgusted. Or are you offended that I'd rather be human than a vampire like you? Don't worry. I accepted my otherness, and who knows, maybe I'll have a shot at beating him thanks to these powers. But yeah, a part of me does sometimes wonder what my life would be like if I had remained human."*

"You'll die, that's what," She could hear the irritation in his voice. *"I'll come to you. Don't do anything. I'll take the first flight to Haiti."*

"Apparently, my grandfather's place is like a fortress in the middle of nowhere, and if you went there, you'd raise suspicion. With your appearance, there's no way you can get in. I can use my

connection to enter. They would never allow you to get close. Whereas, I'm his grandchild."

"You forget that I'm not without power. As a vampire I can also shift into another creature. I'll get in."

"What creature is it? Is it indigenous to Haiti?"

He didn't respond, and just when Erin decided that their telepathic connection must have been disconnected, he replied, "Maybe not. I just want to keep you safe."

She smiled, feeling the warmth in his words as if he was holding her, sheltering her.

"I never should have allowed you to leave," Dane added. "I've been too lenient, too patient. Next time—"

And then the reality was back. "I didn't need your permission to leave, Dane. I'm not your prisoner. I agreed to the blood exchange, but I refuse to act like your blood slave."

"I wish you did. You're not being sensible."

Gripping the armrests in anger, she attempted to keep her thoughts calm while her emotions whipped up into a storm of indignation. "Thank you for showing me why I shouldn't ask you for help. You're such a control freak. You just want to lock me away somewhere, as if I'm some kind of doll who has no will of her own."

"Of course not. I want what's best for you."

"You only want what's best for me if it coincides with what's best for you. If it doesn't, I doubt you'd let me do what I want. I want to do this. Maybe a part of me needs to hold my father accountable for what he's done to me. I need closure."

TOUCHED BY EVIL

"You're just telling yourself that, so you don't feel like Stratton's victim," he goaded her. *"He's your father, your blood. You don't have it in you to kill him. You'll probably end up forgiving him! You shouldn't be seeking out danger."*

Her nostrils flared. *"Well, if I shouldn't be doing that, then I shouldn't be with you either."*

"Good to know that you are not too emotional to realize that I'm dangerous, Erin. You would do well to listen to me."

His threat reminded her of his behavior when they first met. At that time, he had deliberately terrorized her to get her to leave Hope Acres. Sometimes, it struck her how quickly their relationship had progressed within several months. She wondered if she was fooling herself into believing that there was a caring man underneath his predatory exterior or if the blood exchange had affected her thinking. *"No. No more listening. I'll find a way to stop this. I already have too many voices in my head. I can't have you distract me these next couple of days too. Leave me alone."*

"Erin!" Her name was barked out as a command.

"No." The last word Erin spoke aloud in a low, determined voice. She no longer wished to communicate with him telepathically. It felt too intimate. Unfortunately, mere seconds after she uttered the rejection, she regretted her harsh words to Dane and fought her desire to reach out to him and apologize.

I shouldn't have been so angry, she told herself. *It's not that he's too controlling. He just doesn't want me to track down my father because he cares about me. I need him. He's my only ally.*

That last thought hit her like a cold shower. It wasn't true, and deep down she knew it. Dane wasn't her only ally because she had Pauline, and the ghosts attached to her generally tried to help her too. She was lying to herself. This longing to please Dane had to be a side effect of the blood exchange. She shouldn't let doubt poison her. It wasn't real.

Despite Dane not contacting her again for the rest of the flight, her mind continued to be on high alert. She kept waiting for Dane to get in touch with her, but he must have realized that by not doing so, it was harder for her to not reach out to him instead. The longer the silence lasted, the more tempted she was to beg his forgiveness. The other voices were quiet too.

She must have dozed off because when the flight attendant tapped her shoulder, she shot up in her chair, awake in an instant. She blinked up at the woman, squinting against the bright lights inside the plane.

"We have arrived," the flight attendant said.

"Where?" Erin asked sleepily.

"We landed on the West side of the island on a private landing strip in the Artibonite region. It's about a three-hour walk to Petit Espoir, but the hotel is about a forty-five-minute walk where you can freshen up."

The first thing Erin noticed when she stood at the top of the airstairs was the warm breeze as the sun crested the horizon. She glanced at her watch.

"Oh, I forgot to mention something," the flight attendant said as she handed Erin her suitcase. "There's a time difference. It's six o'clock in the morning now. You might want to change your clothes too. The temperatures here are in the high eighties, even in January."

Erin thanked her and went back into the plane. She entered a large bathroom. The air inside reeked of antiseptic. After she locked the door, she opened up her suitcase and looked at the plastic bag on top. Her heart rate accelerated as she reached out. She lifted the bag and peeked inside. She saw what appeared to be a brick of gray clay, some wires, a burner phone and a drawing with instructions.

"*You're a witch,*" Erin heard her mother's voice say. "*You don't need this. They shouldn't force you to work with bombs.*"

"They shouldn't force me to kill my father," Erin said softly. "But I need my friends to be safe. Hopefully, he won't be there, so I won't have to find out if I'm capable of using explosives."

"*I agree with your mother,*" Altman added. "*This is a weapon a human would use, and you're not human.*"

"*Besides, if our grandfather finds this, he might think you're his enemy,*" Leila said. "*He's never done anything to us, but if he sees you're carrying a bomb, he'd want to stop you from using it.*"

"I really can't picture myself cold-bloodedly blowing up someone," Erin whispered. "I can't do this. Should I throw it away?"

"*You only feel that way because you're not desperate enough yet,*" Gideon's dark tone echoed through her mind. "*At the moment you're not feeling threatened.*"

The knock on the door interrupted her discussion.

68

"Yes?" Erin called out through the locked door.

"We need to return now." It was the flight attendant's voice. "Are you ready?"

"Um, almost!" She hurried to take off the clothes she had worn in Las Vegas and chose to wear casual denim shorts and a white tank top with spaghetti straps. Worried that her golden curls would draw too much attention she put her hair in a tight ponytail. "I'll have you know that I feel plenty threatened right now," she muttered.

"Throw the explosives away," Erin's mother said. *"If you hide the bomb at the hotel room and someone searches your room, well, you know..."*

"Yeah, I know," Erin said. Despite her having qualms, she threw the plastic bag in the bin beside the toilet. She turned and stared at her reflection in the mirror. She chose to ignore her pale face and the shadows under her eyes as she gave herself a firm nod. "I got this."

"Do you?" Gideon asked. *"You shouldn't have thrown it away. You could use magic to hide it."*

"But they know magic too, and they may be able to sense it. Don't doubt yourself," Erin's mother countered.

Erin put her winter clothes into the suitcase, and then she left the bathroom. She nodded at the flight attendant, who shot her an impatient glare. Feeling calmer now that she was no longer carrying the explosives, she left the plane with a renewed sense of purpose. She might have felt a whisper of regret, but she told herself she had to let it go. She couldn't enter her grandfather's home armed—not if she used the excuse of a reunion as the reason why she sought him out.

Who knows, maybe he'll welcome me with open arms...

Casting her gaze to the pale pinkish-orange sunrise over the distant mountains, Erin watched the plane take off. When the plane was no longer visible, she turned around to take in her new surroundings. She understood why Margot had said there wouldn't be any problem with customs. Erin couldn't see anything resembling a terminal nearby.

The trees, shrubs and grass lining the road appeared to be lush and full. If she had any doubts about where she was, the palm trees told her that she really was in the Caribbean. She didn't see anyone, nor were there cars nearby. Silence all around, Erin wondered if the hotel really was only a forty-five-minute walk from where she stood. She closed her eyes and listened. Leaves were rustling in the warm air, a chorus of crickets chirped, and there had to be a flock of birds nearby—wings were flapping as the animals let out noisy three-note whistling calls. She could also hear the faint sound of running water. A gentle twitter with a low rattle made her open her eyes, and she spotted a bird with a bright red belly in a tree looking down on her.

She bent down to unzip the front pocket of her suitcase and took out the envelope that Margot had given her. As she went through its contents, she was impressed by Margot's attention to detail. In it, she counted forty thousand gourdes. Fortunately, Margot had remembered to add a note with currency information, which taught Erin that she should have enough money to pay for a hotel and fly back to the US once she had completed her assignment. *If I make it...*

There were also several maps inside the envelope: one of Petit Espoir, one large map of Haiti, and the other appeared to be of where she was now because of the small plane drawn on the road. Behind the maps, Erin found a list with names linked to addresses and telephone numbers. Obviously, Margot had put her grandfather's name on top. In addition, she found contact details of doctors, hospitals, the hotel, motorcycle taxis and the Port-au-Prince airport.

Except for the map, she put everything back in the suitcase. She left the airstrip, dragging her wobbly suitcase on wheels behind her. She had hoped not to draw anybody's attention, but the sound of her suitcase rolling on the road made so much noise that she might as well have announced her arrival with a marching band. She arrived at an intersection and had to decide which way to go. There were no road signs, but the drawing indicated that if she turned right and followed that road she would eventually reach Hotel Magnifique.

She was walking for nearly twenty minutes when she saw the first people. Around two-dozen farmers were plodding about barefoot in marsh-like paddies. Muddy water splashed on their hands and faces as they were dragging rakes beneath the water. They all stopped working and were watching her as she walked by with her shaky black suitcase.

Several farmers walked up to her. One of them

took off his brown hat, saying, "Bonjou. Tout bagay anfóm? Kote ou prale?"

She smiled, feeling awkward. "Ah, bonjour? Je ne parle pas Français."

He shook his head. "Non, kreyòl ayisyen."

She grimaced. "Do you speak English?" When nobody responded, she asked, "Hotel Magnifique?" She pointed in the direction she was headed and repeated the name of the hotel.

He nodded. "Wi."

"Merci!" she said. She waved and moved on. After she had walked for a minute or so, she turned around to see if the farmers had gone back to work. They were still standing there, watching her, the clumsy American tourist with the wrong luggage. When she waved at them once more, they laughed before returning to the field. Reassured, Erin continued her journey.

She felt more at ease after her first interaction with Haitians and was relieved that they had confirmed that she was going in the right direction. *But what if they lied and deliberately sent me the wrong way?* "Isn't that how horror movies start?" she muttered.

"*What? Horror movies?*" her mother asked.

"Never mind, mom. Just my suspicious mind," Erin replied. "Oh, bloody hell!" The suitcase got stuck in a hole for what had to be the tenth time that morning. She pulled it free. Then she opened and closed her hands a couple of times. Her palms were damp, and she rubbed them on her shorts.

"*Maybe you should have a little break. You haven't slept much and might be a bit jetlagged,*" her mother suggested.

Erin scanned the green landscape around her, but she couldn't find any place to sit down. She rubbed the sweat from her brow and sighed. She stood alone on a bad road with a bright sun shining down on her and a dark future ahead.

In the distance, she could make out the glinting water of the river. There were several colorful buildings up ahead too. She took a couple of steps when she spotted the direction sign saying 'Hotel Magnifique', and she let out cheer in elation. When she finally reached the broken fence of the yellow hotel, she exhaled, slightly disappointed. Three people were staring at her as she made her entrance. She chose to carry her suitcase inside, so it would not make so much noise. The lobby was displaying hammers, chainsaws and plumbing supplies. She spotted more building supplies in the room next to the lobby, wondering if she was in a hotel or a hardware store. Or are these tools for protection?

The hotel reeked of grilled fish, stacks of lumber, and then, as she took a deeper sniff, she detected the lemony scent of disinfectants. Thinking of clean bed sheets, she smiled at the front desk clerk who greeted her in French.

"Bonjour. I believe there should be a reservation under my name, Erin Holland."

"Ah, yes," the man said. "But we expected you earlier. You pay upfront and need to pay for last night too."

She frowned. "Just give me a receipt."

After she had paid for the two nights' stay, she walked up the badly lit stairs to her room on the third floor. She put the key in the lock but discovered the door was open already. Once inside, she tried to lock the door behind her, but the key kept turning. She turned on the light that turned out to be a bare bulb. She supposed that this small room with its barren walls and broken sockets was what a prison cell would look like. She opened a door in the tiny hallway and gazed bewildered at the bathroom. The toilet didn't have a toilet seat, and instead of a showerhead, the tub only had a pipe. There was a white cloth on the edge of the tub that reminded her of the rag Pauline used for cleaning, and she didn't even see any toilet paper.

"*Ask for another room,*" she heard Altman advise her. "*And if they're difficult, use my vampiric power of persuasion.*"

"What if the other room is worse?" Erin asked.

"*Hard to imagine, but just in case, put a thrall on him when you demand he gives you his best room.*"

Erin nodded and left the hotel room. She used to be reluctant to use Altman's powers but fortunately he only encouraged her to use them if it was in her best interest. Unlike Gideon, Altman really cared about her and sought to protect her, even if it couldn't always have been easy for a ghost who used to be a vampire to watch over a girl growing up in a mental hospital.

The front desk clerk looked up when she walked up to his desk. "No good?" He laughed without humor.

She stared into the man's brown eyes and guided her power into her voice. "You will give me the best room of your hotel. You are happy to give me this best room. It has a wonderful lock that works, a toilet with a seat, a thick clean towel and toilet paper."

His expression blank, he said, "I will give you the best room." He opened the drawer with keys and gave her another key.

Proud that it worked so easily, she grinned. The rush of power made her feel a little light-headed.

"*You should tell him to carry your bag,*" Leila suggested.

It was tempting to make the rude man act like a better host, but Erin worried that this heady feeling of getting people to act as her puppets could get addictive so she resisted that impulse.

"Thank you," she said and went to look for the best room Hotel Magnifique had to offer.

Erin rolled over for the twentieth time and decided to give up the futile imitation of sleep. She glared at the thunderous air conditioner. "Best room, my ass," she muttered.

She checked the time on her watch and expelled a deep sigh when she noticed she had been trying to fall asleep for two hours now. She opened the bottle of water on her nightstand and had a sip. She got out of bed, grabbed her clothes and walked to the bathroom. When she was washing her face, she noticed the bags under her eyes.

She hadn't seen a phone in her room, and she didn't want to use her cell phone for making a local call, so she went downstairs to search for a pay phone. She didn't see one in the lobby, but she was so tired that she worried she may have overlooked it. After hitting the service bell, she leaned against the front desk like the tired tourist she was. The smell of food was stronger now, but nausea rose up at the idea of breakfast.

"Can I help you?" the front desk clerk asked her.

She moved away from the desk and smiled apologetically. "I was looking for a pay phone. I suppose you have one."

"No, but you can use the phone at the restaurant. Where are you calling?"

She frowned and didn't think it was any of his business. She was about to say so when he added, "Local or international?"

Her face burned with embarrassment, because she had been about to snap at the man for no reason. "Local," she replied while waving the sheet of paper that displayed the telephone number for her grandfather's church.

"Really?" His eyes narrowed as he grabbed Margot's phone list.

"Hey!" Erin protested.

He peeked down for only one second and said, "Oh, Bondye!" He pushed the piece of paper back in her hands, wrinkling it in the process. He stumbled back. "No, no calling from here."

He looks scared, she thought, shocked when a low sound of terror escaped from the man's lips.

"But I need to make a phone call," she insisted. "It's local."

"No. Phone is broken."

She grimaced. "Come on. You just told me that I could use the phone at the restaurant."

"You misunderstood," he said before he left the room.

She decided to go back to her room and use the cell phone Dane had given her instead, but first she was going to use it to find another hotel to stay at. She had been reluctant to use the cell phone for anything other than emergencies. She had never seen any invoices. Dane had to be the one paying her telephone bills, and it made her uncomfortable.

"*It looks like your grandfather has a bit of a reputation,*" Altman said.

She closed the door, grabbed her cell phone and sat down on the bed. She discovered a hotel with good reviews seven miles from where she was. She called them and cheered when they told her they had a room available and that they would send a car over to collect her within thirty minutes. After she completed the booking, she punched her grandfather's number and put the phone to her ear, fidgeting as she waited for someone to pick up.

A man answered after the fourth ring. "Legliz Petit Espoir," he said.

"Uh, hello. I hope you speak English," Erin said. "I'm looking for Emanuel Merenda."

"Who is this?" he asked.

"My name is Erin Holland. I uh, I'm his granddaughter. I'm in Haiti right now, and I wondered if my grandfather would like to meet me."

There was a long silent moment before he said, "I'll call you back." Without waiting for her response, he hung up.

She put down the phone and let herself fall back on the bed, staring up at the ceiling while waiting for the stranger to return the call. *Was that my grandfather's voice? What if it was my dad's voice?*

Would I even recognize his voice?

Her heart skipped a beat when the phone buzzed. Her hand trembled as she picked up the phone and sat up straight. She took a breath to calm her nerves and swiped the 'accept call' button. She cleared her throat. "Hello?"

"Yes, hello. We just spoke. You can come for dinner tonight."

"Uh, okay."

"Be there at eight," he ordered.

"Thank you. What is your na—" He disconnected before she could finish the question.

Uneasy she lay down once more. She hoped that the man's behavior wasn't a sign of how welcoming her grandfather would be that evening.

"*You should try to get some sleep,*" her mother said.

"I'll do that at the other hotel," Erin said. She grabbed her suitcase and left the room.

"*I hope you'll be able to have a proper rest there. You can't have a jet lag dulling your wits,*" Altman said. "*Maybe you can use some kind of sleeping spell.*"

"And risk not waking up before dinner? Besides, I may still need to walk there from the other hotel. Based on that desk clerk's attitude, I doubt that I can find a taxi to take me there."

"*I don't like how he acted when he saw Merenda's name on that list,*" Altman said. "*But don't worry. We'll be with you all the time.*"

She closed her eyes as goosebumps broke out over her skin. "*Thanks. Let's just hope that I won't need you.*"

FIVE

Erin's witchy roommate had finally left the building. Victor watched the brunette with the pixie haircut from the alley across the street. According to his schedule, she was running late. She should have left for Mrs. Beauchamps's place ten minutes ago. She suddenly stopped, her eyes locked on the back of a bald muscular man, who was wearing a blue shirt as he entered the supermarket. She appeared to be hesitating, and then she turned around.

Victor's heart hammered at the thought that he might have to postpone his plans once more. He had been stalking Erin and her friend for weeks, and his patience was nearing its limit. When he first began shadowing Erin, he had done so to record her during a werewolf transformation. When she rode her bike to the Hope Acres forest two weeks ago, he'd thought he'd finally gotten lucky. Only then she had shifted into a leopard. He kept the recording. The video could still complicate her life if he put it online, and he hadn't decided he wouldn't, but for now that was plan B.

He exhaled with relief when Pauline didn't go

back to her apartment but walked on. Curious to find out who it was that she was avoiding, he waited for the man to leave the shop.

He gasped when he saw the face of the man Pauline had been trying to avoid. Recognition sang within him, and he cheered. "Of course you don't want to draw Billy's attention." It had to mean that the witch hadn't managed to get rid of Erin's werewolf. She had to be afraid that Billy would be able to detect her deception and reveal it to the other werewolves. Victor never believed that Erin got rid of her werewolf using magic. If a spell could really cure people from the curse, then this would be common knowledge in his circles. Of course, because of Erin and her roommate, he no longer had any circles to be part of. He clenched his fists, trying to control his anger. He needed to be calm when he broke into Erin's apartment.

He waited until he could no longer see Billy before he made his move. He crossed the street and entered the building with confidence. He had been in the building before, pretending to deliver mail, so he already knew which floor Erin's apartment was on.

When he stood in front of her apartment, he took out his lock picking kit, but before he used his tools he tried turning the doorknob. It was locked. As a private investigator, Victor occasionally had to break into the places of the people he had to spy on, and it surprised him how often they forgot to lock their doors. He remembered the last time Erin had forgotten to lock her door. He had entered her room to find her naked and tied to the bed. His body stirred at the memory of her exposed body, and he pushed the image back. *Focus*.

It took him less than thirty seconds to unlock the door. As soon as he entered the room, he took a deep breath. He could detect lingering traces of Erin's scent, and it drove him a little crazy. He growled. Last month, when he found out that Erin was a werewolf, he had immediately wanted to claim her as his mate. He had given her a little bit of time to get used to the idea because she had been in a relationship with Dane Lynch then, but he'd had no doubt that she would accept his offer. Female werewolves were rare because of the brutal transformation that most men didn't even survive. His cousin's pack only had three female werewolves. Those who weren't mated to a werewolf got passed around in the pack, and Victor had kindly offered to save her from that ordeal.

He had been working for Jonathan Stratton, and he had to put Erin through his sadistic tests to show him how she would respond. When he discovered she had been bit, he should have told his boss about her emerging werewolf, but instead he had decided to protect her. He had sabotaged Jonathan Stratton's final test, and the tycoon had been furious. Victor had to go into hiding at his pack to avoid Stratton's retaliation, but knowing that Erin would be his price, he had thought having Stratton as an enemy would be worth it.

He snickered, deriding his gentlemanly behavior. He thought about the moment he had saved Erin's life when he had found her asleep, naked in the snow, nearly frozen to death. He had shared his body heat with hers without taking advantage.

He now wished he had. He had introduced her to Crispin as his mate, only to have her call him a liar. When he had tried to show Crispin her wolf, she had shifted to her leopard form instead, and Crispin had sent his entire pack after him to tear him apart. Before Erin, he had held a high position in Crispin's pack. Because of Erin he was now considered a rogue werewolf—one without a pack. He saw a picture of Erin and Pauline next to their television, smiling as if they didn't have a care in the world, and he longed to smash it.

Focus, he thought again. He opened a cabinet and saw dishes and cooking pans. The next cabinet had glasses and plastic bins. Instead of continuing to search blindly, he decided to engage his heightened senses. His nose picked up the fragrance of herbs and scented candles, and he tracked down the source of the smell. It led him to the witch's bedroom.

He jumped back when a fat orange cat leapt up from the bed and hissed at him before running out of the room.

After cursing at the ferocious feline for making him jump, he opened the drawer beside the bed. It was filled with candles, herbs, incense and dried flowers. He recognized a familiar-looking purple flower shaped like a helmet. Monkshood. It could be used as poison to kill wolves. He grabbed his phone and took a picture of the flower. It was a sign that they were trying to kill the werewolf, but it wasn't very convincing evidence because they would probably accuse him of planting the flower to incriminate them. Beneath the candles, he saw a notebook. He opened it. The first page listed a spell for gaining confidence. With his heart pounding, he turned the page. Adrenaline pumped through his veins when he realized he had found the evidence he'd been searching for.

"Bingo," he said with a big grin. He put the spell book on the bed and took several pictures. It said the following:

"*With eucalyptus, myrrh and wolfsbane times three,*
No longer shall others sense a part of me,
We seek to hide,
The wolf inside,
No one will smell,
The wolf with this spell,
No one will touch the werewolf's fur,
Instead they will hear the leopard purr,
The werewolf's taste will be concealed.
When called upon, a cat will be revealed.
This cloak will not be lifted,
Into a werewolf will I never be shifted,
Not even silver can tell,
What's been hidden so well,
Hide the wolf, hear my plea,
As is my will so mote it be."

He didn't want to take the evidence with him because it would alarm Erin and Pauline, and he preferred to surprise them. He took some pictures of other spells they had done, so Crispin could compare the handwriting. Then he put the notebook back in the drawer. *How dumb are those bitches that they kept the evidence?* Frowning, he rubbed the back of his neck. *It just doesn't make sense. Unless… they need to repeat it. Maybe the spell only temporarily hides the wolf.* Wicked delight ran through Victor's mind as he again concluded that the witch hadn't really been able to get rid of Erin's werewolf.

He then moved to what had to be Erin's bedroom. He inhaled deeply, and her lingering fragrance smelled good enough to eat. He almost wished she were there, so he could take a bite. He pictured pinning Erin beneath him right there, forcing her thighs open wide to accept him. He would show her the spell he found, and she would beg him to become her mate. Maybe he shouldn't accept it, so she could be humiliated by the pack this time. But he still wanted her, and he hated sharing. As his mate, she would be his, and he'd have the freedom to do whatever he wanted to her. She would do anything… A feral emotion took over, and he felt the wolf pushing under his skin. He took a few steadying breaths and fought to get a grip on his wolf. *Focus.*

It took several minutes, but he finally managed to relax enough for him to check a couple of boxes. He couldn't find anything incriminating in them. He had hoped to find more spells—especially one to mask your scent. He knew that she had to have been the one who killed his asshole half-brother Quentin last month, because she was the only person at Stratton's team building event who was animalistic enough to tear open someone's throat while still powerful enough to use magic that would not leave any scent behind. Another secret he hadn't shared with anyone. No more. *Ungrateful bitch.* Helping Erin had only brought him misery.

But he knew all of her secrets now.

"Erin, I can't wait to expose you," he said softly.

It was tempting for Victor to just pull the door shut behind him and leave the building, but he worried that it would alarm Pauline if she discovered the door unlocked. Fortunately, he could also lock the door in sixty seconds using his special tools. He was about to pick the lock for a second time when he heard someone walking up the stairs. He immediately moved away from the door and walked toward the exit when he heard someone say, "Hey, I know you."

Victor glared at the stranger, a man that he was convinced he had never met before. The man smelled like a corpse, and he looked as if he hadn't washed himself for weeks. His armpits had sweat stains, and he had soiled his baggy trousers with what appeared to be oil. The messy man flashed him a wicked smile, baring rotten teeth. "Yes, I know who you are."

"No, you don't," Victor growled. "Trust me, you don't want to know me."

The man licked his lips as he assessed him. "Oh, yes I do. I love the rage vibe you've got going on."

"And what if I directed that rage toward you. Would you still love it?" Victor asked. He considered grasping the man's throat and choking him, but he didn't want to dirty his hands.

A smug smile appeared on the disgusting man's face. "You could try, but then maybe I wouldn't be so inclined to help you."

"Who are you?"

The man bowed his head. "My name is Ramin Sceledorse. Enchanté."

"I don't know who you are, and I don't care." Victor decided to risk keeping the apartment unlocked and walked past the man.

"I think we both want to teach Erin a lesson," Ramin said.

Victor froze and studied the man. "Why would you want to do that?"

Ramin smirked. "Ah, so that got your attention. I thought it might."

Victor's teeth clenched. *This guy is mocking me.* "Start talking."

"Ooh, are you trying to frighten me?" Ramin laughed. "Let's just say that Erin used me, and when I proposed a partnership, she didn't take me up on the offer."

Suspicion narrowed Victor's eyes. This sounded a little too similar to his own experience with Erin. "What makes you think that I would be interested in teaching her a lesson?"

"Well, that's her apartment you just broke into, isn't it?" Ramin walked toward the door of the apartment and held his hand over the doorknob. Victor's werewolf hearing picked up a clicking sound.

"Did you just lock the door?"

Ramin grinned. "Ah, yes. One of the perks of being a very powerful demon."

"And how did you know about me?"

"I spent some time in Erin's mind when she wanted me to get rid of some evidence. Gideon told me that she had killed someone in my name, but that was a lie. I still helped her because I am a nice demon, and her mind is such a fascinating place. She has so much power and so many secrets."

Victor recognized with an instant of clarity whom the demon was referring to. "Was that when she killed Quentin?"

Ramin's tone was patronizing as he crooned, "Very good. Well done. So, you see that she used us both."

"And how do you think you can help me? You don't even seem to be able to take a shower," Victor sneered.

"Ah yes, the downside of possessing those who call on me. I can't always choose whose body I get to possess, and if I stay in a body too long, it starts to fall apart. It's the stench of decaying flesh you smell."

"Well, I don't want you to possess me, so I think I'll do it alone. But thank you."

For a second the demon's eyes flashed black. "What if I could help you without possessing you?"

Victor wasn't sure he could trust Ramin. "I don't need your help. I already have evidence of her deception." He pointed at his phone.

"Pictures can be manipulated. The way you left the pack will mean that they will probably automatically delete anything you send them. No, what you need is physical evidence. You need her to transform into a werewolf in front of the pack."

Victor sighed. "I already tried that. I even cut myself to force her to shift. Blood always brings out the werewolf, but her spell protected her."

"But you didn't have me on your side. I'll help you get her to the pack, and I'll stop your pack mates from trying to tear you apart, like last time. What you need is bait. I'll help you get bait. And don't worry. I won't have control over you. You can look me up online. Ramin Sceledorse. I have quite a following, you know. Just call out my name after you have made your decision, and I'll help you trap her."

"And you'll help me trap her just because you want to teach her a lesson?" Victor asked again.

The demon nodded and brushed past him down the stairs. Victor followed him out the building. "Well, thanks for the help."

Ramin smiled with sadistic glee as he entered a taxi. "No thank you, Mr. Werewolf. It is entirely my pleasure."

Victor should be happy with the demon's assistance, but Ramin's expression as he drove off sent chills shivering up his spine. Still, he realized that the demon could be useful, and Ramin's words about helping Victor trap her created an image in his head that he couldn't wait to turn into reality.

SIX

Dane scowled as he scanned the small crowd in front of city hall. He had just finished a tiresome meeting with the city council that had questioned whether he and his team were abiding by the building regulations for the structure of the shopping mall he was constructing on the outskirts of New Orleans. He had thought dealing with work would distract him from his fixation on Erin, but instead he resented the time he had to spend at city hall while Erin could be fighting for her life in Haiti.

The municipality had received anonymous information stating that he and his team were trying to cut corners that could potentially risk people's lives. Just thinking about how his integrity had been put into question caused fury to burn inside him, and he had to suppress his instincts to use his vampiric powers of persuasion on the woman doubting his ethics. It was illegal for vampires to use their powers to enthrall humans, and he was usually calm enough to use logic to convince humans. These emotions were out-of-character for him. During the meeting he had kept an extremely calm and imperturbable façade, but the anger churning inside him didn't want to be denied.

TOUCHED BY EVIL

As he watched the demonstrators outside, he wondered if one of them had been responsible for the meeting. The official had shown him confidential papers that had the logo of his company and his signature, but Dane could prove that one of his letters had been altered slightly. Dane had shown the original letter from Maura's file, and when you looked carefully, you could spot the area where a piece of paper had been glued on top of the last sentence. The official believed him, but it surprised Dane that someone was suicidal enough to sabotage him. He had a reputation of burning his enemies to death. *Does someone think I won't retaliate?*

With his vampires catching a mysterious illness and Erin chasing her father in Haiti, this could not come at a worse time. The municipality's building department had already approved the plans for the structure, and they had begun building several months ago. Any delay would cost him money. For now, the officials were appeased, but he didn't want to have a repeat performance. As long as he didn't know who contacted the municipality, he would have to keep an eye on anyone who could have made a copy of that letter.

"Go away," a blond woman in her late forties said to him as he brushed past her.

He turned to her, quirking a brow. "Are you sure you want to do this?" Dane asked coolly.

The woman glanced away, and a man put his arm around her in support. "Leave my wife alone."

Dane crossed his arms over his chest and stared down at the humans. "Sure, if your wife would return the favor."

"Honey, let's go," the man said to his wife.

"His mall is going to put us out of business," the woman cried to her husband. She glared at Dane. "You'll ruin us. But we're not going down without a fight."

"So, you really want to do this?" Dane sneered, baring his lengthening fangs at the couple.

The woman began to shake, clutching her husband's arm. Dane could tell he intimidated the man too, yet the husband didn't want to lose face in front of his wife. "She's afraid we won't be able to continue with our butcher's shop so close to your mall. The bakery has the same problem."

"Just how far are you willing to go to keep your business?" Dane snapped.

The butcher eyed him warily. "We protest?" He pointed at the sign he was holding that said, "Don't let the mall kill small businesses."

Dane took hold of his self-control. He doubted that these humans were responsible for the sabotage, and the real battle he sought to fight was the one where the outcome would be his complete possession of Erin. Her not having accepted their relationship caused a constant restlessness inside him these days. "Don't make me your enemy," he warned before he walked away toward his black SUV.

Dane climbed into the vehicle and sat behind the steering wheel before he slammed the driver's door shut. He was done with distractions. He checked departure times for planes from New Orleans to Haiti on his phone. As a vampire, he could only take flights to Haiti that would fly during nighttime and arrive before the sun would rise. It turned out that there were no direct flights to Port-au-Prince, and he would need to get there during the day. He called his second-in-command.

"Brock, could you please charter a private jet?"

"Ah, a romantic trip. Yes, of course. Where to?" Brock asked. "Paris? Rome?"

"Haiti," Dane said. "And I need to get there as soon as possible."

"Haiti? Isn't that where Erin's father is from?" The alarm in Brock's voice was clear.

"I don't want to discuss it," he said in a tone that brooked no argument.

"At least take me with you. We can't lose you!"

Dane's lips curved in a grim smile. "Thanks. Are you worried you might have to take my place as the next master vampire of Hope Acres?"

"Don't even joke about that! I'm still getting the hang of being the second-in-command after Rafferty got killed."

"You're doing great. Honestly, I would have liked your help in Haiti, but I need you here. With Eve and Maura's mysterious illness, we're too vulnerable right now."

"Okay, well I'm sure that if I throw in extra cash, I can get you a private flight tomorrow evening at the earliest time available."

"Throw in all the cash you need," he said.

If Erin was fine, she may resent his presence in Haiti. He didn't know if it was her refusal to act like a blood slave or the fact that she might be risking her life, but his sense of dread had grown little by little throughout the evening.

I should have locked her up. She thinks I'm a

control freak. I'll show her a control freak, he vowed.

SEVEN

Erin was melting. Her breathing came out in short, shaky puffs. She was used to warm, humid weather because of Hope Acres' sub-tropical climate, but there she didn't have to hike for over two hours in the steamy humidity.

When she left her new hotel, the sun had been up, burning her uncovered arms, legs and head. Now that it was dark, swarms of mosquitoes had tracked her down, eating those uncovered limbs alive.

Great. I'll be meeting my grandfather with my face streaked with sweat and covered in mosquito bites.

She was walking with her cell phone and a nearly empty water bottle in her hands. She was thirsty, but she hoped she could contain herself to use the remaining three sips to freshen up before she would be introduced to her grandfather. During her walk, the thought struck her that she should have brought him a gift. She supposed that not bringing explosives to his house might be considered a gift, but that was not information she wanted to share with him.

She had left her suitcase containing her clothes and toiletries at the hotel, but she didn't trust the people from the hotel not to steal her wallet and passport, so she had put those in the pockets of her denim shorts together with the gris gris that Pauline had given her for protection.

As she passed a ramshackle bar, which had a neon sign for Budweiser in the window, a muscular man with skin like milk chocolate stepped out of the building. He lifted his phone out of the back pocket of his black jeans before he glanced up and noticed her. He frowned as he studied her for a moment, and then he waved to gain her attention as she drew closer.

"Ou se yon bel fanm!" he said. When she smiled and shook her head, he explained, "You're beautiful! Beautiful women should not be walking alone. I will you call you a taxi, wi?" There was a genuine kindness in his eyes.

"Thanks, that's very nice, but I think I'm almost there. Petit Espoir should be nearby," she said. "Thank God!"

Her smile faded at the man's horrified expression. "Don't thank God! It's an evil place," he warned. "Petit Espoir should be called Pas d'Espoir. No Hope."

She licked her lips and swallowed audibly. "Why?"

The friendly man merely shook his head and moved on.

At first, her mind was consumed with worry that Petit Espoir had such a bad reputation. Then comprehension dawned on Erin that espoir meant hope, and she wondered if the name of her father's hometown had been the reason why he had chosen to settle in Hope Acres. *Maybe I'm too sentimental.*

TOUCHED BY EVIL

According to Margot's map, she had to be close. She passed more houses, but the street was deserted, and then she saw the sign for 'Petit Espoir'. She expelled a long breath, feeling the mixture of anticipation and fear that always filled her right before a battle—even though she hoped that tonight's encounter would be peaceful. *Maybe Leila was right about our grandfather taking out our father. Then tonight will just be an opportunity to find out more about my family.*

She turned around the corner, and the formidable church of Petit Espoir loomed over her like a temple of malevolent dark stone. She checked her watch. She was ten minutes early. She let down her curly hair, wanting to look nice for her grandfather. Then she washed her face and arms using the remaining water in the bottle. In vain, she looked for a trashcan. It also gave her an excuse to walk around the building, trying to find other ways of entry or exit. The green gate was the only entrance. She estimated that the robust stonewall around the church was at least fifteen feet tall. On top, she spotted barbed wire. *Is it to keep people out or to keep people in?*

There were four houses overlooking the church, but she couldn't see that there was anyone inside. There was no light and no sound. She couldn't even hear sound coming from the church even though her hearing was usually sensitive enough detect even the smallest possible noise. *Where are the birdcalls? Has he soundproofed his church, or used some voodoo spell to hide any sound? What kind of sounds would he want to hide?*

She told herself she was acting silly and

becoming a little paranoid. "Crazy," she muttered, adding a chuckle when nothing silenced her words. Something rustled above her, and she peered up to see a yellow bird flying by, flapping its wings. *See, it's all in my head.* She sucked in her breath as she reached out and pressed the intercom button at the entrance. *The moment of truth.*

Within seconds there was a buzzing sound, and the door sprang open. She hesitated.

"Not even a friendly bonsoir?" Altman said.

"Maybe he's preparing a surprise. I did arrive early," Erin said. "Don't grandparents like to spoil their grandchildren?" That Leila and Gideon didn't tease her, made her think that they might be worried too.

Her breath hitched as she walked through the entrance, jumping slightly when the gate automatically closed behind her.

The front door opened, and whatever she was expecting, the athletic, military-looking man with skin and hair paler than hers, wasn't it. His skin was like fine porcelain, and even his eyelashes were white. He seemed familiar, but Erin couldn't place him. Her mouth opened, but nothing came out. While she walked toward him, he studied her with an intensity that made her uncomfortable.

"Oh no, Sabas," her mother said.

"Oh hell, I can't stand him," Leila said.

"Ah yes. I remember him from the ritual," Altman said.

Sabas wore glasses, and his eyeballs moved with rapid involuntary movements. "Erin," he said, his voice soft. "You've grown up to look just like your mother."

"Do I know you?" Erin asked.

"Yes, my name is Sabas. I used to live with you in Hope Acres," he said before turning around. "Please follow me." It was cool inside the church, but she couldn't hear the air conditioner. Her footsteps echoed on the tile floor of the hallway while Sabas' step was light, almost silent in spite of his thick army boots. The walls were painted in yellow and red colors. *It would look homely,* Erin thought, *if it weren't for the large mirror decorated with angry-looking masks, snakes, crosses and skulls.*

"It's a bad sign he's here. He used to work for your father," Erin's mother said. *"It could mean that Oliver is still around."*

Erin cleared her throat. "Is my dad here?"

They passed the abandoned place of worship, where she spotted about a dozen pews and illuminated stained glass windows with bright colors. She thought she recognized Jesus and was interested in taking a closer look, but Sabas moved on. He took her to a large living room where a statue of a naked devil with twelve angry eyes was watching her. Against the walls, glass cabinets held skulls, statues and ceremonial drums.

"Please have a seat," Sabas said. He left the room before Erin could repeat her question.

She sat down on the leather sofa and glared at the devil statue.

"Love what they've done with the place," Gideon said.

"Ah, there she is! Pitit pitit fi mwen," a deep voice bellowed. "Akeyi!"

She turned her head to see two men enter the room. One was Sabas, and he held the arm of the second man—a thin black man with gray hair, a mustache and golden eyes, who she suspected was her grandfather.

"Let me look at you," he demanded.

She got up and faced him. His authoritative tone seemed contradictory to his frail physique. It surprised her to see him wearing glasses too. *If he's so powerful, shouldn't he have given himself perfect eyesight?*

He stopped in front of her, and Sabas let go, giving them some space.

"You got my eyes," her grandfather said. He put his hands on her shoulders and kissed her forehead. There was a lump in her throat, and her face warmed.

"Hi, it's a pleasure to meet you," she said, feeling shy.

"Please, call me Granpè. It's good to see you looking so healthy now."

She raised her eyebrows in confusion. "Now?"

He looked away. "I'm sorry. I didn't mean to bring up the sad past. Let's have dinner. Sabas prepared us some local dishes, so you can get a taste of your heritage."

He held out a plate with some baked pastries. "Pate Ayisyen,"

She picked one up while repeating the name of the dish, and her grandfather rewarded her with a large smile.

"Perfect. If you stay here long enough, you will become a proper Haitian." He took a handful of patties and jammed them into his mouth before closing his eyes in rapture. He acted ravenous, and a smile curved her lips as she turned to Sabas. She was imagining him to smile at her in return, but Sabas was watching her grandfather with an expression that could only be described as annoyed. Their eyes met, and then his expression became suspiciously blank.

She took a bite of her pastry, and while she enjoyed the flaky dough filled with meat, she wasn't going to devour it like her grandfather. When he caught her gaze, a faint blush stole up his cheeks. "It's been a while since I had these."

"They're lovely," Erin said politely. "I go nuts over beignets from Café du Monde—not that you're going nuts." Now she felt *her* cheeks heating up.

"Do you want to be seated now, Bokor Merenda?"

Hearing Sabas address her grandfather by his official title caused Erin's mood to change instantly, and silently, she thanked Sabas for the reminder. Her grandfather nodded, and he led her to the dining room.

"So, when did you arrive in Haiti?" he asked.

"I got here this morning," she said. "I got a direct flight from Las Vegas."

"Las Vegas? And immediately you came here to see us, we're honored! But why didn't you visit us before?"

Us? Does he mean Sabas or someone else? "Uh, I didn't know you existed."

Her grandfather's eyes narrowed. "So how did you find out?"

Her pulse quickened. This question she had hoped to avoid. Before she could answer, he continued with a follow up question, "Did the ghosts tell you?"

She gasped in shock while Sabas put a rice dish in front of her. "Riz National with red snapper," Sabas said. She automatically thanked him as the mouthwatering scent wafted from her plate, but fear invaded her mind. *How does he know?* She didn't want to tell her grandfather about her powers and the ghosts linked to her. She thought about Leila's comment that their grandfather had been the one to teach their father how to absorb power from others.

"It looks like the cat is already out of the bag, Erin," Leila's voice echoed in her mind.

No, Erin decided. She first had to know how much he knew. "The ghosts?"

"Yes," he said as he began to eat. He pointed at her food. "Please dig in. You don't want it to get cold. And yes, I know that you hear voices. When I collected your father all those years ago, he told me that the ritual had gone wrong."

"Why didn't you take me too?" she asked in a soft voice that was hoarse with emotion.

"I believed you were dying. You had a sword in your chest and were bleeding out. It was only after we left Hope Acres that I read about your survival. I paid a detective to track you down and found out diplomats adopted you and took you to England. I thought you deserved a second chance in a new country with a family that didn't try to kill their children."

"Uh, okay. Thank you." She picked up her silverware and began to eat too. It was delicious but spicy, and she drank her glass of water all the way straight down.

"A couple of years went by, and I was curious to see how you were, so I contacted the detective to give me an update. It was then that I found out that they had put you in a mental hospital because of the voices."

"So, you know," she whispered, blinking back tears of shame.

"I know," he said, a hint of regret simmering in the depths of his eyes. "Unfortunately, not everyone in our family handles power well. My mother spent some time locked away too, and my wife... My wife killed herself."

"I'm so sorry."

He shrugged and waved his hand. "It is what it is. I didn't go to your hospital because I thought healthcare in England would be better than here in Haiti. I assumed that you were still there, so I'm glad that they let you out. It must mean that you're able to function in the real world. You seem to handle the power well. So, did the voices tell you about me?"

"Uh, actually my boss, Jonathan Stratton mentioned it. I didn't know I had a grandfather in Haiti until he told me. He wanted me to come here to find out what had happened to my dad."

"Jonathan Stratton, the tycoon?" When she nodded, he asked, "Why would he want to know what happened to my son?"

She swallowed. "My dad had invited Jonathan Stratton to join the ritual that night, promising him power. When Stratton couldn't make it, my dad decided to use the vampire Altman as his replacement. Stratton later found out what my father's intentions had been, and Stratton sent me here to find out if you had held him accountable for his actions."

He speared two large chunks of fish at once, chewing them while asking, "Really? After all this time?"

She cringed. "Yes. I think he's obsessed."

He tapped his chin with his finger and studied her with a thoughtful expression. "And after you find out what happened to him, what are you supposed to do then?"

Blow him up, she thought. "Contact Stratton and let him know."

"Hmmm."

She waited for him to explain what had occurred to her father after he had collected him, but her grandfather didn't seem to want to share that information.

Sabas put a creamy off-white beverage in front of her. "I made you Kremas, a Haitian celebration drink."

"Thanks, but if there's any alcohol, I'll pass. It's quite a long trip to go back to the hotel," she said.

"Go back to the hotel? Of course not!" her grandfather snapped, slamming his fist onto the table. "We've prepared a room for you. My grandchild will not be staying at a hotel when we have enough room here."

"Uh, okay. Thank you." She took a sip and smiled at Sabas. "Nice. Coconut and cinnamon?"

"Also, Rhum Barbancourt," Sabas said. Erin wondered if she should ask him to sit down and have a drink with her, but she didn't want to offend her grandfather who seemed to prefer a more formal relationship with his employee.

"So, about your powers—how powerful are you?" her grandfather asked.

"What?" she asked before taking another sip of the Haitian drink.

"Well, you didn't deny that you had powers. So, what are they?"

"Why does he want to know this?" Altman asked. *"I don't think you should tell him."*

Her lids grew heavy, and she blinked a couple of times when the image of her grandfather swam in and out of focus. "I-I'm sorry. I guess I'm a bit more jetlagged than I thought."

"That's possible," he said. "But can you tell me more about what you can do?"

Erin tried to lift her cup, but she couldn't lift her arms. "Huh, strange," she mumbled.

"What's strange, Erin?" her grandfather asked.

"Are you okay?" Erin's mother asked.

She stifled a yawn. "T-tired," she muttered.

"Yes, drugs can do that to you," her grandfather said, the deep voice lightly mocking.

Her heart sank. "D-drugs?" she stammered.

"Yes, there's someone here that I'm sure you'd like to see."

She had a moment of sheer panic. Adrenaline surged, and she tried to get up but the ground under her feet shifted.

"Fuck. You need to get the hell out of there," Altman said.

Erin put her palms on the table for balance, and she swayed as a second wave of dizziness overtook her.

"*Maybe we should call on my demon friend Ramin for help,*" Gideon suggested.

"*Shut up, Gideon! I'll do it. They want to see what she can do, I can show them,*" Altman said.

"*But what if voodoo magic is more powerful?*" Leila warned. "*Wouldn't it be better if she shifts into a leopard?*"

Too weak to hold herself up, Erin collapsed on the table. She couldn't even move her arms to break her fall.

"*They have weapons hanging on the wall. The shift to leopard takes too much time. They expect her to be unconscious, and my attack should come as a surprise. They shouldn't have any defense in place once I use my voice to mesmerize. Also, your leopard is unpredictable, and she can't turn doorknobs,*" Altman said. "*But if I mess up, please try to tear their throats out, Leila.*"

Hurry Altman, Erin thought, as her vision grew blurry.

"*She should have kept the explosives,*" Gideon complained. Those were the last words Erin heard before she succumbed to sleep.

When Altman heard the whispers in a foreign language, he suppressed his desire to open his eyes and check what was happening. He didn't want to risk Emanuel Merenda and Sabas, his albino lackey, finding out that passed-out Erin wasn't as helpless as she appeared. He tried to use his other senses—or rather Erin's other senses. Erin's forehead was touching a hard surface with some fabric on top of it, which he assumed was a tablecloth. He could smell the delicious dinner Erin had eaten seconds before becoming unconscious as if the plate was right next to him. They didn't seem to have moved her.

It was an unusual feeling for him to have a body again. It had been many years since he'd had the freedom to flex his muscles or feel something touching his skin, even if it wasn't really his skin. In more recent years, he had only taken over Erin's body once after Gideon's spell had allowed them to take over her body. At that time, his possession had been to save her from her psychiatrist's twisted experiments. Despite the opportunity possessing her body gave him to experience sensations he had long forgotten—right now his mouth watered imagining what it would be like to take a bite from that dish—he couldn't wait to leave it. It was so intimate that it felt like it was a violation of sorts. He had seen Erin grow up and imagined himself as her guardian angel, watching over her. He didn't want to find any pleasure while he was using her body. There were enough people trying to use her.

He worried about when he should try to escape. He needed them to be off their guard, and the longer he waited, the more likely it was for them to expect that Erin would wake up. The ideal situation would be if Sabas and Emanuel Merenda left the dining room, so he could sneak out, take a car and fly back to the US.

Erin never should have let Stratton bully her into going to Haiti. Dane would have helped her with

Stratton. She should forget about Stratton's secretary, and think about herself for a change. Let Margot Sloane fight her own battles.

Suddenly, someone grabbed his shoulders from behind and pushed him backward. It was hard not to tense up and even more difficult to keep his eyes closed, but he believed he had fooled them when someone lifted Erin's body up. Her feet left the floor as she was tossed over someone's shoulder like a sack of flour with her head hanging upside down. He heard Erin's wallet and passport fall to the ground. This time he couldn't resist a tiny peek, and he recognized Sabas' black shirt and jeans. Each step was agony due to Sabas' shoulder pushing against his stomach. The awkward position and near-crushing hold, made it hard for Altman to breathe. He closed his eyes and swallowed back the rising nausea.

"Altman, do something," he heard Ann say. *"You can't let them take my daughter to a second location."*

How am I supposed to mesmerize them while hanging upside down?

Altman heard Sabas opening a door, and a draft rushed through the hallway as Sabas started going downstairs. The sound of his footsteps bounced off the walls, and he heard Emanuel Merenda's stumbling steps trailing close behind.

When they reached the bottom of the stairs, Sabas lay him down on the ground. Sabas said something in Haitian Creole, and Altman sensed that there was some kind of disagreement due to the sharp tone of his voice. The position they put him in wasn't very comfortable. Instead of having his upper body lean against the wall, they put him against bars. *A cage?* He couldn't risk getting trapped in there. He took a deep breath, calling on his power to enthrall and opened his eyes.

"Atansyon!" Sabas cried out.

Altman locked his gaze with theirs. "You both want to help me." He made Erin's voice sound seductive, deeper, and almost purring as he rose.

"You want to help me leave this house. You will get me transportation to leave Haiti." Altman saw their eyelids fluttering, but they continued to stare at him, unable to look away as he controlled their minds.

He didn't have a lot of experience mesmerizing more than one person at the same time and preferred to control only one mind. Based on their appearance, he would have expected Sabas to be more powerful. However, due to the warnings about the bokor, he chose to treat Erin's grandfather as the one who might be able to break his hold. Altman stepped away from the bars and said, "Sabas, you will open the cell." He turned to look inside before stumbling backward and gasping in horror.

He recognized the muscular man who was lying unconscious on a cot inside the cell while wearing iron manacles on his wrists and ankles that were nailed to the wall next to him. It was Oliver Merenda. Upon closer inspection of the cell, Altman noticed a second cot with two sets of manacles chained to the wall. *For Erin?* There was a stone altar with intimidating symbols and a throne-like chair beside it, facing the wall that had French spells written in blood on it. The table was large enough to hold Oliver

Merenda's body. Erin's father was a big man, tall and broad-shouldered, but his black skin had paled, and he was shaking underneath a thin blanket that barely covered him. Pain pinched his closed eyes.

Altman quickly checked if he still had control over Sabas and his employer. They both had a vacant look, but Emanuel Merenda's eyes were twitching, signaling he was coming out of the trance, and Altman realized that he couldn't let himself be distracted.

"Sabas, open the cell," he repeated. "Emanuel, you want to enter the cage. Join your son."

Sabas held his hand over the lock, murmuring a couple of sentences in Haitian Creole. The lights wavered. Little electric sparks sizzled from his hands until the energy exploded in a loud bang, lifting the dark curse. Sabas took out a key from his pocket and unlocked it. The casual use of magic sent alarm shrieking through Altman, and he worried that being around all this black magic could break his hold.

"Emanuel, you want to enter this cell now. Be with your son," Altman said. It surprised him that he followed the instruction. *Wouldn't a powerful bokor carry some kind of protection against magic, or wasn't he that powerful?*

He suspiciously eyed Oliver Merenda. He was obviously unwell, but Altman didn't dare enter the cell to check on him. The place was giving off dangerous vibes, and he didn't want to linger. He also wasn't feeling too much sympathy for the man who had stolen his eternal life.

Should I order Emanuel Merenda to kill his son? It might be an evil thing to do, and Erin might resent me for using her voice to order it, but she will be safe then.

"Sabas, you will give me the key of the cell and will enter the cell too." Sabas did as instructed and Altman's hands shook as he locked the door. The air around the prison cell door started to thrum as if the dark magic was automatically turned back on. Cold fear slithered up his spine.

"*What are you standing there for?*" Gideon asked. "*Order them to kill each other.*"

"*I agree. It's not murder. It's self-defense,*" Leila said.

"Ann?" Altman asked.

"*Just do it. If not, there will always be this uncertainty that they may come after her. Hopefully, Stratton will leave Erin alone once he knows her father is dead,*" Erin's mother said.

"You want to kill each other. You like the power you feel when life slips away," he said softly using his mesmerizing talent once more while keeping eye contact with the two men.

For a second nothing happened after he said the words, but then power hit him with an excruciating blow, throwing him back with such a force that he fell back onto the stone ground. His breath slammed out of his lungs, and a rush of panic filled him. He opened his eyes. Everything swam in and out of focus while he was gulping in breaths. *The cell wards off my vampiric power,* he concluded. *I need to get the hell out.*

He sat up and winced at the sharp pain slicing through him. Erin's grandfather and Sabas were both blinking rapidly. Sabas was already looking around him as he came out of the trance.

Altman got up and rushed up the stairs. He was about to close the door to the basement behind him, when he heard Sabas cry out, "Erin!" Fear made a lump form in his throat that he had to swallow down. *What if their black magic will set them free?*

He kept the key from the cell in his hand and picked up Erin's wallet and passport from the dining room floor. The cell phone was still lying on the table beside the plate of her unfinished meal. He needed transportation to get to the airport, but he couldn't see any car keys lying around.

"*Come on, what are you waiting for?*" Gideon asked.

"I need keys. They must have a car around here somewhere," Altman yelled.

"*Maybe it's with the car. It's not like people would dare to steal from a bokor,*" Ann said.

"Good point. So, where's the car?" He ran outside and searched the garden around the church. He found a motorcycle with a key. "Thank God!"

"*Uh, guys. The gate is locked. How are we supposed to get out?*" Leila asked.

"*By using magic!*" Erin's mom said. "*We can even use the simple spell Erin created when she tried to escape the psychiatric hospital. Altman, just hold your hand in front of the gate.*"

He nervously cleared his throat. "What if it backfires like when I tried to mesmerize Emanuel and Sabas?"

"*Then it backfires. We must try,*" Ann said. "*And we must hurry up.*"

Altman started the ignition and dragged the

motorcycle to the gate. His hand shook as he held it in front of the lock while waiting for Ann to recite the spell,

"Powers That Be,
Please unlock this door for me,
As is my will so mote it be."

He felt the magic burst from Erin's hands and expelled a sigh of relief when he heard a familiar buzzing sound, followed by the gate opening. He jumped on the motorcycle. It had been many years since he'd driven one, but he remembered the thrill of freedom as he drove away.

"Freedom," he said as he cast one last look at Emanuel Merenda's silent church. *Hopefully, Erin will remain free and not have her relatives hunt her down to finish whatever ritual they intended to perform on her tonight.*

EIGHT

"*rin?*" Altman's deep voice invaded her sleep. She struggled to suppress the haze that engulfed her. Consciousness came slowly. Erin groaned at the half-memory of getting drugged by her grandfather and his helper Sabas. Panic rose in her chest, and suddenly she could barely breathe. *Are we still there? Please tell me we got out*, she thought. With her heart racing, she cracked open her eyes to find herself sitting on a hard bench at what she assumed was the Port-au-Prince airport. She noticed some people mopping the shiny white floor. But other than that, the shops were closed, and the airport appeared to be nearly deserted. "We made it, didn't we?" Erin asked.

"*Well, we got away. But as long as we're still in Haiti, we're not out of the woods yet,*" Altman said. "*I locked everyone in some kind of cell in the basement, but I wouldn't be surprised if they got out and are in hot pursuit. Especially now that they've seen you in action.*"

"So, they could be here?" she asked, jumping out of her chair. She winced at how stiff and sore she felt. "Good grief, how long have I been sitting there?"

"*For about five minutes, but you were out for three hours,*" Altman said.

She fidgeted slightly as she walked up to the window that overlooked the runway. She curled her arms protectively around herself in a nervous effort to draw comfort. "Do you know why they drugged me?"

"*They didn't say, but it doesn't look good. Sabas carried you to some kind of cell that was downstairs in a dungeon,*" Altman said.

Incredulous, Erin asked, "They were going to lock me up in a dungeon?"

"*Well, we don't know if they wanted to lock you up...*"

Shaking her head, "Why else would they drug me and take me to a cell?"

"*Well, maybe it was about, uh... them wanting you to meet someone... someone who was already locked up in the dungeon,*" Altman said hesitantly.

"Someone else was already locked up in the cell?" she whispered. "Who was in the dungeon?"

"*You already know,*" Altman replied.

"My grandfather locked up my dad in there?" She couldn't hide the dejected note of her voice. "That's crazy! Has he kept my father in there all this time? Twenty years?"

"*Honey... Altman, maybe she doesn't need to know all the particulars,*" her mother said.

Erin walked away from the windows and sat down again. "Maybe my granddad couldn't kill his own son, so he locked him up instead... to stop him from hurting others."

"*There she goes again, romanticizing people,*" Gideon complained. "*Come on Erin, you're*

114

forgetting he drugged you! People warned you about his place. He's obviously not a nice guy."

"Shut up, Gideon!" Altman snapped. *"There's no need to be harsh with her."*

Her throat closed up. "No guys. Gideon is right. If my grandfather wants to h-hurt me, I need to know."

"See, she doesn't mind," Gideon said. *"Do you want to tell her about the altar and the words on the wall, or shall I? And they did have another set of manacles chained to the wall. They had to have been for her, right? I mean, I didn't see anyone else in there."*

"Gideon, you're such an asshole," Altman said. *"Is that because you're a warlock, or is this just you? Show some fucking compassion! Just because she says she doesn't mind, doesn't make it okay to bludgeon her to death with the truth!"*

She lied. She did mind. Tears of frustration pricked her eyelids. *Why can't I have a normal father and a normal grandfather who love me? Am I so unlovable?* She thought about the Johanssons who had taken her in and then put her into the mental hospital when the voices in her head had become a problem. "I am a problem," she murmured, her chest tight.

A small group of people in uniform passed her. Two of them were women, who watched her with inquisitive eyes while following a man who ran as if he was late for his plane.

Erin squinted at the TV screen ahead of her, trying to read the departing flights displayed upon it. It was ten thirty at night, and the next flight was scheduled for seven o'clock in the morning.

"Oh God, I have to wait for eight hours until I can l-leave! What if they show up before? They know I'm here!" she cried out, her voice trembling. After being harmed by her grandfather, her father and her adoptive family, it was all becoming too much for her. She was exhausted and scared, and she couldn't hold back the pain building in her throat anymore. Persistent tears blurred her eyes, and she held a hand to her mouth, but she was unable to silence the small sob that escaped.

The hair on the back of her neck rose, and she felt as if she was being watched. A chill ran up her spine. *Oh no, did they find me already?* Out of the corner of her eyes, she spied a familiar figure heading in her direction with a determined expression.

"Dane?" she whispered.

"Ah, yes, I forgot to mention," Altman said casually. *"He called while you were—"*

"Dane!" she repeated, louder this time. Happiness poured through her, a sensation that everything was going to be all right. *He came for me.*

She inhaled sharply as she jumped out of her seat and ran toward him. She stopped in front of him, drinking in the sight of his tall and muscular physique, delighting in the contrast of his midnight black hair and striking cobalt blue eyes that were a blaze of intensity. He looked away for a moment as if coming to grips with the emotion she saw so clearly in his eyes just seconds before. When he looked back at her, his expression had become guarded.

In her mind, she kicked herself, telling herself she had to remember how he had tricked her into making her his blood slave and how he had made her beg for help. She recalled their last conversation, and her fear that she was coming to rely on him too much. But as soon as he reached out, framing her face with shaky hands, she let go of that fear. *He cares. I'm not alone.*

She gave him a thankful smile. Leaning forward, he placed a light kiss on her lips, making her stomach flip. He broke off the kiss while pulling her against his body and wrapping his arms around her. She couldn't remember the last time she had received a hug, but his nurturing touch made her feel safe, and it devastated her at the same time. She finally let go of her defenses as his hands roamed soothingly over her back. Her shoulders shook with uncontrollable sobs, and she found herself tightly holding on to him. His strength surrounding her felt so wonderful as she breathed in his intoxicating, masculine scent.

"Shh," Dane whispered. She cried, leaning against him as he pressed her head against his shoulder. For once, he didn't make any demands and merely gave her what she needed. She had no idea how long he comforted her, but she eventually stopped crying. Her energy was depleted, and she was too exhausted to cry or even remember why she was crying.

He nuzzled her neck before slowly pulling away to study her tear-streaked face. "I want you to stop scaring me like this."

She smiled. She was certain that the smile started out weak and pathetic, but it got bigger with every minute that went by. "I want to stop being scared," she said hoarsely. "So, what's going to happen now?"

He swung her up into his arms, and he carried her to one of the gates. There were people watching them, but she didn't care. Fatigue made her eyelids feel as if they had lead weights tied to them. She let her head glide back against Dane's shoulder. His lips touched her hair, and she was lulled into sleep.

"Now, I'm taking you home," he said.

When Erin opened her eyes again, she found herself once more traveling in style. The private jet seemed even more luxurious than the one she'd used from Stratton. She was strapped into a spacious leather chair. She unfastened the seatbelt and glanced up to see Dane sitting opposite her. He watched her, his piercing blue eyes unblinking.

"Hey. How long was I out?" she asked.

"For about half an hour. How are you feeling?"

She was going to automatically answer that she was fine, but she paused to think about her response instead. "A little drained. I cried all over you, didn't I? I'm sorry."

The muscles in his jaw visibly clenched. Then he leaned forward. "Look at me. Altman told me what happened. Don't apologize for crying after finding out what your grandfather tried to do to you. I'm here for you. I want to be here for you. You're not alone."

She reached out and grabbed his hand. "Thanks."

"It was actually kind of creepy hearing Altman speak with your voice when I called, but I'm glad he took over your body to help you escape. Just remember that you don't only have your ghostly companions to rely on. You needed my help too. I know you told me not to come here, but nothing is more important than your safety. We're not going to fight over this anymore."

Erin didn't say anything. She had called him a control freak, but tonight she would have gladly let him take over her life. She was making such a big mess of it.

"Are you tired? I didn't put you down on the bed because you had to be buckled in during take-off but there's a bed if you want to take a nap."

She smirked. "To have you join me or to have you haunt my dreams again?"

He took a breath as if he was about to speak, but then he hesitated.

Before he could say anything, a flight attendant approached them. "Could I offer you anything to eat or drink?"

Erin withdrew her hand from his and accepted a glass with orange juice while continuing to hold Dane's gaze, challenging him.

After the woman left, he said, "If you prefer, you can also take a shower." He narrowed his eyes. "Maybe you need to cool off."

Her mouth went dry. "Or maybe I just need to blow off some steam."

He arched one black eyebrow upwards. "By arguing with me?"

She felt edgy and wanted him to lose his temper and take it out on her. Knowing she could push his buttons gave her a curious little thrill that tingled down the length of her spine. Tonight, she wanted to live dangerously.

A smile tugged at her mouth. "Maybe I'm just tired of you constantly invading my dreams. Maybe I don't want to play anymore." She held her breath, waiting for his response.

His eyes were gleaming, and his thoughts were unreadable. "Are you ready to stop running, Goldilocks? Does this mean you'll accept me?"

Tonight? Or forever? Uncertainty gripped her. Erin had a feeling that Dane was after her full surrender, and she lost her nerve. "Maybe I'll just have a shower instead."

He said nothing as she fled toward the bathroom. She was taking deep breaths and felt as if she had just run a marathon. She locked the door of the bathroom before changing her mind and switching it back to unlocked. She wasn't ready to tell Dane that she was giving in, but if she forgot to lock the bathroom door while she took a shower, and he decided to take a peek, that would be on him. *Oh, what the hell am I thinking? Am I even thinking?*

With her heart pounding, she slid open the glass door and turned on the water. While stripping, she imagined Dane entering the room and seducing her. The unbidden thrill made her body ache. *Maybe I do need to cool off.*

She hung her clothes over the edge of the bathroom sink, regretting not having a clean set of clothes to slip into afterward as stepped into the shower cabin. *Will he, or won't he?* She was scared he would come in, but also afraid that he would stay away. Conflicted, she turned her back to the door, allowing the warm water to soak into her long, blond hair. She stood there for at least a full minute, eyes closed as she let the strong stream from the showerhead block out any sound.

A draft on her buttocks alerted her that someone had opened the shower doors. It suddenly dawned on her that anyone on the plane could enter. She opened her eyes and was about to turn around when hands clamped around her shoulders, and she was held immobile.

"Actions speak louder than words, Goldilocks," he whispered seductively in her ear. He was naked too, and she felt his cock thick and hard, pressing against her buttocks.

She squirmed. "Actions?"

"Did you think I would not hear you locking the door before unlocking it?"

Her breath caught in her throat. *Stupid.* As a vampire, his hearing was superior too. He let go of her left shoulder and stroked his hand down her back until it touched her buttocks and stopped there. Sighing blissfully, she leaned her head back against his chest.

"You made your decision when you decided to unlock that door for me, but I want there to be no misunderstanding. I want you to say it."

Her pulse began to beat more quickly when she realized there was no avoiding it. *He is going to demand I give him everything.*

"But be careful," he warned as he moved his hand from her buttocks over her hips to her stomach and nuzzled her neck, "because I will hold you to it." The determination in his voice sent a shiver among her nerve endings.

She heard herself moan, imagining his teeth

piercing her skin and his hand moving a little lower—there where she needed it the most.

"After tonight, no more running. You're mine. Admit it." It was an order.

His heavy weight pressed her against the glass, and she put her hands up, her fingers forming fists against the cool door.

She closed her eyes tightly, finding it hard to focus on what he was saying, or maybe she preferred to ignore his words and to only listen to the burning hunger deep inside. Her breath came out in short hard pants.

"This is not just for tonight," he said. "Admit it, or I leave." He took away his hands. As soon as his body no longer touched hers, a strangled noise escaped her, and she turned around to face him. Electrical tension sparkled between them. His eyes showed her he meant it. It was blackmail, but she didn't want to fight him anymore. She didn't want to fight herself either. She was going to give him everything.

"Okay," she whispered.

He rewarded her with a soft kiss on her mouth. "Good. Now, let me take care of you." Relieved that her one-word of agreement sufficed, she was surprised—and slightly disappointed when he didn't pounce on her to finish the seduction. Instead, he opened a bottle of shampoo, poured some of the flowery liquid on his hands and began to work it into her hair.

She grinned, loving the way his strong fingers massaged her scalp. After rinsing it, he put shower gel on his hands. She went from relaxed and slightly aroused, to full on arousal as he started washing her shoulders with his bare hands. His strokes quickly slid down toward her breasts. He cupped them both at the same time, and she gasped, his touch sending a burn straight to her sex. Her hard and erect nipples pushed against the palms of his hands. He pinched one of them, and she let out a soft little cry. He bent his mouth to her breast, and she writhed against him as need clenched in her belly. His tongue curled around each nipple, and his fangs rubbed the areolas. There was a sharp stab when he nipped one of them. She gave a triumphant cry. The pleasure was so intense it hit her right between her legs. She clutched his wide shoulders to keep herself upright. He held her up too, using his right arm while the other moved down, brushing against her thigh.

Trembling under his touch, she pressed her legs together

"Your skin is so soft," he rasped, his voice thick with desire. His eyes studied her with a hunger that made her feel wanted in every way.

His left hand slid higher and higher up her thigh. "Are you ready Goldilocks?" His fingers grazed over the little bud at the apex of her sex, and her knees shook as one finger slid between the folds. She parted her thighs to let his finger thrust in and out of her while he kissed her mouth. She felt the tight muscles around his finger spasm, but she didn't want to be the only one to be swept away by pleasure.

She pulled back from his kiss, released his shoulders to caress his muscular arms and chest. Her gaze flicked to his erection, standing up full and thick. His masterful touch was distracting, but right now, she wanted him to lose control too. When her hands reached his firm stomach, she looked up at him. The water cascaded over his broad chest. Their eyes met, and she smiled. His finger left her sheath when she lowered to her knees in front of him and gently blew over the head of his cock. His breath hitched, and he grabbed the top of her head.

She held onto his hip with her right hand while the other was used to discover his cock. She first touched him timidly, but when she heard him suck in his breath, she became bolder, squeezing his hard flesh in her hand. She considered using the shower gel on him as he had on her, but she didn't want anything to cover his natural scent. His cock dripped onto her palm, and she rubbed its sensitive head with her thumb before bending forward. Her tongue darted out, and she tasted his pearly drops. He jerked at her touch, and his hands tangled in her hair, pulling her closer. She took him into the heat of her mouth. She sucked hard, and her tongue teased him. He groaned, his hips began to thrust between her lips. She loved his response. *"Not so much in charge now, are you Mr. Control freak?"*

He froze. She curled her tongue around him, but he stopped his thrusting. Her senses leaped into full alert. Something had changed. He caught her head between his hands and tilted her head back. His eyes smoldered with emotions she was unable to read. "So even pleasure is a battle with you. No, Goldilocks. You're not going to control me, and tonight I won't control you. We'll both have our pleasure."

Before she could respond, he lifted her up in his arms and pushed her back against the steamed-up glass. His gaze held hers captive, telling her he was staking his claim, as he wrapped her legs around his waist. His chest hair rasped against her swollen breasts, and he lowered his mouth to take control of her lips.

He broke off his ravenous kiss as he pressed the head of his cock against her slick entrance. She struggled for breath while he watched her as he slowly filled her. Once inside, he waited. He locked them together. Erin felt overcome by how long he held them both still as if he wanted to memorize their joining. She whimpered. *Come on,* she thought. *Move. Don't make me beg.*

He grinned as if he heard her thoughts. *He probably has.* She lifted her hips to sate the demands of her body. She wanted him to pound into her hard.

"Together," he said, and then he slammed into her. With his hands on her hips, Dane pinned her against the cold, wet glass as he began to thrust into her. She slid up and down against the door each time he drew his hips back before rhythmically easing them forward. Her nipples raked over his muscular chest, and she tightened her arms around him. Her body gripped his, throbbing and unrestrained, needing to take him deeper.

Each time he surged forward, she moaned in pleasure, her hips undulating along with his slow thrusts. Her body grew tighter and tighter as her pleasure mounted. He moved one of his arms and put his hands between their bodies. He found her sweet spot and began rotating his middle finger in slow circles as he continued to drive into her.

She closed her eyes, focused on the flames that

kept burning higher and higher. His lips brushed over her neck. His pounding sent her soaring, and every nerve ending in her body wanted release. She hardly noticed when Dane grazed her throat with his fangs. *Hardly.* But when he sank his fangs into her neck in the next instant, she shuddered at the bombardment of sensations. As he drank from her, the sensual pressure built until she felt she was about to shatter into a thousand pieces.

"Open your eyes." The deep tone of his voice vibrated through her body. "Together."

She obeyed, and as soon as her eyes met his, his intense gaze locked with hers. Seconds later ecstasy took over. He joined her and threw his head back as he lost himself in her.

Afterward, he dried them both. Then he carried her to the bed and lay her down on it. He clasped her against him so tightly that it was almost painful, but she needed it. She couldn't remember feeling so cherished before. He held her as if he would never let her go. *But one day he will have to,* she thought. The best-case scenario for their relationship was that she would grow old and die while Dane wouldn't age a day. There was no future for them unless she became a vampire too, but she didn't want that. She liked the idea of aging, and if she were to become a vampire and live forever, the ghosts would be forced to stay with her forever too. They would all be trapped together for an eternity. But if she died of old age one day, they would finally be free.

Should I tell him that I don't want to be a vampire like him?

"Uh Dane..." she said.

He nuzzled her neck. "Hmm?"

"I uh, I wondered if you really needed to take m-my blood just now," she stammered.

"Why? It's only a little nip, and it makes the sex more intense. You liked it."

"Uh, yes. I did. But I wondered if there could be side effects, like with the blood exchange?"

He rolled her over until she was lying on her side, facing him. "Is this about the blood exchange? We agreed that you would let that go."

"Yes, I had agreed to that. But that was a one-time event, so I wouldn't have that connection to Stratton anymore."

"Are you telling me that you want me to feed elsewhere? I can always use Sandy as a donor. I haven't before because I thought it would be too intimate, like cheating. I have been using blood bags instead, but it's a different matter to never have fresh blood again..."

Jealousy clawed at her. "No, it's okay. You're right. I did like it."

He narrowed his eyes. "But there's something..."

She swallowed. "I've just been thinking about our future. You mentioned that this is not just for tonight. But is it really possible for us to have a future? You're a vampire, and I'm not."

"You're a lot of things," he said.

"Yes," she admitted. "I have a lot of powers that were forced on me, but nothing indicates that I would live forever like you. Every day, I grow older while you'll look thirty-five forever. And one day I'll die."

"We'll discuss it when it becomes an issue," he

said, his face set with determination.

Her heart pounded. "There's nothing to discuss. I don't want to become a vampire."

"Why not?" He smirked. "Are you afraid of losing your soul?"

"My soul? I was thinking about my mother, my sister, Altman and Gideon. It's one thing if I will never get to grow old, but what about them? I can't force them to be tied to me forever too. They'll never be free then."

The silence that followed her explanation gave her chills. *Will he force me to become a vampire one day?*

"Do you understand where I'm coming from?" she tried again.

He regarded with her with his blue eyes, keeping his expression blank. "I understand where you're coming from."

His wording seemed too careful. She noticed he didn't say he agreed, and she was not reassured that he would not one day overrule her objections.

If that day comes, please let me be strong enough to fight him.

NINE

Doing magic meant that Pauline often had to improvise, but she was confident that the herbs she had bought at the supermarket should help her get rid of Billy's attention. She still needed to figure out what to do about Erin's demon, but her intuition told her that dealing with the werewolf was more urgent. She put the garlic, sage, rosemary and basil in her shopping bag and left the store when she saw the object of her nightmares waiting for her. Panic set in before she remembered that she had been expecting him, and she had not gone outside unprepared. She stuck her hand in her left pocket, and the cool metal of the pair of manicure scissors eased her tension a little.

"Hi Pauline," Billy said.

"Hello. Are you stalking me now?" Immediately after the words left her mouth, she berated herself for them. *I need him to get close before I can start chasing him away.*

"You can't be surprised to see me. I told you that I would be seeing you around," Billy said.

"Why?"

He grinned. "Maybe because I like you. Maybe because you like me too…"

TOUCHED BY EVIL

Not for long, she promised, clenching the scissors. She walked up to him. "Wouldn't the pack mind if you dated a witch?"

"Would your roommate mind if you dated a werewolf?" He kept his voice low, obviously not wanting anyone else to overhear. He grabbed her elbow and guided her to a secluded park. He invited her to take a seat, and Pauline gladly accepted. Her knees felt like jelly, and her palms were sweating. She rubbed her hands on her jeans before taking the scissors out of her pocket. *Don't drop them,* she told herself.

"I can hear your heart thunder in your chest," he growled.

"I'm scared," she said honestly.

"What are you afraid of?" he asked.

She had to get close to him, and she could think of no other way but to lean forward and kiss him. She had never kissed anyone who was dangerous before. Like a predator, Billy's brown eyes were wholly focused on her. His unblinking gaze sent a thrill running down her spine. He was a wolf, and she was his prey. *Not for long.*

The moment her lips touched his, her brains became mush. Her lips were tender against his, but when he licked over her lips with his tongue, he robbed her of breath and reason and brought her into a world of sensation. He took over, his mouth hot and demanding, branded her. She moaned, wanting to grab his head and pull him closer, but then she remembered that she'd had other plans for her hands.

She continued to kiss him, but this time, it was to distract him while her left hand cut a piece of his beard. The metal touched his skin, but he wouldn't stop kissing her, so she thought she was getting away with it. The moment she lowered her left hand, he struck. His hand shot out fast and grabbed her wrist. She froze, stunned that Billy had grabbed her so quickly. He held her tight, and when she struggled to escape, he tightened his hold, telling her without words that he refused to release her without a fight.

He kissed her one last time before he eased backward, but he wouldn't let up on his unbreakable hold on her. She opened her fingers, dropping the scissors and the small clump of hair. *Maybe I can do a spell to track down Billy's hair after he leaves, or maybe I'm just kidding myself.*

"Why are you cutting my beard?" he asked.

"To have something to remember you by?" she murmured, her voice shaking slightly.

His brown eyes flashed, making her squirm. "I'm giving you one final chance to tell me the truth. Choose wisely. Do you understand?"

Pauline nodded mutely. Her mouth was too dry to speak. He gave her a little shake and then released her wrist with a frustrated growl.

"And if you lie, I'll know," he warned.

"Oh yes, Mr. Supernatural-Senses." Too late, she realized that she had spoken her nickname for him aloud. She felt her cheeks grow hot with embarrassment.

His lips curved slightly. "Mr. Supernatural-Senses? Well, I suppose, but don't think that your flattery will soften your punishment if I find out you're lying to me."

She swallowed. "It was for a spell."

"Yeah, I sorta figured that out," he snapped. "What kind of spell? Is it to hurt me?"

"No! Not at all!"

He gave a wolfishly grin. "Is it a love spell? It is, isn't it?" He inched closer, touching the back of her neck and causing goosebumps to pebble her skin. Pauline could feel her nipples hardening, standing out against her thin T-shirt. She wanted to cross her arms over her chest to hide them, but she was afraid that it would highlight how much he was affecting her.

"You want to control me if I love you?" he asked.

She considered agreeing, but she could tell by the narrowing of his eyes that he noticed her hesitation. "No, it was a repel spell."

He frowned. "A what?"

"Uh, a repel s-spell," she stammered. "So that I repel you."

He took away his hand. "You don't want me to touch you? No, that can't be it," Billy observed, nodding pointedly at her nipples pushing against the gray T-shirt.

"No, it was so you wouldn't seek us out anymore. I wanted you to forget about us."

"Because you're hiding something from me... Something you don't want me to find out," he said, his face filled with apprehension.

She avoided making eye contact with him. "No..."

"Yes," he hissed as he grabbed her by her upper arms and shook her. "I told you not to lie to me. I did bite your roommate, didn't I? And you did something to suppress the wolf when she visited the pack to prove she wasn't one of us.

"Yes!" she cried out.

Disgusted, Billy pushed her away and abruptly stood up. "Do you realize how much trouble we're in? Yes, I said 'we'. I thought I hadn't bitten her, and I lied to the pack too. And poor Victor! Our lies got him kicked out! We have to come clean."

"No! Victor told Erin what happens to female werewolves in packs. I won't let that happen to her!" she promised.

"What do you mean? The three female werewolves in our pack are treated fine."

"Are they mated? Because Victor told Erin that if she didn't mate with him, she would get passed around."

"He said what!" His forehead creased in disbelief. "No, that can't be true."

Pauline felt a surge of hope. "Did he lie? Maybe he lied to get Erin to mate with him."

He sighed. "I don't know. I've only been a part of the pack for a couple of months now, and I'm pretty sure they haven't shared all their secrets with me. In Crispin's pack, all the women have mates. There aren't many female werewolves out there, and maybe they have this rule to avoid men fighting over them."

"So, you understand why we had to hide the werewolf, right? Uh, there's also another reason why Erin had to hide from the pack."

Billy looked up at the sky. "You've got to be kidding. What else?"

"Uh, last December Crispin's enforcer attacked Erin. I think his name was Quentin?"

"Quentin Scott? I heard he got his throat ripped out." Pauline remained silent for a moment. "Oh wow!"

"It was self-defense! Besides, Erin used magic to hide the evidence, so nobody needs to know."

He shrugged. "Sure, but Victor was there, and he'll know what she did, or at least he has to suspect what really happened. This could come back to bite her in the you-know-what."

She chuckled. "Bite her in the you-know-what?"

He waved his hand. "Never mind. We need to be prepared and not by doing some repel spells, but by investigating what our options are. I'm the best person to do that."

"You want to help us?"

"Yes," he said, sitting down beside her again. "I will check if Victor told Erin the truth about unmated female werewolves in packs, and if what he said is true, we'll figure something out."

She glared at him. "What, you want to become her mate?"

"Why? Are you jealous?"

A spike of annoyance hit her. "Of course not. But I'll have you know that she already has a boyfriend. Dane Lynch. I see you've heard of him."

"I wouldn't want to be her mate for real, only in name. It's my fault she's a werewolf, so I should protect her from the pack. I'd rather not become her mate. She's not my type." When Pauline snorted, he added, "I'm more into pixy brunettes with sky-blue eyes."

He looked at her with such intensity that she had to believe him. She felt a blush heating up her face again.

"I'll also check what the penalties are for killing the pack's enforcer," he said.

"It was self-defense! Maybe you shouldn't be asking questions about it. They might link it to Erin if you're also asking questions about female werewolves," Pauline warned.

Billy reassuringly patted her hand. "I'll be careful. As long as you don't do any spells to repel me, I'll do my best to protect you both."

"Thank you," she said. She hesitated a second before leaning forward and cupping his bearded cheeks in her palms. She pressed a gentle, real kiss on his full lips. When she broke it off and rose, he let out a low, frustrated growl. She grinned and waved at him as she left the park. "I'll be seeing you!"

Pauline found herself smiling as she walked up the stairs to her apartment. Never before had she been so happy that she failed to do a spell. *He likes me. He really, really likes me.*

She unlocked the door, entered her apartment and then froze. In her living room stood a dirty-looking man grinning at her and exposing his rotten teeth. She exhaled sharply as recognition hit her like a punch in the gut, and she just stood there, unable to move, wondering why Ramin Sceledorse was looking so cheerful. *I shouldn't have waited…*

She opened her mouth to do a spell, but before she could articulate so much as a muffled shriek, a large palm was clamped over her mouth. Panic rampaged through her mind, and she struggled wildly against the man holding her prisoner. He wrapped his other hand around her waist, locking her tightly against his muscular body. Her fear intensified when the demon walked up to her. "Hello Pauline Collins. Yes, I know we haven't met before, but I was in Erin's mind once, and it feels like I know you. I see that you know who I am too." He nodded at the man behind her. "I believe you've run into Victor before."

Shit! Pauline tried to escape Victor's steely grip, but all she could do was utter muffled, furious grunts against his hand.

"Don't worry. We're not going to hurt you…much. Victor wanted to get a little physical on you, but I convinced him Erin might not cooperate if she finds out you got hurt. Right Victor?"

"Don't you ever shut up?" Victor snapped.

Ramin gave Victor an irritated look before smiling back at her. Because of her blocked mouth, Pauline had to inhale through her nose, but the demon's overwhelming stench made her gag.

"Do you have to stand so close? You stink man!" Victor said. "Can we go now?"

"Fine," the demon replied. After waving his hand, the room began to fade in and out. She vaguely heard him add something about how the bait would get the job done, and she briefly wondered what bait they were talking about before everything faded to black.

TEN

The way Dane glanced at her as he drove made Erin's stomach flutter. She was still in a dreamlike state, all warm and soft after their time on the plane. The tender way he smiled at her made her feel loved.

"Do you want to move out straight away, or shall we do that tomorrow?" he asked.

She stiffened, gone was the rosy feeling. She should have known he would start making demands as soon as she slept with him again. "We didn't discuss me moving in."

They stopped at the traffic lights. Dane's fingers tapped the steering wheel. "You agreed that you wouldn't run anymore. You're mine now. What's the confusion?"

"I'm not running. But you can have an affair without moving in together," she said.

He glared at her and punched the gas after the lights turned green. "I was very clear that we would be together from now on."

"And we are. But you can have a relationship, an exclusive relationship, living in separate houses. I just moved into this nice, new apartment with Pauline. We're both sharing the rent. I don't want to leave her like that."

"Fine! I'll pay your half, and I'll pay her share too. She can have the apartment all to herself for free. Everyone happy."

Her eyebrows shot up. "Everyone happy? I'm not talking about money. We're friends. We hang out. At first, I preferred living alone, but now that we have a bigger apartment, it's nice. We help each other. She grew on me."

"I can grow on you too," he said.

She chuckled. "You already did."

"Okay, you mention Pauline. Think of her. You want her to be safe, but you have enemies. You escaped your grandfather. But now that he knows you're out, he might be going after you. Pauline could get hurt just by being near you," he said in a reasonable tone, which annoyed her.

"He's not going to find me. I told him I flew in from Las Vegas. If he's going to look for me, he'll try finding me there."

Dane visibly clenched his jaw as his grip tightened on the steering wheel. "Stop kidding yourself. Hope Acres is where you were born and lived before moving to England. It makes sense that he'll check out Hope Acres, and you're forgetting Stratton. Stratton told you to kill your father. You didn't, so he'll retaliate. He told you he would."

Erin pressed her lips together. *He has a point.* "Yes, that's true. He has threatened everyone in my life. You too."

He shrugged. "We were never really friends anyway. I can protect myself against anyone he sends after me."

"But what if he sends someone after Pauline, and I'm not there to help her? I would never forgive myself."

He sighed. "Well, she can live with us too until we've dealt with the threats against you."

She hesitated as he parked in front of her apartment building. "Thanks. I'm not saying yes, but I'll discuss it with Pauline."

He turned off the ignition. "Good. We'll hear what she has to say."

She unlocked the seat belt in one quick flick and kissed him good night. "*I'll* hear what she has to say. I won't let you browbeat her into accepting your kind offer." She checked her watch. "Good grief, it's already three o'clock in the morning. She'll be asleep by now. I'll talk to you tomorrow."

"I'll walk you to your door," Dane said as he unfastened his seatbelt.

"Right, and have you charm your way in! No thanks. Look, Stratton thinks I'm still in Haiti and my grandfather won't know where I am either, not yet anyway. I'll call you as soon as I have news," she said before she got out of the SUV.

She saw him clench his jaw again, but he did start the ignition. She waved at him, turned around and walked to her building. She opened the door and turned her head as Dane drove away.

After walking up the stairs, she got her keys out when she got to her floor. She was about to jam them in the lock when she picked up the distinct smell of decay. Her nostrils twitched. *I know this smell.* She spun around and spotted the taxi driver sitting on the stairs leading to the next floor.

"I was wondering when you would sensh me, Erin Holland. Took you long enough," he slurred. "Oh shit. I've been in thish body too long."

"I can tell. You stink, and you look awful."

"Careful Erin. You don't want to piss off the scary demon," Altman warned.

The man Ramin Sceledorse possessed had a dripping nose, and he coughed a deep rattling noise. He covered his mouth with his hand, and when he removed it, he looked down on his palm. "Ha, a tooth." He picked it up with his other hand and showed it to her. Pink spit dribbled from his mouth. Repulsed as she was, she couldn't take her eyes from him.

"I don't suppose you're willing to lend me yoursh?" He rose and walked toward her. The smell hit her with the force of a slap, and she swallowed the taste of bile.

"Nothing you can offer me is worth this. What did you give the taxi driver? Obviously not good looks or wealth, unless he likes to dress as a homeless person?"

He shrugged. "He wanted revenge on a former bosh." He turned a black-toothed smile on her. "Join me, and we'll have fun too."

"Thanks, but I'll pass. Please go away and leave me alone, Ramin. It was Gideon's idea to ask you for help. He thought you wouldn't mind helping."

"Hey," Gideon said indignantly. *"It wasn't a bad idea. He did help!"*

"I don't mind helping you, Erin Holland," he said, "but I didn't like you lying to me about the sacrifish. Shit. Sacrifice. You owe me a sacrifice."

"I owe you a sacrifice?"

"Yes, for getting rid of the evidence of that werewolf you killed. Or you can join me. I'll make you more powerful."

"I don't want more power," she said. "I'm sick of it."

"But you need it. You have a lot of enemiesh."

"Enemies?" she repeated. "How would you know?"

He sneered. "I was in your head, remember?" He turned around and walked down the stairs. "I gave you a way out, but you turned me down. What happens next is on you…"

"What do you mean?" she asked while following him down the stairs. But she couldn't see him anymore, and the only sound she heard was that of her own footsteps. She stood still, listening. He'd vanished without a trace. Even the reek of decay had disappeared.

Frowning, she turned around and slowly returned to her apartment while keeping her ears open.

"Thanks Gideon," Leila's voice echoed sarcastically in Erin's mind. *"You didn't think she already had enough creeps in her life?"*

"He did help, and we had to hurry, or those werewolves would have torn Erin apart! Altman agreed!" Gideon yelled.

"Don't remind me," Altman said.

By then, Erin had reached her apartment and opened the door. Feeling nervous, she wondered why Pauline hadn't locked it from the inside. As expected, the lights were switched off. She closed the door behind her and locked it. She rubbed one eye with the palm of her hand and yawned widely. With only the streetlights illuminating the apartment, she moved to her bedroom and froze when she caught the notebook out of the corner of her eye lying open on the dining table. She squinted at it in confusion. It seemed unlikely that Pauline would work on spells and then forget to put it back in her drawer. Her OCD would demand that she immediately put it away.

With her pulse racing, she approached the table and stared at the notebook. The spine looked as if a page had been ripped out. She reached out and touched the rough torn edges. The next page had a spell that Pauline had written titled: 'How to repel someone'.

Erin turned over the previous page and recognized the spell to gain confidence. *Why would Pauline tear out a spell?*

She picked up the notebook and walked into Pauline's bedroom. She pushed open the door, inhaling sharply when she saw that the bed was empty. The curtains were still open. She should be here, asleep. *Did the person Pauline tried to repel come after her?* The worry turned over in her stomach, creating a sour flavor in her mouth.

She felt her cell phone vibrate in her shorts pocket, and she plucked it out before quickly glancing at the screen. Agitation made her hands tremble. She expelled a sigh of relief when she saw Pauline's name on the screen, and her muscles relaxed as she sat down on Pauline's bed before answering the call. "Pauline?"

"Sorry to disappoint you, Erin," Victor said. "Pauline can't come to the phone right now."

A bubble of panic grew in the back of her throat. She covered her mouth with her hand to stop a sob from escaping. She tried to get her emotions under control and not let Victor intimidate her. "Where is she?"

He chuckled. "She's a little tied up right now."

She swallowed. "What do you want?"

"What the fuck do you think I want, ungrateful bitch!" he snapped. "I protected you, and you betrayed me! I want you to pay."

"You were blackmailing me into becoming your mate!"

"I protected you! You could have said 'no'," he said. "Because of your lies, my pack kicked me out. I'm lucky that they didn't kill me last month."

"You told me that without a mate, I would get raped by your friendly pack members! How can you blame me for trying to hide the werewolf?" she asked.

He howled in anger. "You're damn right I blame you! You forget that I also gained an enemy in Jonathan Stratton when I helped you against him. I have to hide from him, and I have no pack."

"I'm sorry, but all this has nothing to do with Pauline. Please let her go," Erin begged.

"That's where you're wrong. I found her little spell book, and I also found the spell she wrote to hide the werewolf. Such a dumb witch not to destroy the spell afterward," he taunted.

She closed her eyes and fought a rising sense of nausea.

"Why did you keep it?" he asked. "Do you have to repeat it? If you do, you're out of luck."

"*You* took the spell," she said. The realization struck her with a numbing blow. He would show it to the pack, and they would know she lied to them.

"Why did you take Pauline? You can show them the spell, and they'll know I tricked them."

"Ah, but I want you there when I show them the evidence. I promised them a female werewolf. If you don't show up, I will have to find another way to deliver a female werewolf to the pack. I've always wanted to sink my teeth into a witch."

She gave a strangled cry of shock and nearly dropped the phone. "You'll kill her!"

"Probably." He sounded bored. "She's not as strong as you. But who knows, she may survive the transformation, and then I'll have two female werewolves to offer the pack."

Anxiety rose in her, but she pushed it down. "Don't bite her. I'll be there. Are you at Crispin's pack right now?"

"No, not at the moment. I thought we should wait three more days. Do you know what night it will be?"

"Sunday night?"

"Full moon," he said. "Be at Crispin's place at nine o'clock on Sunday night, or I will bite your witch roommate instead."

"How do I know you won't bite her anyway?"

"You don't. Be there or lose a roommate," he threatened before he hung up.

She shivered at the rage in his tone.

"What are you gonna do?" Leila asked.

She shrugged. "I have to go. What else can I do? It's my fault he took Pauline."

"They'll want to see the werewolf," her mother

said. *"They'll get angry when they find out that you're still protected."*

She snickered. "I don't regret that we invoked the spell to hide the werewolf last week. It's his mistake that he assumes I would wait until the last minute."

"Maybe you can pretend you've never seen that spell before and let him call your bluff," her mother suggested. *"Do a spell that they can't hear you're lying."*

Erin nodded. "Good idea. I'll call Dane to let him know about the werewolf issue."

"What! He'll never let you go!" Altman said. *"You can tell him afterward."*

"I need him in case it goes wrong. What if they decide to lock me up for a month to see if the werewolf emerges in February?"

"Dane will lock you up instead," Altman warned.

"I can't hide this from him. He'll kill me."

"He'll kill you if he orders you not to go and you go anyway," Altman said. *"But do what you want. That's just my opinion."*

Hoping to prove Altman wrong, she grabbed her cell phone and pressed on Dane's name. He answered immediately.

"Erin. You talked to Pauline already?" he asked.

"Uh no. Uh, Victor took Pauline. He wants me to pay a visit to Crispin's pack on Sunday. If I don't, he'll bite Pauline."

"Bloody hell! Have you told him that you're not going?"

"Uh no. Aren't you listening? He'll bite Pauline. She could die!"

"I won't let you put yourself in danger anymore," he said in a low tone.

She jumped up and started to pace. "Don't make me regret calling you. It's not as if I don't have a plan. Victor took Pauline's spell, and he thinks I'm helpless now. He doesn't know that Pauline and I already performed the spell to hide the werewolf last week. It doesn't matter that it's going to be full moon on Sunday."

"He'll show the spell to Crispin. They'll know it's a lie."

"I'll pretend that I don't know it. I'll say it's fabricated, that he forced Pauline to write it under the threat of being bitten. I can think of several scenarios. I have a couple of days to prepare. Maybe I can create a spell for convincing werewolves."

He sighed. "Erin, it's too dangerous."

"That's why I'm asking you to join me. I trust you to help Pauline and me. Together, like you said."

"You're using my words against me, now?"

She smiled and sat back down. She could tell she was getting to him. Now, all she had to do was convince the werewolves. "Pauline tried to help me. I would never forgive myself if she got hurt because of me."

"Alright. I'll allow you to visit Crispin's pack Sunday night. This is the last time. I will make it clear to them that you're my mate and that Victor must stop harassing you. Are you sure that your werewolf is subdued?"

"I'll be fine this cycle, but I might have a problem if they make me stay there for a whole month."

"Then I'll make sure that won't happen," he promised.

"Thank you," she said.

"Don't thank me yet. After Sunday, I'm taking you home, and I will keep you locked up until I know that all your enemies are gone."

She laughed and hung up. The amusement quickly faded when she realized he hadn't laughed with her. She sat still, more than a little worried by Dane's last comment. *He had to be kidding, right?*

Emanuel Merenda braced his hands against the steel railing as he stared over the ocean, watching the sunlight sparkling on the water. Seagulls' cries cut the morning air as the birds swooped over the large container ship. A warm breeze ruffled his gray hair, filling his nostrils with a salty tang. He deeply inhaled the fresh air. The medication against motion sickness always made him feel a little lightheaded, and the sea breeze usually helped him clear his head as he focused his gaze on the horizon.

Despite the constant rumbling of the ship's engine, he heard footsteps, and he turned to see Sabas come up from below deck. Emanuel clenched his jaw. He despised the albino and knew the feeling was mutual, but circumstances had forced them to work together. At the beginning of their binding collaboration, disgust, rage and bitterness had driven him. But now, most of those feelings were directed at himself.

"Oliver is asleep in the cabin," Sabas said. "He

probably won't wake up before we arrive. The captain expects we'll arrive in New Orleans on Monday morning."

"Are you sure we shouldn't be traveling to Las Vegas?"

"The hair we collected when she was passed out will help us track her down, but it makes more sense that she would go home," Sabas said. "Also, she talked about the beignets at the Café du Monde as if she recently had them."

"New Orleans it is. So… Oliver asleep for two whole days," Emanuel murmured. "Maybe the journey will be too rough on him."

"Maybe it will be. Do you care?" Sabas snapped.

Without saying anything, Emanuel eased around and faced the water again. He heard Sabas return to his cabin. He didn't need to reply. Emanuel had stopped caring about his son a long time ago. Sabas believed he had betrayed his son, and Emanuel agreed. Emanuel thought about his grandchild, the woman they were tracking down. The girl looked nothing like him except for her golden eyes—eyes she inherited from his son. It didn't matter. He was going to betray her too. He supposed he should feel sorry for her, but when Emanuel had decided to dedicate his life to Kalfu, it had killed something inside him. In his quest for power, he had sought to please his loa, but he hadn't served him properly, and he lost his immortal soul. As he got older, the fear of that loss began taking over his life.

Five years ago, he had experienced a heart attack, and the brush with death had forced him to awareness. Terrified of being powerless and vulnerable again he'd decided that he would do whatever it took to delay his death. He sighed, knowing he was delusional. He realized with a numbing sense of defeat that his fear of death made him weak.

No wonder I disgust Sabas. I disgust myself.

But even that understanding would not make him protect his granddaughter. It wasn't about power. It was a matter of survival.

ELEVEN

Erin saw Dane's car pull into the parking lot in front of her building, and she walked up to the passenger's side. He frowned when he saw her outfit—or maybe he just frowned because he would be driving her to Crispin's pack. She had decided to wear a pair of gray cutoff sweatpants with a gray full-zip hooded sweatshirt. It wasn't a flattering outfit, but she needed clothes she could easily remove, in case she needed to shift. Dane drummed his thumbs on the steering wheel as she climbed into the passenger seat beside him. He nodded at her, strain etched into his face and his jaw clenched tight.

"Hi," she said. "Are you okay?"

"No," he replied. "My instincts are telling me that this is madness, and I should take you as far away from Crispin's pack as possible." He raised his right hand when she was about to open her mouth, "Don't worry. I won't."

A part of her wished he would take her away, but she couldn't forget Pauline.

"I fooled them last time," she said. "To prepare, I used a deception spell and a confidence spell on top of the spell that hides the werewolf. I should be fine."

"Don't let your confidence spell fool you too.

Victor will be prepared for your deception this time," he warned. "And he has evidence."

The spell. Nerves coiled in the pit of her stomach. She shivered despite the heated seats. It took every ounce of willpower she possessed not to open the door and get out of the car. *Think of Pauline.* "Yes, it sucks that he has the spell we used to hide the werewolf. I wish we had memorized it now. Then he wouldn't have any evidence."

It was only a fifteen-minute ride to Crispin's place. Her tension increased the closer they got. She opened the window and inhaled the scent of the forest, forcing herself to relax. As she stared at the trees, she tilted her head back and gazed up at the patches of night sky that were visible through the Spanish moss covered, interlacing branches overhead. She could see the full moon, but Pauline's spell protected her from its grip. Still, she felt restless. The forest used to call to her, serving as a sanctuary for her leopard, but tonight her leopard couldn't relax. She was agitated, pushing to be free. Her skin itched, and her cat needed to run. *Not yet.*

"Don't worry. I won't let them take you," Dane said.

She sent him a faint smile. "Don't make promises you can't keep, Dane. We're clearly outnumbered."

"That's true. Even if I had the four vampires of my clan with us, we would still be at a huge disadvantage, especially now that nearly everyone is sick. Brock actually suggested adding more members."

"Well, don't look at me!"

He raised his eyebrows. "Maybe I should be

looking at you. If you were to become a vampire, you might lose the werewolf."

She glared at him. "Is this some kind of trick to get me to become a vampire? We've discussed this."

His teeth flashed. "No, I said that we would discuss it when it became an issue."

"You also said that you understood my position. Nothing has changed. I won't force my mom, Leila, Altman and Gideon to be tied to me forever," Erin said.

His expression turned pensive. "Maybe they wouldn't be. You would first need to die before you are transformed. They may be able to cross over then."

"Well, you don't know that for sure. I don't want to talk about this anymore."

Complete silence followed. A few minutes later, they pulled into the parking lot of Crispin's house. She saw that the alpha was waiting for them with his muscular arms crossed over his chest. His expression was grim, and the look in his brown eyes was deadly.

"Here comes the welcoming committee," she murmured.

As soon as Dane turned off the engine, Erin got out of the car. Crispin ignored her, walked up to Dane and shook his hand first. Both men were tall, but the alpha towered over Dane with his seven feet height. Despite Crispin's military physique, Erin decided then that she would put her money on Dane if it were to come to a fight between the two of them. Crispin was alpha, physically in top condition, but Dane was Hope Acres' master vampire, lethal if someone stood in his way, and he wouldn't let morals stop him.

"Dane Lynch. I wasn't expecting you here, tonight," Crispin said. "Although Victor told me last month that you two were dating."

"Not dating," Dane said. "She's mine."

"Are you?" Crispin asked Erin as he stuck out his hand toward her. She shook it. Crispin lifted his nose, sniffing the air

"And he is mine," she said as she placed her hand possessively on Dane's back.

Dane's mouth curved. "And I am hers," Dane acknowledged.

"Well, that remains to be seen, doesn't it?" Crispin said. "I don't smell the wolf on her, but Victor has shown us something a little disconcerting. He had to send me a picture because he couldn't come here anymore. Well, not unless he wanted his throat ripped out."

Her mouth went dry, and she swallowed, "Right. So, uh, what picture did he send you?"

"I think you know." Crispin's voice hardened.

"Well, when Victor called me last night, he said he was going to make me pay. He would show you evidence that I was faking it. He said something about a spell."

Crispin gave her a tight smile that didn't quite reach his eyes. "Are you telling me that you don't know what evidence he has?"

She shrugged. "Some kind of werewolf spell?"

He narrowed his eyes. "We'll see. We have arranged an open-air court, where I will allow you both to present your case to the entire pack."

She cleared her throat. "Is my roommate Pauline here? Victor told me that he kidnapped her. He threatened to bite her."

This time Crispin sent her an uneasy glance. "Yes. He told me she was a witness."

Dane and Erin followed him on a path leading away from the town and into the thick, lush forest. The wind tugged at her clothing and whipped through her hair. The forest was alive with insects, and in the distance, she heard a wolf howl for action.

Dane grabbed the alpha's arm. "Crispin, are you sure that this is the right time to have this confrontation?" He pointed at the full moon.

Crispin waved his hands. "It's the best time to see if she's one of us. Of course, if the pack discovers she lied to us, and that they attacked Victor because of it, their emotions could become more animalistic with the full moon. Don't worry though," he said, looking at Erin. "A female werewolf is far too precious for our survival. I would never allow any permanent damage."

Oh my God. Fear gripped her, but her footsteps never faltered.

They stopped in a clearing beside the bayou. At least two dozen men were watching their arrival. The air smelled of shape shifters and something else. *Something familiar, something rotten. What is it?* Erin turned to Dane, who stared at the crowd with a blank expression.

She studied the werewolves. Some were giving off hot angry waves with their anticipation of violence while others did not attempt to hide the predatory lust burning in their eyes. On the edge of the clearing, she spotted the three female werewolves. One of them was a blonde whose features were drawn tight with what appeared to be seething hatred.

She wanted to say something, to pray perhaps, but she knew that the werewolves would hear anything she whispered, so she stayed quiet. That resolution was immediately put to the test when she spotted three people standing beside a big rock at the end of the clearing.

Victor was holding Pauline's upper arm. Duct tape covered her mouth, her wrists were tied in front of her and her roommate's eyes were puffy and red-rimmed with misery. On her other side stood Billy. His hand was on her shoulder. His expression was as wretched as Pauline's. *He must be worried about the punishment for biting me.*

Movement caught her eye, and she glanced at the trees on her right. A dark figure flitted through the shadows. When she recognized the shape, panic welled up, closing off her airway. *What the hell is he doing here?* She felt as if she was about to faint as she reached out telepathically to Dane. *Hold me,* she thought. He moved closer, and his hand curved around her upper arm, supporting her.

Grateful for his assistance, she managed to walk forward.

"What is it?" he said in her mind.

She met Dane's gaze. *"The demon Ramin Sceledorse is here."* She pointed her head to the area where she had seen him, but he was gone. *Perhaps he was just a figment of my imagination.*

"Who?" he asked telepathically.

"Never mind, I guess I'm just seeing things. My nerves must be getting to me," she thought.

He frowned, but he didn't argue. It wasn't the

time and place to argue anyway. Instead, he focused his attention on Victor.

The werewolves moved aside to let them walk through. Crispin led Erin and Dane to the rock, which was about three feet high and seven feet wide. The alpha werewolf climbed on top of it. From above, Crispin peered down at Erin.

Erin smelled blood. Its distinctive odor was unmistakable, and it was coming from her roommate. With hot rage rushing through her bloodstream, she ran toward Victor. She punched him in the chest, and he released Pauline's arm. Erin then tore the duct tape from Pauline's mouth and watched her friend spit out a piece of cloth.

"You're wounded!" she said to Pauline. "Show me where. Did he bite you?"

Pauline shook her head and raised her bound wrists. "It's the rope. My wrists started to bleed when I tried to get it off. Erin—"

She raised her hand to stop Pauline from talking. Whatever it was, it had to wait.

"Fellow pack members, Dane, Pauline and Erin." Crispin's voice rose strong above the murmur of the other werewolves. "Tonight, we listen to Victor Nichols, who claims that his banishment from our pack was unlawful and was caused by Erin Holland's lies. Victor declares that he has evidence to substantiate his accusation, and if proven right, he demands retribution."

Erin glanced at Victor who locked onto her with a deadly glare. She inhaled deeply, and then slowly exhaled. *Confidence.*

"Dane," Crispin continued. "You're here as a courtesy, but this is pack politics, and as you know, you're not allowed to interfere."

"Yes, I know," Dane said, but there was a hiss of resentment in his voice. Erin realized that if Victor exposed her tonight, she couldn't let Dane risk war with the pack because he wouldn't survive it. Not only that, if he retaliated, he would also jeopardize the other four vampires in his clan.

"I will give the floor to Victor," Crispin said before he jumped off the rock.

Victor climbed onto the rock and faced the crowd. "Fellow pack members," he called out, and then he paused for dramatic effect while making eye contact with each werewolf. "I have been wronged! Because of this woman's lies, I lost the only home I've ever known. Worse, when I was banished, I nearly lost my life when I was chased by the entire pack. Billy bit her the first time he shifted, and he made her one of us." He pointed at Billy, who stared at the ground displaying a guilty blush on his cheeks. "I have seen her transform into a werewolf," Victor went on. "I offered my protection, but instead she and her witch friend used magic to suppress the werewolf within, never allowing it to run!" From the horrified expressions of the crowd, she could tell that according to Crispin's werewolves, there was no greater sin.

Victor held up the piece of paper he had torn from Pauline's notebook with a cry of triumph. "And I can prove it to you! Here is the spell she used to suppress the werewolf." He then looked at Crispin. "Do you have any questions?"

"No. You may step down." Crispin waited for Victor to jump off the rock. Then he gestured for Erin to climb onto it. She got there in one jump, and heard someone say, "See, only a werewolf could make that jump!"

She met the eyes of the man who had talked and said, "Wrong, I'm a leopard, and we're known for being great jumpers." She shot Victor a hostile glare before looking down at the others.

"Good luck," Dane's voice echoed in her mind. *"You've got this."*

"Hi y'all," she said as casually as she could. "I hope that tonight is the last time that I have to be here. Victor claims that he's been wronged, but the only ones wronged here tonight are my friend Pauline and I. I'm not a werewolf. I have shown you this before, and I have to say that as a leopard, there's no place worse than having to go to a werewolf pack."

There were some chuckles, and Erin found it easier to breathe. *I can do this.* "You all saw my leopard the last time I was here because of Victor's accusation."

"It doesn't make sense. Why would Victor lie?" Crispin asked.

She shrugged. "I don't know. He told me that I had to be his mate, but he knew I was with Dane, and that I didn't want to leave him. Maybe he wanted me to be a werewolf, so I had no choice."

Crispin's eyes were on her, full of speculation. "But he must have known that as soon as he took you to the pack, we would find out that you weren't one of us. Unless, he didn't know…"

His statement caused low murmurs to float over

the crowd.

Shit. Crispin is right. She saw by the grin on Victor's face that he thought he had won. She needed a reason why Victor would think she was a werewolf, while still convincing the other pack members he was wrong. Inspiration struck. "The reason he thinks I'm a werewolf is because he knows I was bitten by one. Victor bit me."

"What!" he yelled. "No way! It was Billy!"

She sighed. "He's been obsessed with me ever since Jonathan Stratton ordered him to spy on me. When I told him I wasn't interested, he bit me. He told me that if I didn't mate with him, I would be forced to sleep with all the other pack members who weren't mated."

"You bitch! You lying bitch!" Victor screamed. "It was Billy."

Crispin raised his right hand, and Victor shut his mouth. "Then by your own admission, you were bitten. You must have shifted into a werewolf or is Victor right, and did you use magic to suppress it?"

She shook her head. "I didn't need to use magic. I have the leopard that is part of me. When the full moon came, so did the leopard. I don't think my body could handle more than one animal. I expect that if Victor's bite had infected me, the battle between both animals would have torn me apart."

Crispin took the spell from Victor and sniffed it. "It smells like your roommate and here it says, 'The werewolf's taste will be concealed. When called upon, a cat will be revealed.' This is very specific."

The idea briefly crossed her mind that she could admit that they had written it as a precaution, when she remembered telling Crispin at her arrival that she didn't know what spell Victor had sent him. "I don't know who wrote that spell. Pauline hasn't mentioned it to me, but maybe he had a witch write one and then when he kidnapped my roommate, he made her hold it while she was unconscious. Come on," she bluffed. "We're close to New Orleans. That town is overrun with witches. I'm sure he could have paid someone to make up a spell to make his lies sound more convincing. Also, if I had created a spell to suppress my supposed werewolf, do you really think I would be stupid enough to keep it?"

Crispin was now suspiciously eyeing Victor.

Victor's hands had balled into tight fists of anger, and his nostrils flared.

"But wait, the werewolf curse, it's a virus, right?" Erin asked, but she knew the answer. "If I were a werewolf, the virus would be in my blood, right? I think I know an easy way to prove I'm not a werewolf. You can check my blood."

"Ha!" Victor growled. "You think you have it all figured out, don't cha? The only person here who is able to check your blood is your pal Billy. And it's not in his interest to prove that you're a werewolf because then people might find out the real reason why you're one of us!"

"I'm sorry, Victor," Crispin said. "But you're the only one accusing Billy here, and so far, he's been a great asset to our pack. Erin risked a lot by admitting to us that she's been bitten. Even offering us her blood seems very risky if she were lying."

"Well she is," Victor snapped.

Crispin narrowed his gaze on his cousin. "Prove

it. And don't point at that spell because what Erin said about you finding other witches to write this for you, and then making her roommate touch it, is all very plausible. I can't help but think about what you told me the first time you mentioned her. You said she was perfect and that you wanted to mate her despite her being with Dane Lynch. I need more compelling evidence."

The sound of twigs snapping behind her announced the arrival of another party. A whisper of unease raised the hairs on the back of her neck.

"And that is what I'm here for," a male voice said.

Erin spun around, and her breath was caught in her throat as she realized that it really had been Ramin Sceledorse she had seen in the shadows.

"Oh shit," Gideon muttered. *"I'm so sorry."*

"Hey Erin," Ramin said as he wiggled his eyebrows. "Don't you wish you had said yes to my offer earlier?"

"What?" she said.

"Who is this?" Dane asked aloud.

Ramin Sceledorse giggled, his rotting face, which was now covered with puss, shone with glee. "Erin didn't tell you? I'm the demon who helped her get rid of the evidence when she killed Crispin's enforcer."

Crispin shot Erin an incredulous look. "Did he just say that you killed our enforcer? You were the one who killed Quentin last month?"

"He tried to kill me." She nearly choked out the answer. "I had no choice."

"I knew it!" Ramin said. "You owe me a

sacrifice."

She glared at Victor. "Will he do?"

"See," Victor said to Crispin. "Not such a victim after all, right?"

Dane flung his body in front of hers, attempting to shield her from anyone seeking retribution. She put her hand on his arm and moved next to him, refusing to hide. "I'm sorry you lost your enforcer. I didn't want to kill him, but he went after my leopard in wolf form. He was rabid. This proves werewolves and leopards shouldn't be around each other."

Crispin made a show of studying her slim body. "Are you telling me that your leopard was stronger than our strongest werewolf?"

"No! I just got lucky, that's all," she said quickly, hoping he wouldn't make her prove her prowess in a fight.

Crispin turned to Ramin. "And you're here to testify that you helped her get rid of the evidence?"

"No, he's here to prove to you all that she is a werewolf," Victor answered for Ramin. He raised his voice. "And that I've been telling the truth all along."

"Really? And how would he do that?" Crispin asked.

"Ah, such fun we could have had," the demon mused. "Oh well. I'll remove the protection spell Victor found."

She winced. "It wouldn't prove a thing. He's a powerful demon. I'm sure he could turn me into a unicorn if he wanted! It wouldn't mean that I'm a unicorn."

Ramin gave a chilling laugh. "Thank you! I'm indeed powerful, but I'm not a liar. If I lied, people wouldn't summon me anymore. I need an impeccable reputation. You really should have looked me up online before rejecting me."

"Show me," Crispin ordered the demon.

"You can't take him seriously," Erin whispered. "I mean, look at him!"

"I am looking," Crispin said. "He looks gross, not powerful at all. I doubt he could turn you into a unicorn, but I want to see if he can do what he claims."

Shouts of encouragement told her the crowd agreed with him. Dane grabbed her arm and pushed her behind him again, but she knew that no matter what he did, the outcome would be the same. She would be exposed. She didn't want him hurt too. She cared about him too much.

I love him.

"I'm sorry, Dane," she said telepathically. *"I underestimated tonight."* The demon wanted a sacrifice, and she was going to give him one. She stepped away from Dane's protective hold and walked toward the demon. She glanced over her shoulder, her eyes searching Dane's. She felt a sharp pang of regret.

"Erin, no!" Dane shouted as the demon touched her collarbone. There was a sudden unnatural silence. The demon's stench was forgotten. Her pulse thundered. She met Ramin's gaze. "Here's your sacrifice," she said solemnly. If she managed to survive tonight, she didn't want to see him ever again.

An eerie blue glow lit up his hands before it began to cover her entire body like electricity, causing little pinpricks of pain. Ramin stepped away and she collapsed. The blue glow was gone and with it, her protection.

She glared up at the sky when every part of her began to ache. She managed to unzip the hoodie and take it off, but then the pain became too strong to think about practicalities.

"Erin?" She recognized Dane's voice, but she couldn't respond. She fought to ignore the full moon, but its call became too strong for her to resist. Shivers rippled through her as if she was burning up with a fever. Her muscles contracted. Her wolf was rising to the surface, becoming frantic to claw out of her.

Her body contorted, her jaw throbbed, and agony exploded in her mouth as if all her teeth developed at once. A deep rumbling growl escaped from her chest. Her wolf struggled to escape the confinement of her clothes but succeeded without tearing them in the process.

She looked down at her wolf form. Yellow gold fur covered her body. She remembered being in this form before, enjoying the freedom of digging her claws into snow as she ran, hunting prey, but then Erin had fought her wolf, suppressing it. She growled in anger. She had never been allowed to run in this region.

The wolf peered up and saw the large crowd surrounding her. Some were still in the process of taking off their clothes, but most had already shifted. One lifted its snout and let out a bloodcurdling howl. She sensed they were going to lunge at her, and she was about to flee when a hand grabbed her by the scruff of her neck, pushing her down.

"No," a deep voice growled. It was the alpha, his strong hold preventing her escape. The wildness took over. She snarled, twisted her head and sunk razor-sharp teeth in his palm. He released her with a yelp, and she charged him.

"Erin, stop!" Dane's voice echoing in the wolf's mind caused confusion, distracting her, and the next instant a powerful blow struck her, knocking her out cold.

"She shouldn't have been able to disobey me," Erin heard a male voice say. She opened her eyes, but her vision was blurred. Trying to get her bearings, she blinked several times. She saw Dane, Pauline, Victor, Billy and Crispin standing by the rock she had been standing on earlier. She sensed a pair of eyes on her and turned her head to see the demon watching her with a sadistic grin on his face. A sharp breath escaped her lips, alerting the others that she was awake.

Pauline ran toward her and got down on her knees. "Oh my God. Are you alright?"

She looked down and saw that someone had put her clothes back on.

"Hey, they released you," Erin said hoarsely. "Did you put on my clothes?"

"No, that was Dane. Oh Erin, I'm so sorry you had to come here. It's all my fault," Pauline said softly. Her voice trembled.

Erin tried to smile. "No, it's not. I should have known that Victor would never stop coming after me. Here," she said, lifting her arms, "Could you please help me up?"

On wobbly legs, she walked over to the men discussing her. She scanned the clearing. "Where is the rest of the pack?"

In the distance, she heard howling. "I sent them away," Crispin said.

Erin noticed the dried blood on his hands. "I bit you, didn't I? Sorry about that."

"Yes, you shouldn't have done that. Or rather, you should not have been able to attack an alpha. New werewolves always follow orders from alphas. It's instinct."

"It doesn't matter. She'll learn to follow orders," Victor sneered. "Now that the demon stripped her of her camouflage, she'll have no choice but to obey pack law."

"No, she won't," Dane said.

"Dane, you know how important female werewolves are to our survival. Our packs all agreed with your council that we wouldn't interfere in vampire matters under the condition that you wouldn't interfere in ours. If you break this rule, you'll have a war on your hands," Crispin threatened.

Dane stood grim-faced, his expression ice-cold, saying nothing

"Erin, your lies caused a werewolf to get kicked out of his pack. According to pack law, this werewolf gets to decide your future."

Victor looked at her with an evil curl to his lips.

"He wronged me first!" she said.

Crispin frowned. "How so?"

"A couple of months ago, he got a job as a security guard at the hospital. We were working together, and he pretended he wanted to help me find out more about the night my father tried to kill me. Instead, he set me up. He collaborated with my psychiatrist, so he could kidnap me and take me to a remote area where Doctor Quirkhart tortured me. Victor should compensate me!"

Victor waved his hands. "It was before she became a werewolf. I was working for Jonathan Stratton who ordered the kidnapping. It wasn't my idea. But all this isn't relevant. Pack law doesn't apply for the time prior to her being a werewolf. So Erin, your ass is mine."

Crispin sighed, not contradicting Victor.

"Wait," Billy said. "Crispin, you were complaining before that you still hadn't found an enforcer. Shouldn't she become the pack enforcer?"

"A woman?" Crispin asked.

"Not just any woman. The woman who killed Quentin, right? Shouldn't the werewolf who kills the enforcer take that position?" Billy suggested.

Pauline touched Billy's arm, smiling affectionately at him. "I think that might be an okay alternative."

Victor smirked. "Erin as the enforcer of the pack? You're crazy. She said she got lucky. She'll get killed in the first fight!"

Crispin stood with his head bowed, staring down at the dried blood on his hands. Then he raised his head, his brown eyes gleaming in the darkness as studied her. "Billy's right. I need someone to replace Quentin. I've never heard of a female enforcer before, but I've never heard of a one-month old werewolf disobeying an alpha's order either. As enforcer, you couldn't be given to Victor unless Victor would like to challenge the new enforcer?"

Erin stiffened, waiting for Victor's response. The idea of being given to a vengeful Victor was a lot less appealing to her than a position where she had to enforce pack law—even if it meant she would probably get killed during her first fight. From Dane's hard expression, she could tell that he realized that too.

"This is ridiculous," Victor said, his voice thick with anger. "Sure, I could fight her and kill her, but I don't want to be the next enforcer. But fine, let her experience life as the enforcer here. Let's see how long she survives."

"Erin?" Crispin asked.

"I accept," she said.

Crispin smiled. "Good." He stuck out his right hand and when she shook it, he said, "Welcome to the pack, Enforcer. I'll see you tomorrow."

TWELVE

Dane had just dropped Erin off at her apartment before driving to New Orleans. He had to keep busy and stay as far away as possible from Erin before the fear of her new role at Crispin's pack drove him over the edge of sanity. He had promised her—and himself—that he wouldn't let Crispin's pack get her. If he didn't have the responsibility as Hope Acres' master vampire, he could take her and run. The grip of his left hand tightened on the steering wheel while he ran his other hand through his black hair in frustration. He forced his temper under control. Crispin had read his intentions properly when he had warned Dane not to interfere in pack matters.

You'll have a war on your hands. Think about your clan.

He parked his car at the deserted construction site of the mall he was building. He checked out the status of the build and saw it was progressing nicely before walking a couple of blocks to the Napier butcher shop. Brock had given him the contact details of the butcher and the butcher's wife who had been protesting the arrival of his mall when he had met them outside of the municipality two days ago. Dane's conversation with Brock had been short.

TOUCHED BY EVIL

Whatever virus Maura and Eve had caught, had now also spread to his second-in-command. Brock had told Dane that he had been throwing up blood for the past hour.

What a mess. Vampires sick, Erin having all these problems, and now I must stand idly by while she is forced join Crispin's pack in a role that will probably kill her within a week. The idea of losing her consumed him. Especially because for a second that evening, it had seemed that he was finally going to get what he wanted most of all. He ground his teeth as he remembered picking up Erin's thoughts at Crispin's pack. *She loves me again, or maybe she never stopped loving me.*

He had almost messed things up when she had come to him last month to help her break off her blood bond with Jonathan Stratton. If only he hadn't felt so betrayed when she had chosen to connect with Stratton over him. But Dane acknowledged that had happened because she had wanted to lash out at him when she discovered that he had exchanged blood with her while she had been unconscious. They had both been angry, but he had betrayed her trust first. After she realized what a monster Stratton was, she had begged Dane to reconnect with her, so that the connection with Stratton would be broken. He loved her, but she had told him her request wasn't romantic at the time.

He had felt used, and it had hurt, but he had not given up. She had told him she loved him before she had discovered the blood bond, and he had been seducing her, wanting to hear her say those words again. To hear them telepathically tonight—only to let her be taken away because of an agreement the council had made with the werewolves many years ago—was too cruel a fate.

He stopped in front of the butcher shop. The sign said it was closed, and the lights downstairs were switched off. But the couple had an apartment above the shop, so Dane rang the doorbell. He checked his watch. It was nine thirty, and he doubted that the couple had already gone to bed. He could hear the TV upstairs and heavy footsteps walking down the stairs. The middle-aged butcher opened the door.

"Uh h-hello," the man stammered.

"Good evening," Dane said.

"Pooh bear, who is it?" the wife asked as she followed him downstairs. "Oh, it's you," she said.

He raised his eyebrows at the blond woman. "Yes, it's me. Aren't you going to let me in?"

"No! Don't invite him in," she told her husband.

"Mrs. Napier, vampires don't need to be invited if they really want to get into your house. They just push against the door and step inside. Just like this," Dane said as he forced his way in.

"Get out!" she yelled.

"Now, honey. Let's just listen what the m-man has to say," Mr. Napier said.

"Thank you," Dane said. "After you." He waited for the couple to go upstairs before he joined them in a cluttered living room. The husband turned off the TV and put the remote on the wooden coffee table that stood on a thick orange carpet. The centerpiece of the room was an overstuffed cabinet that displayed cat and clown figurines that were nestled between framed photographs. Two landscape paintings

171

decorated the walls along with a painting featuring a crying clown. The sound of two grandfather clocks ticking interrupted the uncomfortable silence in the room.

The woman aggressively glared at Dane while the husband gestured for him to sit down on the sofa with a resigned sigh. "Would you like to drink? Er…" He cleared his throat. "Do you drink?"

"No, thank you. Don't worry." Dane faced the wife. "I won't stay long." He didn't sit down. Mr. Napier stood beside his wife and put his arm around her back.

"You protested against my mall at the municipality two days ago. While I was there, I found out that someone had been forging documents, sabotaging my work. I want you to tell me what you know about it," Dane said. The husband squeezed his wife's arm, and Dane narrowed his eyes at the gesture, ignoring Mrs. Napier's exclamation of alarmed protest.

"Who told you I would be at the municipality that evening?" Dane asked.

"Er, we heard that you would be there. Everyone here was talkin' about it. I don't remember. Do you, honey?" Mr. Napier asked his wife.

"Uh no," she whispered.

"Listen, I know you're lying. I can hurt your husband, so I can make you talk, but I am willing to give you one chance to be honest here," Dane said. "Take it."

She kept her head down before saying softly, "I discussed it with the baker's wife, Stella."

"You discussed it with her. Was she the source?"

Dane asked.

She looked up, her hands shook, and tears of guilt slid down her cheeks. "I eh…"

Mr. Napier's grip on his wife's arm became more forceful. Dane walked toward the couple to separate them when he noticed the framed photograph of a young woman with short curly hair. Feeling instant recognition, he grabbed the picture and showed it to the couple. "Who is she?"

"Honey…" Dane could tell by the tone of the butcher's voice that he warned his wife to keep quiet.

"This woman has been in my house for the past three months. I know her as Sandy. Is that her name?"

The woman nodded silently while she continued to cry.

"Is she your daughter?"

The woman nodded again, and Dane frowned at the butcher. "You were letting your daughter spy on me, so you could protect your shop?" The man paled visibly, and Dane noticed a sheen of sweat on his face.

"You're an old man. Couldn't you just retire if you were so afraid of a little competition?" Dane sneered.

"I couldn't let you chase us away!" the wife cried out.

"It was your idea? Well, congratulations for risking your daughter's life for money!" The mysterious illness crossed his mind. "What the hell has she been doing at my house? Poisoning us?"

"It was only to temporarily weaken you," Mr. Napier admitted. "Her blood wouldn't permanently harm any of you."

"And because I didn't drink from her, I never got sick," Dane said. "Did she intend to find another way, to make me sick?"

"No, we had given up," the butcher said. "You were supposed to miss the appointment at the municipality, so they would withdraw the application."

"That was two days ago. She's still in my house now, making my second-in-command sick!" he snapped.

"Well, I thought she couldn't leave immediately after that meeting, not without raising suspicion," Mrs. Napier said. "We're sorry. We'll do as you say. We'll retire. Sandy will leave your house straight away."

"No," Dane said. "I'm not letting you get off that easily."

"What!" the mother shouted. Dane took little satisfaction from seeing her horrified expression. He was used to people fearing him, and he couldn't let such an attack go unpunished if he wanted to stop it from happening again.

"I'll think about punishment. Right now, I'm not inclined to kill her, but she'd better not have fled the house once I get home because I don't feel like chasing her. If she makes me track her down, then that's what I'll do, but my method of punishment will be a lot more painful," Dane warned. "Knowing that you are responsible for your daughter's pain should be punishment enough, but I might change my mind." He didn't want to have that woman continuing to poison his clan, so without saying anything else, he left the couple to ponder their sins.

As soon as Dane entered his mansion, he went to Sandy's bedroom. He found her sitting on a chair, facing the window. He heard her sniff.

"Tears won't sway me," Dane said. "It didn't work for your mother, and it won't work for you."

She turned to face him then, and he saw stark fear in her eyes. She blinked back tears. "I know. I'm sorry. My blood was only supposed to make vampires sleepy and weak, so you would be too tired to go to that meeting, but I think the people at the magic shop understated the side effects."

Fury burned through him. "You came into my home, poisoned those in my care, intended to poison me, and you forged documents that could have gotten me in legal trouble if your skills had been convincing enough. Tell me, why shouldn't I kill you?"

"You could use me!" she said desperately. "I have skills. I got in here, didn't I? You said my forging skills weren't convincing enough, but they were good enough to fool Maura when she checked my background."

"What are you suggesting?" Dane asked.

"I'm suggesting that if I can get in here, there might be other places where I can get in. Maybe where your enemy is?"

That caught his attention. "And which enemy are you talking about infiltrating for me?"

She breathed a sigh of relief. "I can infiltrate Jonathan Stratton's workplace for you."

"Why would I want you to do that?" he asked.

She snorted. "When you live somewhere, you overhear things. I can overhear things for you if you let me go to Jonathan Stratton."

"How would I know that you wouldn't end up helping Stratton instead? You're obviously not very trustworthy."

She cleared her throat. "I uh, I suppose I could write a confession, so you could show that to the police if I don't comply."

And if I do end up killing her, the police would have a motive written by the victim. "That won't be necessary," he said. "I know where your parents are. If you betray me, I'll just pay them another visit."

THIRTEEN

"**A**re you really moving out?" Erin heard Pauline ask. She glanced up to see Pauline hovering in the doorway. Her roommate's eyes filled up with tears as she watched in misery while Erin packed what she could before Dane came to pick her up.

"I'm afraid so." For a second, Erin felt tears swimming in her eyes too. She blinked several times and focused on packing her clothes. "God, we only just moved in here, and now I have to move out again," Erin complained. "We shouldn't have thrown away those boxes." She rolled up her clothes and tried to put as much as possible into her suitcase and several plastic bags, but she knew she would have to leave the majority of her possessions behind.

"Forget about those boxes!" Pauline sat down on the edge of the bed. "I wish you didn't have to go. Can't you tell Crispin you'll be his enforcer from nine to five and that you want to go home after work?"

"I wish. You were there last night. Did he sound like he would allow something like that?

Pauline shook her head. "I... I guess not. Oh Erin, I'm so sorry." Her voice broke.

Erin shrugged. "I suppose it's not that bad. At least he didn't give me to Victor. But I'll miss you You're like a sister to me. A nice one."

"I'll miss you too." Pauline inhaled a trembling breath. "And not just because I'll now have to find a way to afford this apartment on my own wages."

Erin frowned. "I forgot about that. I haven't discussed wages with Crispin, but they should pay me. I will continue to contribute to the rent for the time being. I might think of a way out. I'm hoping that Dane knows how. When he drove me home, he mentioned that he would talk to vampire lawyer who knows about the deal the vampires made with the werewolves." During that ride, Dane had also repeated his offer of making her a vampire, but she didn't want to argue with Pauline about it in case she agreed with him.

"Where will you live?"

"Crispin said I could move into Quentin's old house, but that it might be easier for me to live with him and his wife for a while, so he can teach me a bit about the pack's dynamics."

Pauline's eyes glittered "His wife? Was that the blonde who was glaring at you?"

"I guess I don't have any friends at the pack."

"Billy's a friend," Pauline said softly.

Erin's lips curved. "Really? I remember a time when you suggested I kill him. You said I'd be putting him out of his misery.

Pauline's blue eyes widened with horror. "I didn't mean that. Please, promise me you'll never tell Billy I said that. If you do, I'll never forgive you!"

Erin chuckled. "Don't worry, my lips are sealed.

But what happened? The last time we ran into him, you weren't exactly on friendly terms."

Pauline blushed. "I ran into him a couple of times after that. He offered to help us."

"Help *us* or help *you*? I saw you wrote a spell about repelling someone," Erin began.

Pauline raised her hands, cutting her off. "Yes, well, now I don't need to repel him anymore."

When Erin raised her eyebrows, Pauline added, "Oh shut up. If you must know, he kissed me, and I kissed him back."

"You like him, then. Don't get me wrong, I would love it if we were to live close together, but you could get hurt. If he bites you, you could die. The first shift is so tough on your body that most people don't survive it. It's harder on women," Erin warned.

"Thanks, but we haven't even discussed that. It was just a kiss. Don't make a big deal out of it."

"Oh, I'll miss our conversations," Erin said before throwing her arms around Pauline and hugging her tight. She kissed her cheek and got up to grab her toiletries. "I've got to run. Dane said he would be here at ten, and he's always very punctual."

When she returned from the bathroom, Pauline was still sitting on her bed, staring into nothingness. In a voice laced with sadness, she said, "Please find a way to come back."

"I'll do my best," Erin promised as she picked up her suitcase in one hand and carried the two plastic bags in the other.

"Here, let me carry the plastic bags. I'll wait with you outside," Pauline said, blinking back fresh tears.

"No, you stay here. We already said goodbye. If

you join me outside, you'll start crying, and then I'll cry, and then Dane won't let me go to Crispin, which will cause a war between the vampires and werewolves…"

"Okay," Pauline said. She opened the door, and moved aside so Erin could walk down the stairs. "Be safe!"

Erin glanced over her shoulder and waved the plastic bags at her friend. Sorrow washed over her as she wondered if she would see her friend again or if the pack would kill her before she had the chance to.

Once Erin was outside, she dropped the bags and suitcase on the floor and waited for Dane to arrive. Across the street, she noticed that the supermarket was still open, but it didn't appear to have any customers. She wondered if she could buy some chocolate before Dane showed up. She had a feeling she might need some comfort food while staying with Crispin's pack, and she couldn't remember seeing any shops near her future home.

My future home… A stab of apprehension shot through her.

"Are you okay?" her mom asked.

"Hey mom. It's been a while," Erin said.

"We thought we'd give you some time alone with Pauline, and we didn't want to say anything at the pack. We didn't want to distract you, and we weren't sure if the werewolves could also hear us," Altman explained. *"We didn't want to say anything that would give you away."*

"No, Gideon's friend did," Erin muttered.

"Yeah, he's an asshole," Gideon said. *"I*

promise I'll never call on him again."

She could hear the vibrating sound of her cell phone. She sat down on the sidewalk and zipped open the suitcase beside her. She was so busy searching for the cell phone that she paid little attention to the white van parked close by, even when she heard the door slide open. She found the phone, and the screen lit up, displaying a foreign number starting with fifty. *Shit, what is the country code for Haiti? Should I answer?*

Footsteps approached. Erin glanced up, expecting to see Dane, but her stomach flipped in shock as she stared up at Sabas. He aimed a strange-looking gun at her. She heard a muffled sound and something sharp smashed into her chest. She screamed as it sent an explosion of white-hot pain through her. She grabbed the dart in her chest. Without thinking, she pulled it out, drawing blood. Appalled when she saw the red-tipped dart in her hand, she dropped it to the ground. She managed to stagger to her feet, but muscles turned to jelly. The world spun as a lightheaded feeling overwhelmed her, and her legs didn't support her anymore. *Too late.*

She dropped to the ground with a crash. Her heart pounded in her ears.

"Let me help you up," Sabas said as he wrapped his arm around her. She tried to push him away, but she no longer had any control over her body.

"Erin, call out to Dane for help," Altman's voice echoed in her mind.

She wanted to open her mouth, but her jaw didn't seem to be working anymore.

Sabas had a tight grip on Erin as he dragged her

toward the van. The side doors were still open as he roughly shoved her into the vehicle. Not able to move her arms, she hit the floor of the van with her face. She heard Sabas slam the door shut behind them. "Drive!" he shouted, and she jerked forward as the vehicle took off at high speed.

"Erin, use telepathy. Reach out to Dane now," Altman insisted.

"Dane!" she thought.

"Erin?" she heard a male voice. *Dane?*

Sabas pinned her face down, pushing a knee on her back as he clamped a pair of heavy manacles onto her wrists. Then he flipped her over.

"Let's see if you can use your magic in these," he said. Her eyes widened when he pulled out a knife, but she could do nothing to protect herself. Her limbs were like rubber, and everything in the back of the car seemed to be growing darker.

Sabas put the knife down, and he grabbed some kind of device that he held over her body.

The van hit a bump in the road, and Sabas glared as he grabbed the door handle to balance himself. She saw his lips move, but she couldn't hear anything. Her eyelids felt heavy, and it was too difficult to keep them open. She stopped fighting the drug and let everything fade to black.

FOURTEEN

For the first time Dane could recall, he was running late. He didn't want to deliver Erin to Crispin's pack, but he also didn't want her to go there without him. If he wanted to avoid getting his clan killed, he had to follow council rules and not interfere in pack law, but he still wanted to show Crispin that Erin would be under his protection. It crossed his mind that vampires being forbidden to meddle in pack business, also meant that Jonathan Stratton wouldn't be able to touch her anymore. His smile dimmed when he thought about the other threats to Erin's life. *Will she survive the macho werewolf culture? Will werewolves accept a female enforcer? What if they challenge her just to prove their manliness?* He clenched his jaw. *That vampire lawyer had better find a way out soon for Erin, or I am going to do something irresponsible...*

The last traffic light before Erin's street went red, and as he hit the brakes, he heard Erin reach out telepathically. *"Dane."*

"Erin?" He briefly closed his eyes. *"I'm on my way."* He frowned when she didn't respond. *I will see her soon enough,* he told himself, ignoring his rising

agitation. *She's probably just wondering why I'm late.* But then doubt began stealing in. *Had there been a sense of panic in her tone, or was it impatience with me being late?*

He thought about calling her, but then the light changed to green. He expelled his breath and revved the engine, driving as fast as he could. He couldn't shake an instinctive warning to hurry up.

He pulled into the parking lot in front of Erin's building and killed the engine. He couldn't catch sight of her. Frowning, he glanced at his watch. It was seven minutes past ten. He got out and waited in front of his SUV when he noticed the open suitcase and the plastic bags. *Why would she leave her stuff out on the street like that? Anyone could steal it.*

He lifted the suitcase and the bags and put them in the trunk of his car. Then he grabbed his phone, brushing his finger over Erin's name before putting the device to his ear. The vibrating sound of a cell phone came from the trunk. He tossed his phone in his pocket and ran up the stairs, heading for Erin's apartment. Impatiently, he banged on the door. Seconds passed that felt like minutes before Pauline opened the door.

"She's not here, is she?" he asked.

Pauline shook her head. "No, she was waiting for you downstairs. Do you think the werewolves picked her up already? I think Crispin was worried she might not show up."

"He was right to worry—the idea of running off had crossed my mind—but no. The werewolves wouldn't have left the suitcase and bags behind."

She stared at him in shock. "Someone kidnapped

her before she would go to the werewolves? Maybe Victor?"

He ground his teeth. "Possibly. He wasn't happy with Crispin's decision, but he would never openly challenge him. I doubt he would openly challenge Erin either. If he took her and hid her to make it seem like she ran off like a coward, Crispin would take away the enforcer position, and she would be given to Victor."

"It might be someone else. She has other enemies," Pauline said. "Jonathan Stratton had her kidnapped before too."

He sighed. "Yes, but he probably thinks she's still in Haiti. Unless he's tracking her somehow..." Dane thought about Erin's comment about Stratton caring enough about her to arrange for her to get vaccinations. *What if the shot hadn't been a vaccine?* "Okay, you might be right. I'll look into it. Also, her grandfather had tried to drug her, but I doubt he could have found her so quickly."

"Maybe his black magic can help him locate her too," Pauline said. "But time wise, it makes more sense that Victor is responsible, and he just kidnapped me, so he has experience with it. Come to think of it, that time that Stratton arranged for Erin to get kidnapped, Victor was assisting him."

"I'll drive to the pack and see if Victor is there. I will have to inform Crispin that she's gone missing, and hopefully he'll believe me when I tell him I'm not responsible."

"I can create a truth charm," Pauline offered. "The stone will light up if Victor's lying."

"There's no time," Dane said, turning around.

"I already have the material," Pauline insisted. "It should take fifteen minutes, tops. It would also show Crispin that you're not lying—you know, to avoid a war."

Dane turned his head, watching her with ill-disguised impatience. "Okay. Fifteen minutes, and then I'm out."

"I also know a location spell, but it's gone wrong in the past," she said, walking toward her bedroom to grab the ingredients.

"Try it," Dane said. "I have a feeling we'll need all the magic we can summon."

Something was dramatically wrong. Erin stretched with her eyes still closed and discovered that something heavy was secured around her wrists. She tugged, but it was like yanking against steel. Her eyes flew open, and she found herself lying on her back on a narrow bed, staring up at a concrete ceiling. She turned her head a little, and for a second, she wondered if she was back in Haiti. She wondered if she had ever left. Right now, it felt as if she had only dreamt about escaping. The room she was in looked just like the basement Altman had described.

Dry-mouthed, she fought her rising panic, but it wasn't easy. Someone had put iron manacles on her wrists and ankles. She was behind bars. Through the small rectangular window on the other side of the bars, she could see lawn and the base of some shrubs, which told her that she was in a basement of some kind. She shivered in the chilled, damp room while trying not to choke on the musty smell when she inhaled.

She closed her eyes, but she couldn't ignore the stone altar and the throne-like chair beside it. She was afraid to sit up and find the chair facing a wall covered in blood-written French spells.

The faint sound of breathing betrayed the presence of someone nearby. Her heart lurched. With dread pumping through her veins, she pushed herself up, swallowed back the rising nausea, and turned around. She shrank back against the rough surface of the brick wall beside her, staring in mute horror at her shackled father sleeping on the bed behind her. She took in the wall behind him, and the red French text on it made her gasp. She immediately checked her father's face to see if he had heard her. But if he had, he didn't show it.

She started rocking her body while rubbing her arms up and down in a comforting manner, trying to quell her rising terror. Her hand touched a gauze pad, and she froze. A blood-spattered bandage had been put on a cut in her arm. She took it off. This time her leopard genes had not completely repaired the skin. She frowned at the wound. *At least it's not bleeding anymore.*

She recalled Sabas holding a knife in the back of the van, and she frowned. *Why would Sabas deliberately cut my arm, but still care enough to clean the cut and put a bandage on it to avoid infection? Maybe they don't want me dead.* She looked at her father and realized that death might be preferable to whatever they had done to him.

She hadn't seen her father in twenty years, but it

was strange to see him looking so vulnerable. He had always seemed larger than life to her—not because she had been much shorter when she was seven years old—it was because her large, muscular father had towered over everyone. He was bald now, and his shivering black skin appeared gray. His blanket had slipped to the floor, and she thought about picking it up and covering him with it. She saw that her chains were long enough to go to him. *No,* she told herself. *He's a murderer.*

She glanced at the bandage in her hand and threw it through the bars. There was no mysterious force field that prevented it from falling on the other side of her prison.

"When he put you in the car, Sabas held some machine over your arm," Altman explained. *"It beeped, and then he cut your arm open."*

"Why would my arm beep?" she asked, her voice hoarse.

"We believe it was a tracking device. It looked like a chip," her mom said.

"Someone was watching me? Da—? No, it had to be Jonathan Stratton," she said. "It's on the same spot where that doctor gave me all those vaccinations. I should have known that those shots had nothing to do with protecting my health." She sighed. "I can't believe I didn't think of it before, but how did they think to check?"

"Well, you told him that Stratton had sent you to Haiti to find his son. If a billionaire celebrity is trying to locate his son who tried to kill him, you would know that he's rich enough to keep tabs on the person tracking him down too," Altman suggested.

"Everyone knows that Oliver tried to kill you, so a chip could be seen as an extra precaution in case he tried to finish what he started."

She stared at her father, wondering if he ever regretted that he killed her mother and sister. *Do you regret trying to kill me, or do you only regret that you didn't succeed? If you had succeeded, you probably would have been strong enough to fight your father and not end up in here.* "Although, I did get the powers, and I wasn't strong enough to fight him either," she mumbled.

"What?" Altman asked.

"Never mind," Erin said as she stood up and walked toward the door. The chains rustled and clanked as she examined the lock. "I'm surprised the chain is long enough for me to get this far."

"Be careful," Altman warned. *"The last time I tried to use my power in your grandfather's basement, it exploded."*

"I have to do something. Have you tried taking over my body while I was out?"

"Yes, it didn't work," Altman said. *"We think it's those shackles. Sabas has stopped you from using your magic in them. Maybe they are specifically designed to block you from using your magic. It's probably also the reason that your father hasn't escaped."*

"I have to try, even if it kills me," she said.

"Wait. You're still linked to Dane. Reach out to him," Altman said. *"Hopefully, the black magic can't interfere there."*

She closed her eyes and took a long, trembling breath. *"Dane,"* she thought as she pictured him. She fell backward when a jarring pain sliced through her head. "Okay, that hurt," she said through gritted teeth. She opened her eyes and glared at the symbols on the altar. "Is black magic blocking our connection?" She waited several minutes for Dane to respond. Even if he hadn't heard that telepathic call, he would have tried to reach out to her as soon as he arrived at her apartment and found her missing.

Afraid to try again, she thought about using magic. With Altman's warning in mind, she took another deep breath to ward off her fear, and she called on her magical power instead

"Powers That Be,
Please unlock these manacles for me,
As is my will so mote it be."

She closed her eyes, flinching at the thought of more pain, but nothing happened. She peered down, staring down at her bound hands. Nothing happened.

Instead of feeling relieved that she hadn't been hurt physically, not experiencing any effect of the spell somehow made it worse. The hopelessness of her situation hit home. She saw a bucket with toilet paper in the corner of the cell and worried that she would have to use it soon, right in front of her father.

I am powerless. Helpless. As helpless as my dad. She studied her father and wondered what they had done to him to make him look so ill.

Will they make me sick too? Why did they take me?

Dane considered flying to Crispin's pack in his

eagle form, thinking he might see more from above, but he didn't know if the werewolves knew about his extra powers, and he would rather not share it with them. Instead, he drove at high speed while continuously trying to reach out to Erin telepathically. *"Come on, Goldilocks. Talk to me."*

This time, there was no welcoming committee when he arrived. As soon as he left his car, he inhaled. His sense of smell may not be as advanced as that of werewolves, but it was more developed than that of humans. He cursed under his breath when he detected Victor's scent as well as that of Crispin's, but there was no sign of Erin.

He then focused on his highly evolved hearing skills. He heard several conversations, including an argument between Crispin and his mate. His mate was not looking forward to having Erin stay at their home. There was no indication that Erin was there. Victor could of course have taken her elsewhere—as he should have if he had kidnapped her. *Perhaps he had that demon help him.* The demon had helped Erin mask her scent after she had killed the werewolf, and now that the demon had joined forces with Victor, it would make sense that he would do the same.

Dane's fingers tightened around the red stone Pauline had given him. As soon as Erin's friend had finished reciting the truth charm, the stone had felt hot to his touch. She had told him to tell a lie and see how the stone reacted. He said he was thirty years old, and then the stone gave off an orange glow while heating up so much that he nearly dropped it. He had asked her if Victor had to hold it for it to work, but she had then demonstrated that wasn't necessary.

He believed that Victor had kidnapped Erin, and he was looking forward to fighting him. A hint of a smile teased Dane's mouth. He wasn't allowed to get in the way of pack matters, but Victor kidnapping his partner and making it seem as though Dane was responsible could bring about a war between the werewolves and his clan, and then Dane would be justified in defending himself by attacking the werewolf. As long as the fights were conducted in a fair manner, he'd always come away the winner.

Dane debated whether to go to Crispin and explain the situation or to go directly to Victor and see if he could strangle the truth out of him. The choice was made for him when he saw Crispin walking out of his big, white house. The alpha was frowning at him, obviously displeased when he didn't see Erin.

"Please don't tell me what I think you're about to say," Crispin said.

Dane showed him the stone, "Do you know what this is?"

Crispin narrowed his eyes on Dane's hand. "A rock?"

"It's a truth charm," Dane explained as he gave Crispin the stone. "Take it. It will get warm and glow if anyone lies. I did not take Erin. I believe that Victor took her and hid her with the help of that disgusting demon. I want him to tell me he didn't do it, and if the stone shows he's lying, I want to fight him and kill him."

Crispin turned a gaze of deep suspicion from the stone to Dane. "How do I know that this thing works? Or if it works on anyone but you?"

"I am a werewolf," Dane said, and the stone lit up in Crispin's hand.

Crispin sighed. "I believe you, but I doubt that Victor took her. He wouldn't dare challenge me like that. It means that someone else must have her now. Unless she decided to run…"

"She didn't run!" Dane snapped. "Her cell phone and suitcase were left behind on the street."

"She could have make it look like an abduction," Crispin said. "She didn't want to join us from the beginning. She lied to us and hid that she was a werewolf."

Dane's clenched his hands into fists, digging his nails into his palms. "The only reason she hid the werewolf was because Victor told her that as a female werewolf, she had no rights and that she would get raped if she joined your pack. As an enforcer, she would have a different role. She had accepted that role."

"I hope you're right Dane. These rules are there for a reason. You know that if you want there to be order in a pack, we need the women to be mated to the men as soon as possible. Otherwise the men would be fighting over them all the time."

"She's mated to me," Dane growled.

"A werewolf and a vampire," Crispin said. "It's against the law. Have you discussed it with a lawyer?"

"We're looking into it," Dane said.

"Please do," Crispin urged. "Her getting kidnapped may make it seem like she wouldn't be a very powerful enforcer, and if she can't fulfill that role, I'm afraid that I'll have no choice but to give her to Victor. I don't wish that on her."

"Then don't do it," Dane said. "You're the alpha."

"Yes, and alphas have to follow rules too if they don't want to be replaced. Let's go to Victor. I hope I'm wrong and that you can prove Victor did take her. But if he didn't, then either she ran off on her own, or someone else took her."

Let it be Victor.

They found Victor leaning against Dane's SUV with a grin on his face. "So, where is our little enforcer?" he asked.

"Like you don't know!" Dane sneered. "And get the hell away from my car!" Victor shrugged, but he moved away.

"Erin has disappeared," Crispin said. "Dane says you're responsible, and that demon might have helped you."

"Of course, he would say that," Victor drawled. "He obviously hid her from you, so she wouldn't get killed as the enforcer, and now he's putting the blame on me."

Crispin gave Victor Pauline's truth charm. "Hold this."

Victor accepted the stone, warily eyeing it. "What is it?"

"It will light up if you lie," Dane explained, giving Victor a smug smile.

Victor glared at Crispin. "You believe him? Maybe it's set up in a way to light up when I tell the truth."

"I'll know if you're lying, cousin," Crispin said.

"I don't need the stone, but it's just an extra assurance for Dane. So, tell me now if you had anything to do with Erin's disappearance."

"No, I didn't. I didn't kidnap Erin, and I don't know who did," Victor said. "I doubt that demon took her. He didn't say he would, and I haven't asked him to."

The stone didn't glow, and Dane's smile faded from his face. *Shit.*

"But I'm pretty sure that he knows. He must have hidden her away somewhere," Victor continued. This time he gloated as he met Dane's gaze and gave him back the stone. "Happy now?"

"I believe you," Crispin answered. "Dane, you know what this means."

Dane nodded.

"I know you used that stone, but I'll have to search your mansion anyway," Crispin said.

Victor gave a short bark of laughter. "Well, I'm sure you'll let me know if you find her, Crispin. You know you can't let her get away with this."

Dane itched to wipe Victor's smirk off his face, and his fangs lengthened.

"Victor, you're not helping," Crispin said. "Go away. I'll keep you posted." Victor left.

"I'll gather my team, and we'll all go to your house straight away."

"It's a waste of time, Crispin. You know it," Dane said.

"Yes, I know. But if I don't do it, Victor will use it to stir up trouble." Crispin put his hand on Dane's shoulder. "I'm sorry she's missing."

A chill ran through Dane. "She didn't leave of

her own volition, and she has a lot of people out to get her. All this is taking up time that we can't afford to lose."

"I promise you that after we have searched your house—and it will be done quickly—we will do everything in our power to track her down. We'll need to check her bank account too. Just in case. We'll combine our efforts. We will find her."

"Erin, please let me know you're okay," he thought, reaching out to her.

Despair welled up in him when again there was no response. *"Please, fight back."*

FIFTEEN

Erin jerked awake when she heard the jingling sound of keys, and her eyes snapped open to find Sabas and her grandfather standing in front of the cell door. Sabas said some words in what she assumed was Haitian Creole that caused the lights in the basement to flicker, before sticking one of the keys into the lock. It clicked open, and they entered the small dungeon. She briefly considered closing her eyes and faking sleep, but Sabas' eyes met hers, and she knew that she was too late to fool him.

"Hello Erin," Sabas said. "Don't worry. Today, you're only an observer."

Observer of what?

Her grandfather didn't even glance in her direction as he marched toward her father's cot. "Hello son. Have you seen your new companion?"

Erin pushed herself to sit up before turning her head to gaze at her father, who was still lying on his back. He appeared to be too weak to lift his head. She knew the precise moment she entered her father's line of vision because he gasped in shock. "I-is that Erin? Erin, is that you?" Her father's deep voice was hoarse with emotion.

197

Erin nodded mutely. The cry of anguish building in her throat made it hard for her to swallow.

"Yes," Sabas said. "She traveled all the way to Haiti to find you and have you killed."

Erin stared at the floor, feeling the burn of shame in her heated cheeks.

"You're not going to deny it, I hope," Sabas said. "We know that as soon as you informed Jonathan Stratton that you had found your father, he would have sent someone after him to kill him. Oliver tried to get him to commit suicide, after all. No man would forgive that."

"No w-woman would forgive that either," her father stammered. "S-she shouldn't forgive me. I don't deserve it."

"He's right," Altman said. *"He doesn't deserve forgiveness."*

"Why did you take her?" Oliver asked.

Yes, why did you? Erin thought.

"A couple of reasons. We noticed that it's been getting harder to force you to cooperate. We had to hurt you pretty badly the last time in order to convince you to recite the words. We thought we had killed you, and we don't want that to happen. So instead of torturing you, we thought of torturing someone else."

Sabas' nod in her direction raised the hair on the back of her neck. Her hopes plummeted when she thought about Sabas believing her father would sacrifice himself to avoid seeing her suffer. It was insane for anyone to believe that since her father had been the cause of a lifetime of suffering for her.

"Also, if we do accidentally kill you one day, it

will be nice to have a back-up source of power that Mr. Merenda can drain." The casual way the man talked about torture and murder made her gut churn.

Her grandfather positioned himself behind her father's neck. "Shall we?"

"Here we go," Sabas said, walking up to her father. Sabas's large hand gripped her father's left arm and used it to lift him up from the bed while her grandfather took the arm on the other side, just above the elbow. Her father stumbled as they dragged him toward the stone altar. Sabas put him on top of it while her grandfather sat down on the throne beside the altar.

Her father shook his head. "Please don't make me read the spell."

Sabas glanced at Erin, and he must have noticed her frightened expression. "Don't worry, Erin," he said. "It doesn't kill him. It only weakens him."

He then grinned at her father. "Of course, if you don't read the text, she *will* have something to worry about." His blasé tone sent a shiver of dread up and down her spine.

"Try to call on the leopard," Leila suggested. *"Attack them."*

Erin closed her eyes and envisioned her leopard, but she couldn't feel her leopard's presence anymore. She opened her eyes to discover Sabas aiming a gun at her, his expression determined. Terrified, she stared down the barrel of the gun. The manacles blocked her leopard, and without her powers, she was helpless against a gun.

"You wouldn't kill her," her father said. "You wouldn't go through all this trouble just to kill her

199

now."

"I didn't say I would kill her. I mentioned torture. Shall I shoot her in her leg?"

"And risk hitting an artery? I don't think s-so," her father said, but he sounded uncertain.

Sabas shrugged, "Okay. Her foot then." He cocked the gun, aiming it at her feet. "Don't move, Erin. I might miss and hit your leg." He chuckled.

"No!" her father said. "I'll do it. Please lower the gun."

"Huh-uh," Sabas taunted. "Not until you start reciting."

Her father lifted his arms over his head and waited for his father on the throne to grab his wrists before he looked at the words written in blood on the basement wall.

Erin suspected that he had said the words so often before that he knew them by heart, but he was reading them so that he didn't make a mistake. *To protect me?*

He spoke, "*Je demande aux esprits*
De donner mes pouvoirs à celui
Assis sur le trône à côté de moi
Je suis de bonne foi
Il peut me vider, s'il le desire.
Entièrement, si c'est son plaisir.
Il peut même me rendre immobile
Comme c'est ma volonté, ainsi soit-il."

The tension in the basement increased until Erin felt as if she was suffocating. She leaned back against the wall, staring appalled as her father began to have a seizure. Her grandfather looked old, but he was strong enough to dig his fingers into his son's flesh, holding him in a pinching grip. Her father's aura started to glow with magic. It was energy shimmering with all the colors of the rainbow that flowed into her grandfather.

A soft, weak scream escaped her lips, and her father opened his eyes, peering down at her intently. "I'm sorry," he mouthed. Tears of regret and guilt coursed down his cheeks.

Her eyes stung and burned as she witnessed her father weaken in front of her. She wanted to squeeze her eyes shut, but she felt she would be letting him down if she did. She forced herself not to look away while hoping her father wouldn't die. Even though she had agreed earlier with Altman's statement that her father didn't deserve forgiveness, watching him die was unbearable.

"Okay, that's enough," Sabas said putting away his gun, and her grandfather released her father's arms. Her grandfather rose and carried his unconscious son to his bed together with his lackey, the manacles clinking with every step they took. She stared down at her hands. They were curled, almost like claws. Rage welled up inside her, and she jumped up from her bed, launching herself at them. Because of the noise from her chains, they heard her coming. Sabas dropped her father on the bed and whirled around, punching her full in the face. Her head snapped back, and she saw stars. She collapsed onto the cold stone floor, and they left her lying there, leaving the cell and locking the door behind them.

She waited for them to go up the stairs before she

moved. Her face felt as if it was on fire. Rubbing her jaw, she pushed herself up off the ground and stumbled toward her father's cot. His face was too pale, but his chest slowly moved up and down.

"They didn't kill him," she whispered.

"Too bad," Gideon said.

"They were going to shoot me," she said as tears spilled out of her eyes. "He didn't want them to hurt me."

"Erin, just because he's protecting you now, doesn't mean he's not a bad person," Altman said.

"I know," Erin said, but she pulled out the crumpled blanket from beneath her father's body and covered him with it anyway. The voices in her head were silent as she returned to her cot, thinking about the sorrow in her father's eyes.

SIXTEEN

Dane stood in the doorway, watching the werewolves leave his mansion before he turned to face Brock. "I need to call Stratton and see if he's responsible for Erin's disappearance. Could you check if there are any surveillance cameras on Erin's street that may have recorded what happened?"

"Yes, of course," Brock said.

"How are you feeling?" Dane asked.

Dane's second-in-command grinned. "Wow, she must really have a positive effect on you to ask me that! Well, I'm fine Dane, thank you very much."

"It has nothing to do with Erin. It's about safety," Dane bit out. "You've been drinking poisoned blood from Sandy for a while. I want to make sure you've fully recovered."

"Oh, right. Of course. Sorry. I'm fine," he mumbled. "I'll uh, I'll go check for cameras." Brock hurried to his room while Dane moved downstairs. He sat down at his desk and dialed Jonathan Stratton's direct number. Instead of the Las Vegas' master vampire answering his phone, a woman answered, saying, "Jonathan Stratton's office. Margot Sloane speaking. How may I help you?"

"Margot Sloane? Are you the woman who gave Erin that evidence, so she could use it against Stratton?"

He heard a gasp. "Don't say that!" she hissed. "He knows, but he doesn't need any reminders."

"Is he listening in?" Dane asked.

"Could be. He has excellent hearing," she whispered.

He wished they could talk freely, but he realized that Stratton's secretary would be safer if she wasn't involved in any plans against her boss. In this case, ignorance really was bliss. He also wasn't convinced that having Sandy Napier work there as a spy would be the solution, and he didn't want to give her false hope.

"I thought that this was Jonathan Stratton's direct number," he said.

"It is, but he's in a meeting right now. Oh wait, the door has just opened. I'll see if I can put you through."

He was put on hold for at least thirty seconds before he heard Stratton's smug voice say his name.

"Where is she?" Dane asked immediately.

"Not even hello? You know, I didn't have to take your call," Stratton said. "I can always hang up."

"Hi," Dane snapped. "Did. You. Take. Her?"

"I assume we're discussing our mutual friend Erin Holland here." As usual, there was a smile in Stratton's voice, but Dane failed to see any humor in the situation. "I flew her to Haiti, but you already know that because she called you from my car during the ride to the airport. If she's gone missing in Haiti, then I recommend you check out Erin's grandfather."

"She came back home," Dane said. "She's not in Haiti anymore."

"Hmm, she returned without informing me. We'll need to have a little talk about that. But you're saying I can't because she's gone missing, right?"

"Right," Dane said.

"It seems rather obvious what happened. She's gone into hiding. I asked her to do a job, she didn't do it, and now she's gone. I wonder if she considered her friends when she 'disappeared'." Stratton's tone turned deadly.

Dane tightened his jaw, flexing it in anger. "She didn't run off. Someone took her. If it's not you, then surely you have a way to track her."

Stratton chuckled. "Not anymore. You should be the one able to track her since she chose to have a blood bond with you. Although, she didn't show the usual behavior of a blood slave when she was bound to me, so tracking may not work."

"What about that vaccine?" Dane asked.

"What about it? You need vaccines when you fly to Haiti, so my secretary arranged it," Stratton replied.

"You don't give a fuck about vaccines! I bet that you used that excuse just to put some tracking device in her."

"Hmm, I wish I had. That sounds like a clever idea," Stratton drawled.

"If she dies, you're dead," Dane vowed. "I don't care how many bodyguards you have to hide your cowardly ass behind."

"Well, Dane. I've got to go now. I'm afraid I can't help you. Do let me know if you find her. She's still working for me, you know. As always, it's been a pleasure." Dane's fingers tightened on his phone when he heard Stratton's laughter right before he disconnected.

Dane put the phone on his desk, frowning at it. Stratton sounded truthful when he claimed he didn't know where she was. *If it's not the werewolf and not the vampire, could it be the voodoo priest?* He closed his eyes, concentrating with all of his strength to try to reach out to Erin once more. *"Who has you? Is it your grandfather?"*

Again, there was no response.

Jonathan Stratton stopped laughing as soon as he hung up on Dane. His fingers tapped the desk in frustration. *How could Erin have returned from Haiti without anybody telling me?*

He hit the speed dial for his second-in-command. Edward picked up the phone after the second ring. "Sir."

"I just got a call from Dane Lynch telling me that Erin Holland has already returned to Hope Acres and that she's gone missing!" Stratton yelled.

"She returned? When did she leave Haiti?" Edward asked.

"You're asking me? Isn't that your job?"

"Uh, yes. We can find her of course. I'm sorry, sir. I didn't realize we had to monitor her all the time. I just thought it was a precaution in case she disappeared."

Stratton ground his teeth in annoyance. "Well,

she's disappeared now, so find her for me!"

Stratton stood up and began pacing his office in frustration while he waited, listening to the clacking sound of Edward rapidly typing, which was emanating through the phone.

"Uh sir. We see that the signal has been cut off. It was last active yesterday evening around ten o'clock, just in front of her building. I'm sorry, sir. It seems that we've lost her too."

Stratton closed his eyes and began rubbing his temples as he tried to calm down. "So, you need to find out what happened, don't you?" he chided.

"Uh, right sir. There are shops in that street. Maybe there are cameras or witnesses. Shall I see if there are cameras?"

"Do you need to fucking ask?" he snapped.

"No, sir. I will check and get back to you."

Twenty minutes later, Edward called him back. "We're lucky. There were several cameras," he said. "I sent you the videos."

"Lucky." Stratton sighed. "Just tell me what you saw."

"Ms. Holland went downstairs just before ten o'clock with her luggage. There was a white van nearby. Some really white dude shot her with what appeared to be a tranquilizer dart, and he dragged her into the van. We saw the license plate, but it turned out to be stolen. The van drove into an alley, and that's where they got rid of her tracker before driving off."

"This white dude, was he an albino?" Stratton asked.

"I don't know sir. Do you know him?"

"Probably. See if you can find her without the equipment," Stratton ordered.

"Yes, sir," Edward said before Stratton disconnected the call. He opened his email and clicked on the videos Edward had sent him. He chuckled when he saw the luggage. *No wonder Dane is pissed. She was going to move in with him.* He then saw the abduction and recognized Sabas straight away.

He heard a knock on his door and saw Margot Sloane enter his room with some documents. He stiffened, resenting that his secretary would soon find out that his mission to keep an eye on Erin had failed. He hated failure.

She put the two contracts on his desk, and without meeting his gaze, she moved toward the door. "Not so fast, Ms. Sloane," he growled at her back. "Did you know that your friend is in trouble?"

She slowly turned around. "What friend?"

Stratton glared, his lips thinning into a tight line. "The friend you'd hoped would get you out of working for me."

Ms. Sloane stood rigidly in front of him, her fingers balled into tight fists at her sides. He could sense that she wished she had the strength to fight him.

"You seem angry, Ms. Sloane, almost rebellious. I can give you something to really get angry about if you'd like. Do you want me to teach you another lesson?" he snarled.

"No, sir." His secretary's voice was cool, but he could see her hands shake.

"You may leave."

As the woman left his office, Stratton's mouth spread into a triumphant grin. *At least there are some things I can control.*

Margot Sloane stormed out of Stratton's office. She dropped into the chair at her own desk before taking several long, steadying breaths.

She had to hide the slow-building rage beginning to twist inside her when standing before her evil boss. She knew that she needed to control the trembling of her hands, but she also knew that he had noticed them. He thought he had her completely subdued, and why wouldn't he think that. She didn't need to use the cane anymore, but she was confronted with her severed toe every morning as she put on her pantyhose, and she didn't want him to cut off any more body parts.

"Are you okay?" she heard a soft voice ask. Margot looked up to see concerned brown eyes peering into her own. Pity creased her new colleague's face. Margot wanted to tell her that she should worry about herself. She knew Sandy was a mole and worse, she knew that Stratton was aware of it too. The young woman had dyed her brown hair red and had changed her name to Sarah, but Edward had recognized her from the file he had on everyone in Dane's surroundings.

Stratton was just playing with Sandy, just like he was playing with her. *They play with our lives, while they get to live forever,* she thought.

"We're nothing but pawns to them," she said

aloud. Immediately, she regretted the words.

"What do you mean?" Sandy asked, approaching her.

Margot glanced at Stratton's office. She had left his door open. *Shit.* "Never mind," she said. "I'm just a little too busy at the moment. Did you have a question?"

The woman shook her head, and Margot watched her walk away. *Dane Lynch must have had a lot on his mind to think he could fool Stratton that easily, and soon Sandy too would become one of Stratton's victims.*

Margot was tired of all of Stratton's victims. *I'm tired of being his victim too.*

What Jonathan Stratton didn't understand was that every time she left his office, she felt something die inside of her. It was her sense of self-worth.

She couldn't live with herself anymore, but she didn't want to end her life without trying to do something about Stratton either. *I will only have one moment,* she realized. *If I fail, then at least it will be over. I would rather be dead than risk another one of Jonathan Stratton's 'lessons'.*

SEVENTEEN

abas placed two plates of food on the floor at the entrance of the cell while holding Erin and her father at gunpoint. The delicious smell of food made her mouth water. Her stomach gave a loud growl, and Sabas gave her a wry glance before adding a bottle of orange juice and several bottles of beer.

He backed out of the cell and locked them in once more before he left after saying a couple of words in Haitian Creole. When Erin could no longer hear Sabas, she stood up, picked up one of the plates of lasagna and salad with one hand and a beer with the other before taking them to her father.

"You're being too nice," Gideon said.

"No, she's not. It's called self-preservation, Gideon. If her father dies, they'll do to her what they've been doing to him," Altman warned.

"Thank you, ma petite," her father said, trying to meet her gaze as she handed him his plate. She avoided looking at him. She felt bad that he had sacrificed himself for her, so she wouldn't be tortured, but she found it difficult to forgive his past actions.

To her surprise, their captors had been feeding

them well. The food tasted good, and she drank the orange juice with an unquenchable thirst. She wondered if she should worry if they were condemned prisoners being offered their last meal, but when she noticed her father's physique, she concluded that Sabas and her grandfather had to have been feeding him well throughout his captivity. After they had finished their meal, she put the dirty dishes by the door and went back to work on breaking out.

Despite the iron manacles chafing her skin, Erin kept pulling on them, hoping she could somehow loosen them from the wall they were nailed to.

"You're hurting yourself," her father said. He had finished his meal, but he was still very pale, lying on his left side and looking tired and worn as he watched her feeble attempt at escape.

She ignored him, yanking harder on the chains until she smelled blood. She peered down at her wrists and noticed she had cut herself. She waited for her skin to reknit, but she frowned when the wound continued to bleed. She touched her face that still hurt after Sabas's punch. Her right cheek had begun to swell

"It has to be those shackles," Altman said. *"They seem to block any magic, including your ability to heal quickly."*

"I think you'll make it out of here. You're a fighter," her father said. He sounded proud.

"Well, I've had to be," she snapped. "People keep trying to kill me."

"Oh, you shouldn't talk to him, Erin," Altman said. *"Don't let him get into your head."*

"I don't know, Altman," Erin's mother said. *"It*

may be cathartic."

Her father closed his golden eyes as if he couldn't meet the accusation in hers. "And I'm the one who's responsible," he mumbled.

"Yes, you are. I still have the scar to remind me of what happened. The irony is that if I hadn't been so weak as a seven-year-old, I wouldn't be here today. If I'd been older, I would have had the strength to stab myself through the heart with that sword you gave us. But thanks to my weakness, I now hear the voices of those you killed that night, and I got the powers you wanted to steal from them. Are you jealous?"

"God no! I'm glad you survived. I hate what I did to Leila and to the only woman I ever loved." Shame made his voice raspy.

"You're forgetting Altman and Gideon," she said.

"Thank you," she heard the male voices echo in her head.

He raised his gaze, and she swallowed hard when she read the desperation in his eyes, the pleading. "You think I'm a monster, and you're right. I am. Being in here has helped me see that. It may not look like it, but being locked up by my father while he constantly drains my powers has been a blessing. I'd like to explain what happened, if you'll let me."

She frowned. She didn't want to hear his excuses, and she didn't want the others to hear them either.

"I don't mean to justify my actions, because I can't do that, but let me explain. You can call it a confession if you like. These rituals are slowly killing me, and I know it's what I deserve. When you escape, could you please put me out of my misery? I just want to die a swift death. It would be justice. I deserve it. But before I die, I would like to tell you the truth so that you understand why it happened. Maybe it will serve as a warning not to mess with voodoo. Are you willing to hear my confession?"

She heard him inhale deeply while waiting for her response.

"It wouldn't just be me you would be telling it to. Altman, mom, Leila and Gideon are here too. Do you think they want to hear your confession?"

"Actually, I want to hear what our dad has to say," Leila said.

"Me too," Erin's mom said.

She heard someone sigh, *"Am I the only one here who thinks it's dangerous to let this guy talk?"* Altman asked. *"Remember the last time he talked to us?"*

"I'm curious," Gideon said. *"I want to hear his story. Just look at him. He's not that powerful voodoo priest from twenty years ago. All he can do is talk."*

"Fine," Erin said. "Go ahead."

"Thank you," her father said. He cast up his eyes in what appeared to be a prayer of gratitude, which made Erin feel very uncomfortable.

"When I was fourteen, my parents were accused of being traitors against our government. We were being watched. One day, when my dad was out, the soldiers came. They weren't alone. Three men, who held high positions in the government accompanied them. My mom tried to send me away, but they told her they needed me to witness her punishment, so I could tell my father. I... I fought, but I couldn't protect h-her as they tortured her. I was powerless." His words held despair, and the lump in Erin's throat grew so big that she couldn't say anything.

"Powerless as I watched my mom... She didn't die then, but they broke her. Two weeks later she just gave up," he continued. "I wanted to hurt those men so much. When my father came back, he let me have my revenge. He lured them to us, and he showed me how to drain them. He took their energy, so it wouldn't go to waste as they died, and that energy made him stronger when he needed to fight the next evil that we encountered. There was a lot of evil where we lived. The police were corrupt too. There was corruption everywhere. One day, my father got ill, so he asked me to hunt down the evil men in his stead. I was so proud that he asked me to help him. Unfortunately, absorbing all that darkness had a side effect. It altered my personality. I traveled to new places to hunt down the darkness within mankind. I went after pedophiles, serial killers and human traffickers. Your mom knew about my mission to stop these monsters from making more victims, but she was afraid of how it affected me, and she wanted to leave me."

"Mom?" she whispered.

"It's true. At first, he only went after criminals," Erin's mom said. *"But that doesn't explain why he killed us and tried to kill you."*

"We weren't criminals," she protested.

"I know that, but absorbing the energy of those people had warped my way of thinking. In my twisted mind, your mom was taking you and Leila from me.

She was taking herself from me, and I didn't want to let go of the only family I had. My dad had only cared about getting more power and having me help him get it. With your mom, I experienced love, but I couldn't let go of my mission. When I found out she was taking steps to leave me, I got crazy. I knew that if she left, I would never see you again, and I wanted you to become a part of me, forever. For the ritual to work, I needed five people—one for each corner of the pentagram. In my delusion, absorbing you with your spirits made sense."

Erin raised her eyebrows. "And now this doesn't make sense anymore?"

"My dad has been draining me, and thanks to that, he also took away all the poison I had acquired over the years as I was punishing the worst of the worst. I saw warlocks and vampires as evil too, and that's why I had decided that they deserved to die. I wanted Jonathan Stratton because I had heard of his wickedness, but he canceled. Altman, I didn't know, but I thought all vampires were bad."

"Thank you very much," Altman said.

"And Gideon did black magic. You can't summon demons without performing some kind of sacrifice," her father said.

"You wanted your family to be forever tied to creatures you considered evil?" Erin asked.

He shook his head. "I needed five people, and I wasn't thinking clearly with all the energy I had taken from the monsters. I didn't realize I had become the monster I had been chasing all my life until my dad brought me back home. In a way, this has been good for me. I feel empty now, but clean. You can't forgive me, but I hope you understand how it happened. Perhaps, after I'm gone, you won't only feel hate for me."

Erin didn't say anything. She saw her father close his eyes as he began to fall asleep. She thought about her mother's comment about listening to her father being cathartic. She watched her father's face. His pallor seemed to have lessened. It was as if peace had washed over him, softening his features. *It was cathartic for him.*

She thought about how her father had been forced to witness his mother being tortured as a child and how that powerlessness had formed him in life.

"I hope he didn't get to you," Altman said. *"I know, it was a sad story, but he did kill us. He's still a murderer."*

"Do you think it's possible that my grandfather took away the poison during these draining sessions?" she asked.

"You think he's a changed man?" Altman asked.

"I doubt it," Gideon said.

"Why would he lie? There's nothing for him to gain," Erin said.

"Maybe he really does want our forgiveness," Erin's mom said. *"And he encourages you to escape."*

"And kill him swiftly," Erin said softly. "Maybe that's what he wants. His father has been torturing him for twenty years. He just wants it to end."

"I say, let him be tortured," Gideon suggested. *"Besides, you're not strong enough to kill your own father, even if he did murder your mother and sister."*

"Let's stop discussing murder and start talking

about escape. Maybe you should try the spell again to unlock the manacles," her mother said.

Erin closed her eyes in concentration and recited the spell again.

"Powers That Be,
Please unlock these manacles for me,
As is my will so mote it be."

There was no effect whatsoever. She was afraid to reach out to Dane because of the horrible headache that had followed the last time she had tried it. She opened her eyes and glared at the manacles. She couldn't summon the leopard.

I would even be happy if I could get the werewolf to show up, she thought. Her lips curved. *Such irony.* She had been fighting so hard to think of ways to repress the wolf only to discover that there was no magic that could suppress it. She could only hide it. *If I had been walking around with these manacles as badass bracelets, it would have solved many of my problems.*

As soon as she thought it, she wondered if she was right. *Could the werewolf really be gone?* The shackles suppressed magic, but the werewolf wasn't a magical creature. It had become part of her because of a virus in her blood. *Wolf, are you there?*

She groaned, when again, there wasn't any response. For a second, she could have sworn that she'd had the solution, but apparently the manacles could even prevent werewolves from shifting. *Unless… Unless she's angry with me for using magic, so she wouldn't be free to run.*

Erin didn't know how to communicate with her wolf. When she had been in wolf form, she had become all instinct, and it had been difficult to get her wolf to do anything Erin wanted. *Uh, if you're there, wolf. I'm sorry I suppressed you. I was really afraid of joining the pack. I heard some pretty awful stories about it. I'm not going to hide you anymore. But if you don't help me, we'll have to stay locked up in here until they decide to drain the life out of us.*

She wondered if the wolf would be able to understand her if she really was still in there. She then thought of a simpler way to reach out to her. She focused on the tiny window that didn't show the sky, but she imagined the full moon. She thought about being outside, running under that moon in her wolf form. She wanted to be there so badly that when she envisioned the face of a yellow gold wolf, she first thought it was part of her imagination.

But then she sensed the excruciating cramps that she had experienced the first time she had shifted into a werewolf. Her body temperature shot up, and she felt her skin stretch. Erin panicked.

No, she thought. *Not now.*

She sensed the werewolf's confusion. She pictured her grandfather and Sabas holding her down, draining her. She imagined biting them as a wolf and the surprise on their faces.

The wolf retreated, but it didn't leave completely. Much like a wolf on the hunt, it hid in the shadows of her mind as if stalking its prey before it would attack and reveal itself.

Erin and her wolf waited for her jailors to arrive.

EIGHTEEN

Dane knocked on Pauline's door, clenching and unclenching his fists as he waited. Pauline opened the door and peered up at him. "Hi! Did the truth charm work?" she asked.

He gave her back the stone. "In a way, it did, but it didn't get the results I'd hoped for. We could see that Victor was telling the truth. It's just that he's not the one who kidnapped Erin, and then I became the suspect. The werewolves came to my place to make sure I wasn't hiding her there." He snorted. "As if I would hide her there if I didn't want her to be found."

"So we don't know anything?" Pauline's tone sounded lifeless as her shoulders slumped to match her dejected expression.

"Actually, we do. Brock checked if there were any surveillance cameras on your street. He found footage on the surveillance cameras outside your building. Her grandfather's aide took her."

"So her grandfather is responsible? This is such a mess!"

"You mentioned that you could do a location spell. Do it," he ordered.

She nervously cleared her throat. "I already tried,

but it's not working. It's like they made her invisible."

"Try again!" he snapped. "Right now, your magic is all we have."

"I will try again, but they must have put up wards to make her invisible." Pauline managed to keep her voice even despite her obvious unease. "I'm not sure how I'm supposed to make the invisible, visible."

Frustration throbbed beneath Dane's skin. He rubbed the back of his neck in an attempt to relax the muscles in his tense shoulders. "Can you try again now? Is… is there anything you need that I can give you—some ingredients, anything?"

"No, uh. I think I have everything." Pauline seemed to search for words. "Sorry, but you make me nervous. I'd rather be alone for the spell, so I'm not distracted. If you give me your number, I will call you as soon as I get anything."

Dane saw a notepad on the kitchen counter, so he strode toward it and quickly jotted down his cell phone number. "Call me anytime, even if it's during the day. I'll get you anything you need. We can't afford to waste any time."

Pauline gazed at him with surprise in her expression before she offered him a hesitant smile. "You really care about her…"

It was the truth, and he saw no reason to pretend otherwise. "Just find her for me, okay?"

She nodded. "I won't give up."

He left as the sense of urgency arose within him along with a feeling of trepidation. *Please find her.*

Erin and her wolf had waited for at least ten hours before her grandfather and Sabas came back. She had pretended to be asleep at first, but then she got so tired and worried that she would actually fall asleep that she sat up straight instead while continuously eyeing the stairs. She knew she had to sleep, but she didn't want to risk losing her wolf's cooperation. She stayed awake by feeding on a combination of adrenaline, grit and pure terror.

Sabas first collected the bucket that they had been using as a toilet, looking disgusted as he mentioned something in Haitian Creole to her grandfather. Her grandfather stepped out of his way to let Sabas pass while turning his back to Erin, and she saw an opening. *Do a fast shift,* she told her wolf. *And be quiet.*

Bracing herself, she shifted. Heart pounding, her body jerked upward as her skin stretched. Agonizing pain tore through her as her body rearranged itself. Joints popped and muscle stretched while she fought to not utter a sound. Her jaw cracked and elongated to a snout. She kept her eyes on her grandfather's back, praying he wouldn't notice that his granddaughter now had yellow gold fur covering her body. As her arms and legs transformed, the manacles became too big to hold her and she stepped out of them. The chains clanked, alerting her grandfather. He stepped forward and slowly turned around. *Too slowly.*

Her paws dug into the hard cot before she launched herself at her grandfather. She bit down onto his shoulder, her fangs cutting through his skin like a knife through butter. She allowed herself to savor his flesh, which was seasoned with the coppery taste of blood. She scratched his back with her claws as her grandfather howled and collapsed beneath her.

She heard footsteps running toward her. Without releasing her prey, she looked up and saw Sabas aiming a gun at her head.

"No!" her father yelled as he ran toward Sabas. He stood in front of Erin, shielding her with his body. "Don't hurt her! If you need to punish someone, punish me," he pleaded.

Sabas' eyes were hard. "As you wish," he said, and he shot Erin's father in his stomach. The loud noise resonated in the basement, hurting her ears. Her father let out a bloodcurdling yell as he clutched his abdomen before falling on his back and narrowly missing landing on Erin.

Stunned, Erin's wolf opened her jaw, letting go of the shoulder. The wolf whined as she walked up to her father's shivering body. Her snout sniffed at the hot blood that was gushing over her father's hands. Her tail wagged in distress. Sensing Erin's need to touch him in human form, the wolf shifted back. This time she did yelp when she experienced the excruciating pain of her transformation.

Erin was on her knees, pulling up her cutoff sweatpants when the sound of the door being slammed shut made her look up. She saw that Sabas had dragged her grandfather out of their cell and had locked them in again. His expression promised retaliation, and she bared her human teeth at him. He leered at her naked chest, and she quickly put on her sweatshirt.

She heard coughing and peered down to see her father using one hand to cover the gunshot wound on his stomach while he held the other in front of his mouth. His hands were covered in blood from the wound, but the amount of blood leaking from his mouth made her realize he was coughing up blood, choking on it.

Her father's ebony skin had quickly turned clammy as he gulped in air, panting. His entire body was shaking. He took the hand from his mouth and reached out, gripping Erin's wrist. He was weeping, and tears were seeping out the corners of his eyes.

"Is okay," he said. His voice was hoarse. "I deserve this."

"No, it's not okay," Erin whispered.

He let go of her wrist, raising his trembling hand to her face. He dropped it when he had a coughing fit that swiftly became anguished gurgles.

"Don't c-cry," he said. She rubbed a hand over her face and was surprised to find her cheeks wet.

"Q-quick death," he stammered. "B-better."

She stared into his pleading eyes, eyes that were so much like her own. Apart from her sadistic grandfather, he was her only living relative, but not for long. She put her hand on his shoulder and the other on his hand on top of the wound. He was dying, because he had protected her when Sabas was going to shoot her. *I should have shifted to get out of the manacles and then used magic to escape. Why did I think I could attack my grandfather and get away? It's my fault he's dying.*

"I can't let you die," she muttered.

"Erin, no!" Altman said. *"He's right. He*

deserves to die."

"But it's my fault. He protected me," she insisted.

"Well, good for him. He finally did something right!" Gideon said. *"That doesn't negate all the killing!"*

"But he was under influence of all those evil people he drained, and now that's no longer part of him," she said. "I don't have the shackles on anymore. Maybe I can use a healing spell. Remember mom, when I used one on Vincenzo last year?"

"Oh honey, you had special herbs and other items to call on the elements then. I think you need to let him go," her mother said.

"Not that I want you to do this, but you could call on Ramin Sceled—" Gideon started saying.

"No!" all the other voices shouted at once.

Her father's coughing had stopped as slow, wheezing breaths replaced it. The gurgling continued.

She stared down at her hand, on top of his. Her eyes moved to her wrists that had been cut by the manacles before. The cuts were gone, replaced by smooth skin. *If only I could give him some of my healing powers...*

The altar behind them drew her eye. She saw the throne where her grandfather had been sitting to absorb her father's powers. She looked back down at him. He tried to smile at her. "Is okay," he said again. "I'm proud of you, daughter. Escape."

"We'll escape together," she said. "First, I need to get you out of these shackles." Now that Erin had lost her own manacles, she could sense the magic inside her, wanting to be released. She closed her eyes and called on the power she had inherited from her mother.

"Powers That Be,
Please unlock these manacles for me,
As is my will so mote it be."

The shackles fell off her father's wrists and ankles, and she got up.

"Hold on." She stood behind her father, slid her arms under his armpits and pulled him up, using her leopard's strength. *Or is it my werewolf's strength?* She grabbed her enormous father and dragged him to the throne. Then she lowered him into the seat.

He panted while looking at her in confusion.

"Do you think you can grab my arms, like grandpa grabbed yours?"

"No. Dangeroussss," he said, shaking his head.

"Just take a little of my energy, so you can heal," she said.

"What the hell? Erin, this is crazy," Altman said.

"He's right. It's too dangerous," her mother said. *"It's probably healthy that you can forgive your father for what he did to all of us, but don't risk yourself."*

"Why not, he sacrificed himself for me," she said.

"Some sacrifice," Gideon sneered. *"He was going to die anyway. Only now it's faster, just what he wanted."*

"Just let me go when you feel that the wound is healing," Erin said to her father. "Do you think you can do that?"

He nodded, swallowing heavily.

"No, don't do this Erin," Leila said. *"What if he*

can't stop? What if he doesn't want to?"

Erin ignored her sister as she climbed on top of the altar and held her arms over her head. She gasped when her father's wet hands grabbed her wrists, holding them tightly. She frowned at the text on the wall in French. She only knew a couple of words, so she had no idea if she was pronouncing it correctly. She swallowed hard, licking her dry lips and spoke.

"Je demande aux esprits
De donner mes pouvoirs à celui
Assis sur le trône à côté de moi
Je suis de bonne foi
Il peut me vider, s'il le desire.
Entièrement, si c'est son plaisir.
Il peut même me rendre immobile
Comme c'est ma volonté, ainsi soit-il."

As soon as she uttered the last word, she was hit by full-blown seizures. Magic vibrated though her. She bit her tongue and tasted blood as it trickled from her mouth. She choked on a sob as she tried to get off the altar, but her father's viselike grip wouldn't let go, his fingers were biting into her wrists. It was as if her body was on fire, burning from the inside out. Spikes of pain were shooting across her skin and jolts of energy were pushing their way out of her, causing a golden glow to rise from her chest.

The sound of her strained breathing roared in her ears as she watched her aura light up and flicker. Her aura glowed brightly, but it was no longer touching her. Her body had rejected it. She squinted at the light. It hurt when it drifted away toward her father.

TOUCHED BY EVIL

Tears ran down her face as her father was stripping her of her aura. The power being torn out of her caused her body to convulse again and again.

"S-stop," she stammered. "Enough."

Her lungs began to ache, and she couldn't talk anymore. It was almost as if he was stealing her soul too. She pictured it enfolding him. She recalled her sister's warning, and a wave of hysteria swept over her. *What if he doesn't want to stop?*

Agony beat at her temples, and her legs felt numb. She thought about Ramin Sceledorse, but she didn't have the energy to say his name. A sinister wave of darkness dimmed her vision, and she shuddered. She was suddenly so cold. The chill made her skin pebble with goosebumps. She realized her father was completely draining her, but she was too tired to fight him and too exhausted to care.

Her eyelids fluttered, just like her heartbeat. She closed her eyes and gave up the battle to stay conscious.

Pauline's hands shook as she dialed Dane's number on her cell phone. Willow was sitting on her lap, but despite the concerted effort to relax, the petting didn't decrease the tension in Pauline's shoulders. Her heart thudded as she was thinking about her discovery. "Come on, pick up, pick up," she mumbled. It was six o'clock in the evening, so he should be awake.

When Dane answered the call, all he said was, "Yes?"

"I think I found her!" she cried out as soon as she heard his voice.

"Pauline?" he asked.

"Yes," she said, exasperated. "No guarantees, but I think I found a way to track Erin down."

"That's great," he said. "So, where is she?"

"I found her by searching for paranormal energy."

He snorted. "I hate to burst your bubble, but there should be paranormal energy everywhere in Hope Acres with all the werewolves, vampires and witches!"

She sighed. "Yeah, well. You're right. It is everywhere, it's almost as if it's become part of the Hope Acres' air. But then I noticed a blind spot. Whenever I tried to look at a specific part of the map, there was nothing."

"Maybe nobody lives there," Dane suggested. "Or it could be humans."

"No, even the bayou was completely lit up, and I doubt alligators are paranormal. I believe someone wanted to hide paranormal energy deliberately, and if you want to be successful at that, you need a lot of power. Of course, whoever is doing this could be hiding something or someone else, but I think it would take someone extremely powerful to pull this off. By all accounts, her Haitian family is very powerful, and they sure seem to like that location for rituals."

"What do you mean?" he asked. "You know it?"

"So do you. It's where you met her for the first time," she said.

"Please don't tell me it's the Devereaux Church,"

he ground out.

"Then I won't tell you, but we do need to tell the werewolves and your clan where to meet us."

"Bloody hell." His voice was a deep, angry rumble that vibrated through the phone. "I should have known. I can't believe we wasted so much time. We should have checked out that location straight away. It's where he did the first ritual."

"But it's not her dad this time. He's a prisoner too," she said.

"Is he?" he cried out. "Erin getting kidnapped and ending up in the same location where her father tried to kill her twenty years ago seems too coincidental."

Terror slithered through her. "Oh God, we need to hurry," she whispered.

"I'll call Crispin and bring along my clan. How quickly can you meet us at the church?"

"But I'm not prepared!" she said. She took a deep breath while struggling to hold back the fear that was threatening to suffocate her. "I could be there in fifteen minutes, but I haven't created any spells to protect us against voodoo magic."

"There's no time. I'll invite the werewolves, but if they're not able to go there right now, I'm going in with my vampires without their help."

"Yeah, you're right," she admitted. "We shouldn't wait. I'll be there."

"I'll leave as soon as I talk to Crispin. If I don't see you outside the church I'm going in."

"I'll be there," she repeated, but Dane had already hung up. Trying to control her panic, she walked into her bedroom and grabbed her spell book.

She leafed through it, but she couldn't see anything useful. "Maybe I'm just not a great witch," she told herself. After all, her gris-gris hadn't been strong enough to keep Erin from getting taken by her grandfather. Despite that failure, she placed the extra gris-gris she had created when she had made Erin's into the pocket of her jeans. Then she picked up a bag and randomly threw different kinds of herbs and candles into it, in case they needed her to do some magic. She left the apartment without searching for any additional protection against voodoo magic. Dane was right. There was no time. She told herself it would be fine. After all, they outnumbered the kidnappers by many.

However, as she ran down the stairs, the sense of urgency increased, turning into a sense of gloom.

In Erin's foggy brain, she detected that something had changed. She no longer felt her father's fingers forcefully circling her wrists. She wondered how much time had passed since he had released her. She briefly considered lowering her arms that were still stretched out above her head, but she couldn't muster the energy to move them. Her entire body was numb, and cold sweat ran down her back. The dense chill of the stone altar was seeping through her clothes. She couldn't stop shaking.

Her eyes cracked open when she heard footsteps approaching her, but she couldn't even turn her head. Breathing hurt. Her lungs were burning, and she had to gulp air.

TOUCHED BY EVIL

"Thank you, ma petite, for saving me," her father said.

She stared at the ceiling. Tears were leaking from the corners of her eyes, sliding down her temples into her hair while the tears she had yet to spill blurred her vision, making it hard to focus. She blinked a couple of times before her sight improved. Suddenly, she saw everything so much more clearly.

Twenty years ago, her father tried to steal the powers of a witch, a warlock, a wereleopard, a vampire and whatever the hell she was. Today, he had finally succeeded. He had drained her completely. He probably took her ghosts too. She realized she wouldn't recover this time. Her body was shutting down, and she wouldn't even have the voices to give her comfort as she was dying.

Like a shadow, her father edged closer. His face took shape as he hovered over her. He looked so strong, so powerful. He didn't look like a victim anymore. Here stood a man who commanded attention, or a bokor commanding an army of zombies. He'd lost his hair, but he hadn't lost his charisma. She could understand why her mother had fallen for him. He was still tall and muscular. His golden eyes seemed so sincere. He put his hand on her wrists that were still positioned over her head, and he pushed down her arms. His lips were pressed tightly together.

"I'm sorry. As soon as I got a taste of your energy, I wasn't able to stop myself from taking it all," he said. "I'm afraid I can't stay. I've got to arrange the trip home, but don't worry. You won't be alone."

A little gasp of surprise escaped her when she heard her grandfather say, "You got what you wanted. Just go."

Her father grinned maliciously, and the hairs rose on her skin. "Yes, I did, didn't I?"

She frowned and tried to talk, but only air emerged.

"Shh," her father cautioned. His expression shifted to caring once more. "Don't speak." He wiped the tears from her cheeks, but she saw through the pretense of the gentle, nurturing moment. She wished she had the strength to push his hand away. He must have seen the rage in her expression because he dropped his hand.

Her chest strained with effort, but only a few incomprehensible sounds came out.

"Annoying isn't it, when you're drained?" he asked coolly, no longer pretending. "Makes you feel weak and vulnerable. I'm lucky my dad didn't decide to bleed me dry while was I fasting. I'm sure he wanted to—payback for having locked him up for twenty years. Fortunately, I had Sabas watching my back. Not that I think you would have had the balls to stand up to me, papa."

She squinted at him in incomprehension. *Did he just say that Sabas had had his back?*

"Ah, you're confused because you saw Sabas shoot me. Those weren't real bullets, petite. He shot me with blanks, and then combined with special effects, pig blood and a little acting—voilà, you want to save me. It was a lot of hassle to get you to say the words, I know, but the devil's breath I used on you during the first ritual wouldn't have worked here. Oh,

TOUCHED BY EVIL

I'm sure the white powder would have made you want to do whatever I wanted, but you wouldn't have been able to read the words. Since my father emptied me of my powers beforehand, it meant that I could absorb all of yours at once. It really was like fasting." He chuckled. "I've never felt so energized before. I can't wait to hear Ann again. She's finally a part of me. I missed her. She thought she could escape me, but now she really is mine," he added with an air of satisfaction.

Her stomach knotted at his words, and she continued to cry silently. She shouldn't have believed the fantasy. *Oh, why was I so blind to drop my defenses?*

His smile became predatory. "I'm so full that I need to wait before I can take back my powers. I'm sure you're happy that you won't need to feed me for a while, papa. Or maybe you would like me to drain you too…"

She inhaled a ragged breath. Her grandfather answered him, and she sensed her father leaving, but she couldn't stay focused anymore. The uncontrollable trembling had intensified while she felt that everything else in her body was slowing down. She imagined her heartbeat becoming uneven and faint, her blood sluggish and her breath non-existent.

She wished she could talk to her mom, Leila and Altman. *I hope they got away, but if not, they'd better give you hell—Gideon especially.* It was her last rebellious thought. She closed her eyes. She felt a warm hand on her shoulder, but her eyelids were too heavy.

"I'm sorry, pitit pitit fi mwen."

She recognized the sound of her grandfather's voice. *No more power to steal.*

For a second, she thought she heard Altman say, *"Don't give up."*

Altman? Not real. Just wishful thinking. If only Dane were here, holding me close. Have I told him I loved him?

She was so tired that she didn't even have the energy to shiver. The cold didn't touch her anymore either. While every limb was heavy, she could feel herself drifting away. She didn't feel pain anymore. Her blood slowed down. She exhaled one final time.

Then her heart stopped beating.

NINETEEN

Dane raised his eyebrows at Pauline in disbelief when he was able to push open the door of the Devereaux Church without having to break the lock. *If something evil were happening here, wouldn't Erin's family lock the door?*

Pauline shook her head and shrugged in response.

Behind him, about a dozen werewolves from Crispin's pack and Brock from his own clan were waiting for him to enter while Crispin was leading his men into the church through the other side.

"Can you sense her?" Pauline asked softly.

"Erin, are you here?" Dane sent out telepathically.

She turned to Billy. "Can you?"

"No, sorry. I don't hear her." Billy closed his eyes and concentrated. "In fact, it's like I don't hear anyone outside our tiny group."

Pauline frowned. "Nothing? Isn't that strange? As a werewolf you should have some kind of super hearing, right?"

"Vampires are supposed to have super hearing too," Dane said, "but I can't hear Crispin or any of his men on the other side of the building. It's like

236

everything is on mute. And no, Erin's not responding." He nodded to the others to indicate that they should follow him before he entered the hallway of the church. The ominous silence that reigned caused a cold sweat to pepper his skin. He thought back to the first time he had entered this church, the first time he had laid eyes on Erin. Unlike that evening, he couldn't detect a discharge of power tonight. There was no indication that a ritual had taken place. *But why do I feel that tonight is worse?* The answer came to him immediately. *Because tonight my heart's involved.*

His hand shook slightly when he pushed open the door to the room where twenty years ago he had found the bodies of Erin's mother and sister, the body of Altman—his old second-in-command, some young warlock and seven-year-old Erin as she lay on the ground, bleeding to death.

Please don't let me be too late.

Relief rushed through him when he discovered that the room was empty. It lasted but a second, when he realized that if she wasn't here, they had no way of knowing where she was, especially now that their senses were somehow unable to function properly.

Crispin burst through the door in front of the room with some of his men following him in their werewolf form. His brown eyes glittered as he stared at Dane. "You'd better not be wasting our time while she's running away to avoid having to join my pack."

Dane met the alpha's glare without blinking.

"We have to search the grounds," Pauline said urgently. "My intuition is shouting at me that she's here. Come on!"

"Can't you guys smell her?" Dane asked Crispin urgently.

Billy closed his eyes and sniffed the air, inhaling deeply. He opened his eyes and pointed at the floor. "I think she's beneath us, but she's not alone…"

"Okay. There has to be a door leading to the basement somewhere," Crispin said.

Dane had just opened a door leading to the kitchen when he heard someone yell, "Found it!" He ran to the man and pushed him aside, so he could dash down the stairs. He didn't care about Billy's warning that there was someone with her. As soon as Dane reached the bottom of the stairs, he let out a horrific scream. "Erin!"

Panic erupted through his body when he saw Erin behind bars, lying motionless on an altar with an old black man standing beside her, holding her hand.

"Get the hell away from her," he roared.

The man dropped her hand and took a step back. A clinking sound made Dane look down. That's when he noticed the iron manacles on the man's wrists and ankles.

"You're too late," the man said.

"No!" Dane said as he tried to rip open the door. As soon as he touched it, an electric shock hit him, throwing him backward.

"They used black magic to lock us up. It's too powerful." The man sounded defeated.

"No!" Dane repeated as he got up. He refused to let a little voodoo stop him from reaching Erin.

"I can try to open it with magic," Pauline said shakily.

"If you do, you'll get electrocuted too," the man

said.

Dane didn't want to wait anymore, and he looked at Crispin who nodded at him. Together they ran toward the door again and threw themselves at it, only to be knocked back again.

"Oh, you are all incompetent," a whiny voice said behind them.

Dane turned his head and glared at Ramin Sceledorse.

"What the fuck are you doing here?" he snarled.

The demon sighed. "Helping you apparently. I was bored." He waved his hand. The door swung open. Dane ignored the demon and rushed into Erin's prison. He grabbed her limp body on the altar and shook her, paying no attention to the werewolves who had followed him into the cell. There was a lump in his throat, and he blinked back tears. "Don't leave me!"

"Call 911!" Pauline shouted.

It didn't occur to him that as Hope Acres' master vampire, he could not appear weak. She was the only one he cared about. He lifted her from the altar and laid her down on the ground. He fell to his knees beside her and took hold of her wrist to check her pulse. There was no sign of a heartbeat. Worse, her skin felt cold to his touch. He would have given her his blood, but she needed to be alive to swallow it. Saying obscenities, he titled her head back and began CPR. Her body stayed lifeless despite the air he poured into her mouth.

"You blow air into her lungs and let me do the palm presses," Pauline said tearfully as she joined him on the floor. Her face was wet with tears as she locked her fingers together and started pushing down her hands onto Erin's chest.

"Come back, Goldilocks," he whispered between breaths. "Fight for me!"

"She's gone, Dane," Crispin said.

"No!" he bellowed like a hurt creature. "Come on, Erin!" He blew into her mouth once more, while he tried to telepathically reach her. "*I'm begging you! Come back to me. I need you!*" Then, instead of blowing air into her mouth, he swooped down to kiss her with a desperate hunger as he tried to reach her soul, calling her back with his touch.

"*Dane,*" he heard. He lifted his head and stared down at her. Suddenly Erin's body shuddered and arched. Pauline continued performing CPR and gasped as Erin coughed. Erin's eyes opened wide while she was fighting to drag air into her lungs.

The shallow breaths Erin drew sounded terminal, and her teeth started to chatter. He wished he could lift her body into his arms, but he had heard Erin's ribs break during CPR. "Stay with me," he whispered as he kissed Erin's temple. He couldn't detect the leopard anymore—the werewolf was gone too. It was as if all her powers had been sucked out. She had the scent of a human being now—a human being who was dying. He sliced his fangs across his wrist and held the wound to her mouth. She hated him for forcing her to drink blood before, but he couldn't let her die without a fight. He knew that this time she would need more than a few sips of his blood to survive. "Please drink, Goldilocks."

"*Bye Dane,*" Erin said telepathically. "*I love you.*" He sensed her sliding away, the breath stilling in her lungs as the color drained out of her face.

"No! Fight!" he ordered. *"Please Erin. I can't go on without you. I won't. If you die, you're taking me with you."*

The ache in Dane's voice made Erin open her eyes one final time. He held his head so close to hers that he was just a breath away. Fear creased his brow, and his gaze was filled with shadows.

"Hurts," she thought.

"If you love me, you stay, damn it! Please let me keep you," she heard Dane say in her mind. It sounded as if he was hurt too. She saw tears welling up in his eyes, and she wished she could reassure him, so he wouldn't be upset anymore.

He had lain down beside her while holding her, but he was careful not to move her. His left hand stroked her upper arm, offering her comfort when she felt she should be comforting him. She could smell the blood on him. *"Another blood exchange?"*

"Please, let me sire you," he muttered huskily into her hair. "I know you'd rather be human, but you're not going to make it, Goldilocks. Not even if you drink a little bit of my blood to strengthen you. Besides, I don't sense your ghosts anymore, so you don't need to be afraid about them being forever connected to you if you were to become a vampire. So please, let me sire you."

"Let? You're letting me decide?" She looked at him in confusion, and for one minute, their minds were one. She became him, sensing his determination

to allow her to decide whether she lived or died, and also sensing his fear of not being strong enough to let her go. Mixed with that fear was the anger he felt toward her father and his desire to tear him apart.

"Don't give up," he whispered. Hearing the desperation in his voice, she thought she was beginning to understand. His arms almost squeezed the life out of her, and the agony she experienced due to the pressure on her broken ribs made her vision turn black. He let go as his body began to convulse against her as if he suffered from epilepsy.

"Shhh," she managed to say, and his body calmed down. He studied her face before he covered her mouth with his lips, kissing her with such a lasting love that she felt her eyes burn with emotion.

When he interrupted the kiss, she inhaled deeply, her heart breaking at the sadness she saw in his eyes. She knew there was only one way she could soothe him.

"Yes." Her word was a bare whisper in his mind, but she knew he had heard her because she could sense his surge of hope. She knew he wanted to check if she meant it, but he choked down the urge in case she changed her mind.

"Yes," she repeated. *"But let me fight my dad."*

"No!" His howl was utter outrage. "I can't let you live just so I can lose you again!"

"I see who he is now. He won't trick me again. I need to do this for me, my mom, Leila, Altman and all his other victims. You can sire me, but I have to go after my dad too."

His stomach lurched. *"You're not strong enough,"* he protested.

"You're right. I'm not. I need help. Just don't exclude me. Please. I'm exhausted." She had no air left in her lungs.

"Fine," he said. She could tell he thought he would get her to change her mind, but she was going to prove him wrong.

"I can hear the ambulance," Pauline said.

"We won't stay," Dane said. He turned to his second-in-command. "Brock, can you enthrall those ambulance people, so they leave happily? Erin agreed to let me sire her, and I don't want anyone stopping me when I take her away with me."

"Okay," Brock said. Then he left the basement.

Dane peered down to see that the wound on his wrist had healed already, and he had to bite it once more to get the blood to seep out. He put the wound against her mouth. She hesitated to drink his blood. "Come on, Erin. You don't want me to sire you here, right? It's just a sip so that you're strong enough for the trip out of here. Don't worry, I'll send you to sleep before I move you."

She gave a short nod, but she grimaced as she swallowed several drops. It soon sounded as if it was easier for her to breathe.

Crispin let out a disappointed noise. "She's going to become a vampire?"

Dane glared. "Yes. As you can smell, she's no longer carrying the werewolf virus, so you have no claim on her anymore."

Crispin raised his hands in the air and stepped away from them. "Fair enough." He nodded at her grandfather. "What should we do with him and all this voodoo stuff?"

"I propose we watch the church," Dane replied. "Her father is bound to come back to pick up his altar and that throne. You still want to help?"

"Yes, he nearly killed a female werewolf. In a way, he *did* kill her. He's not getting away this time," Crispin vowed.

"What do you want us to do with your grandfather?" Dane asked Erin. "Should we release him?"

For a moment, there was silence as she watched her grandfather. He defiantly thrust his chin out. In his expression, she read that he believed she was going to abandon him. He had gotten her kidnapped, but he seemed to be a victim like her. *But is he?* She also had believed her father had been a victim. "Can you bring him with us?" she murmured. "I don't know if we can trust him, but if he stays here, my dad will probably drain him too."

"I'll ask Maura and Vincenzo to take him. We'd better leave before the effect of my blood wears off," Dane said. "Erin, are you ready to go home?" His voice was low and seductive. *I will follow you anywhere,* she thought while staring into his eyes. She began to relax as he compelled her to sleep. She felt peaceful in his protective hold and allowed her eyelids to drift shut. She was aware of him lifting her into his arms and carrying her upstairs while she was wrapped in a cocoon where pain couldn't touch her. She refused to worry about the upcoming transformation.

He'll keep me safe, Erin thought heavy-eyed and snuggling against his broad chest, she fell asleep.

TWENTY

"Wake up, Erin." The compelling voice forced its way into her sleep, making Erin reluctantly open her eyes. After glancing around, she realized that she was lying on her back on Dane's imposing four-poster bed. After taking a deep breath, she found herself under Dane's piercing blue gaze. He had taken his shirt off, and her eyes were automatically drawn to his wide shoulders and muscular chest. *Is he trying to distract me, or is he afraid the blood is going to stain his shirt?*

"I know you're exhausted, but we need to do the transformation now. Unfortunately, I need to bleed you dry so my blood can replace yours." He raised his hand and caressed her cheek before pulling her into his arms.

She could sense that her strength was waning. She felt so weak that she could barely keep her eyes open.

"Stay with me, Goldilocks," he whispered into her ear, "You promised." His warm breath blew tendrils of her hair around her neck, tickling her and creating anticipation in her body. His fingers stroked along the fine line of her jaw before he bent his head.

TOUCHED BY EVIL

She felt his mouth softly touch her skin with affectionate kisses. Then his teeth grazed her throat, and her pulse began to race. At the first touch of his tongue, fire burst through her. He readied her for his bite, but he didn't make her wait long. Seconds passed before he sank his fangs into her flesh. A jolt of pleasure swept over her body as she drowned in sensation.

She moaned as his left hand swept down to cup her breast. His expert touch drugged her senses. Her nipples throbbed and need ran through her, tightening her body while her blood was pouring into him. Desire climbed when his other hand glided down her body, over her slim waist, before opening her legs to explore the heat between her thighs. Her stomach clenched with arousal, when his fingertips separated the engorged lips of her sex, massaging her clit. Her hips lifted, and when he pressed inward, a shudder passed through her. She let out a little noise in the back of her throat, and her body shook before it shattered into a million pieces.

Suddenly she was in his mind, experiencing his delight at her orgasm as he continued to swallow her blood. He wanted to give her some happiness before the process of her becoming a vampire started. She also sensed his dread that the transformation would be too much for her body to handle in its weakened state. He had already decided what he would do if that were to happen. *He'll really follow me into death,* she realized. She had been worried that he was too possessive and too controlling a lover. But in his mind, she saw a love so pure that it meant he would let her die a human if that was what she truly wanted.

I want us to have forever, she thought.

The desire subsided as the life force left her. Her body felt so heavy that she couldn't move anymore, not even to breathe. Her heartbeat grew fainter. She couldn't even hear it anymore. *Of course, daddy took my super hearing too.* Her eyes fluttered shut as darkness blotted out her vision, which was quickly replaced by a dazzling light that was so pure she forgot all about the pain.

The air was filled with the cheerful melody of birds singing. A warm breeze caressed Erin's body. Utterly relaxed, she could smell the wonderful aroma of lavender when she took a deep breath. After expelling a sigh of contentment, she stretched her arms and yawned widely. The movement didn't hurt. It was as if all the pain had been drained out of her. Feeling mellow, she was floating on clouds of bliss.

"You're not planning on sleeping the whole time you're here, I hope," an amused male voice said.

Her eyes flew open. She gasped when she recognized him. "Altman?"

Seeing the tall, redheaded vampire grin at her filled her with joy. She got up and ran into his arms to give him a long hug. Tears welled in her eyes when she realized that he had been the father who loved her since she was a child, and he'd chosen that role. "It's so wonderful to see you! Are you visiting my dreams again?"

"Maybe," he replied.

She let go of him and took a step back. He looked radiant, a luminous smile spread across his features. In wonder, she took in her surroundings. She was standing in the middle of a field that was covered in summer flowers. Brightly colored butterflies were sunning as they sipped on asters while honey-scented blooms attracted bees. She could feel the warmth of the sun on her skin, and Altman had to be feeling it too. The vampire's face was lit up. In the distance, she saw a bright light that hit her with the full force of its beauty. The sight soothed her, and she experienced a perfect peace.

Her heart thumped with a small shock. "Is this what my mom calls the Summerland? Are we dead?"

"Maybe," he repeated, his gray eyes intent on hers. "Or maybe we're both dreaming. Well, I'm obviously dead, but I've been dead for twenty years. You're dying, and I think we're dying with you. But whereas you'll go back, it seems like we're moving on this time. I feel that light pulling at me."

"I thought my father took you too—that you were now a part of him. I couldn't hear you anymore."

He smiled. "Thank God that didn't happen. Although, we could have tried taking over your father's body and have him kill himself. I wish we could protect you. Fortunately, Dane and Pauline are still there."

"You're really leaving?" she asked hoarsely.

He shot her a look of regret. "I suppose we might be able to stay if we fight it, but I think it's time for you to be free of us too. You'll have a great future with Dane." Awe washed over his face as he gazed at the brilliant light. "Can you feel it? It's amazing!" He chuckled. "I'm not sure Dane is worth giving this up."

She raised her hand to wipe the tears from her

*eyes before she smiled too. "Easy for you to say.
You've lived longer than Dane!"*

*"I wouldn't say 'lived'," he teased as he winked
at her. "But Dane seems like a changed man. Who
knows, maybe you'll get married. He's the type of
man who would want to bind you to him every way he
can think of." He sighed. "If you get married, I wish I
could be there to give you away."*

*She closed her eyes for a moment. She felt him
touch her shoulder before pulling her close for a final
embrace. He kissed the top of her head. "Don't let
Oliver Merenda's actions poison your life," he
whispered. "I've been more of a father than he ever
was. You were a wonderful daughter to me, even
though I've been terrible at protecting you."*

She shook her head. "Don't say that."

*"I'm sorry your mom and Leila can't say
goodbye in dreams. I hope they'll let us visit
sometimes. Ah, I hear Dane calling you."*

"Dane? I don't hear—"

"Erin, open your mouth." Without thought, she
obeyed Dane's command. He was cupping the back
of her head in the palm of his hand, pushing it down
onto the wound in his chest. She could taste blood,
but she didn't have the energy to look. *"Drink
Goldilocks,"* he said, his mind continuing to take
control of hers. She realized that he had moved their
bodies. This time he was lying on his back while she
was on top of him with her face positioned above his
heart. She swallowed his blood. She was surprised at
how thirsty she was and that it felt so natural. Even
the taste seemed heavenly. The last time she had

drunk blood from someone's chest, it had been Stratton's, and that experience had been awful.

"Forget Stratton. Don't let him ruin this moment, Erin," Dane said telepathically. *"This is about us having forever."* The more blood she took, the less control of the thirst she had. The thirst flowed through her with desperation as if she knew instinctively that his blood was essential to her. It was life.

She was still sucking at his wound when pain slammed into her like a tidal wave. She gasped when her muscles twisted. She let out a long wailing scream.

Dane pulled her up, his arms surrounding her in an almost vice-like grip while she was in the throes of never-ending spasms. She could hear him in her mind, but she couldn't understand what he was telling her.

Her mind was filled with chaos. The pain was all she could think about. It consumed her. The torment seemed to last for hours. The excruciating agony surged through her, ravaging her body as the human Erin died, and Erin the vampire was born.

At last, Erin could make out Dane's words. *"Sleep, Goldilocks."*

TWENTY-ONE

With trembling knees and her eyes tightly closed, Margot stood beside Jonathan Stratton's door. She had left it slightly ajar the last time she had left his office so that she could hear it as soon as her manager was on the phone. He had to be distracted and not be using his vampiric super hearing. She silently counted. *Sixty-five, sixty-four...* She inhaled a long, shaky breath. Then bracing herself, she entered the room.

"How can there be no footage?" Margot could hear Stratton's anger. "All you had to do was reactivate the fucking cameras. They were already there!"

She failed to control her shaking fingers, but she tried to keep her face expressionless as she walked toward his desk. He glared at her when she placed the files in front of him. The envelope was hidden at the bottom of the pile. *Fifty-nine, fifty-eight...*

"I could have seen Dane siring Erin, but because of your incompetence—" She turned around before walking slowly toward the exit. She came to an abrupt halt when she heard the whistle. Her stomach lurched, and she swallowed away her nausea as she faced her enemy. He leaned back in his chair with one hand holding the phone to his ear while his other hand had his index finger pointing up. "Wait. Ms. Sloane?"

Her heart thumped loudly in her chest, too fast and too loud. *Please don't let him hear it, or worse. What if he heard the ticking of the bomb?* "Yes, sir?"

"What's this?" he asked, picking up the first folder.

My resignation letter, she thought. *Or my death warrant.* She remembered Erin's comment about collateral damage when Stratton had forced her to take the explosives to blow up her dad. She felt her lips curve, suddenly accepting her fate. She lifted her chin slightly. *I guess that this time the collateral damage is me.*

"I haven't got all day," he snapped.

No, you have about forty seconds. She covered her mouth before a hysterical giggle could escape. She shook her head. *Focus.*

"It's the contracts you needed to sign for extra security, and the report you wanted on that gambler who was caught cheating here last Thursday." It surprised her how calm she sounded. She wondered if his cold gray eyes would be the last things she would see before dying. Goosebumps of revulsion rose on her arms, and she gazed at the lights outside. She would rather die watching the Las Vegas Strip.

"Can I have some privacy?" he asked.

She turned to Stratton, who was frowning at her. "I know you and Erin Holland used to be bosom buddies at one point, but I thought that I taught you better than for you to continue your interest in her."

Oh, thank God, she thought. She nodded and left the office as quickly as she could without raising suspicion. She closed the door behind her and rushed to the stairway when Sandy passed her.

"Sandy," she said automatically, not wanting Dane's spy anywhere near the bomb.

"What? No! My name is Sarah." Margot caught Sandy's sense of panic.

Shit. There was no time to explain. Margot put her finger to her lips, grabbed Sandy's wrist and pulled her toward the exit.

She had just thrown the door from the emergency exit shut when the world shifted. The explosion rocked the top floor, sending them down the top flight of stairs. Sandy slammed hard into her, and Margot cried out in pain. The fire alarm went off, blaring through the stairwell, triggering a sprinkler system that drenched them within seconds. She lay still on her stomach with her eyes closed as her body went numb.

Sandy groaned as she pushed herself off Margot. Margot heard Sandy grasp the railing and pull herself up before bending down to turn Margot over. Margot opened her eyes and narrowed them when the water hit her face. She studied Sandy. Her red hair was plastered to her face. "Can you move?" Sandy yelled. "We're getting soaked in here."

Margot didn't know if her legs would be able support her, but Sandy didn't have the patience for her to find out. She pulled her up, put Margot's arm around her neck and started to walk down the stairs.

"I think I'm okay," Margot said. When Sandy continued holding her as she hurried downstairs,

Margot called out, "I can walk."

Sandy stopped and released her while watching her. Margot leaned on the railing and hesitantly took a step. She expelled a sigh of relief when she didn't collapse. It took them nearly five minutes, but they eventually reached the ground floor of the hotel, just in time to see the fire fighters enter the building.

Sandy was shivering. Margot noticed that the young woman had paled noticeably, but her brown eyes were bright with speculation. "We could have died," Sandy said

"Yes, we could have," Margot said, keeping her voice calm. They shared a look of understanding.

"You knew my real name," Sandy said. "I guess Jonathan Stratton did too?"

"Yes, he did." *And I stopped him from turning you into another one of his victims,* she thought.

"Thank you," Sandy said as if she had heard her. "You'd better get out of here."

"Yes," she agreed, then she turned and left the building. She drove home, let herself in and then turned on the TV. She stopped flicking through the channels once she found the local news channel. All her hopes were pinned on hearing a confirmation of Stratton's death. She thought it would have a nice touch of irony if Stratton died by the same weapon he had forced Erin to use on her father. Margot grinned, recalling Stratton telling Erin that nobody could survive an explosion. Not a voodoo priest. "Not even a vampire," she mumbled.

Poor Erin, turning into a vampire now too, she thought. *I can't imagine a worse fate than having to spend eternity stuck with these monsters.*

There was no use running. If her manager had miraculously survived the blast, he would kill her, but Margot had finally realized that death was preferable to being his slave.

Dane eased himself onto his side and lay watching Erin. She looked so beautiful that he was amazed by his good fortune. Her long blond lashes rested against her cheeks while an abundance of curly hair was draped across the pillow. She was in a peaceful, healing sleep. He wished peace would descend upon him as well. He reached over and plucked his cell phone off the bedside table. After glancing at the screen, he let out a disappointed sigh when he realized there were no calls yet from Crispin. He put the phone down shaking his head, and then wrapped his arms around Erin and nestled close.

Her body temperature wasn't as warm now that she was a vampire, but she still felt soft like Erin. His fingers stroked her hair, gently smoothing it.

What if Crispin decides not to call me when Oliver Merenda and Sabas return to the church? What if he wants to go after them himself? Erin would hate being excluded, but at least she would be safe. Unless Crispin and his pack fail, and they get away again... Alarm burned deep in his chest at the thought. *No, he better not forget to call me.*

Despite Erin's desire to fight her father, Dane had already decided not to wake her if Crispin called. As a newborn vampire, she would be too vulnerable. Cradling her, he knew that he couldn't stand to see her go after such evil. The risk of losing her would be too much of an ordeal for him. He also knew that he wouldn't be able to convince her to let him fight this battle for her. The only option was to keep her in the dark until it was all over. She might resent him for a while, but at least she would be alive. He would have eternity to make it up to her. *I will—*

His cell phone buzzed, interrupting his line of thought. *Finally.* But he frowned when Sandy's name popped up on the screen. Curiously, he accepted the call. "Yes?"

"Hey, it's Sandy. I'm uh, calling from Las Vegas. I-I have some news," Sandy stammered.

"Okay," Dane said softly. He kept his gaze locked on Erin's face as he left the bed. She continued to sleep.

"There was an explosion in Jonathan Stratton's office just now," Sandy said. "He's dead."

"What?" Disbelief filled him. "Are you sure?"

"Yes. I heard someone say they found bits of him all over the office. Besides, there's only one way out, and we didn't see him leave. You can't open the windows on the top floor, so people can't commit suicide," she explained.

"Do they know who did it?" Dane asked as hope surged through him. *If Stratton is dead, it's one less thing to worry about.*

"No, but he had a long list of enemies."

He heard what Sandy didn't say. *And you're one of them.* "True. I heard he has kept trophies of all his victims. The police might be interested in that."

A sound of disappointment escaped her. "You want me to stay anyway? I don't know where those trophies are. Also, I got hired using a fake ID. The police might end up thinking I'm a suspect!"

"Okay, you can go home now," he said. "Goodbye, Sandy." He disconnected, shocked that his enemy, who had always been so well protected, could have been killed that easily. *How did they get through all the security?*

He joined Erin on the bed again. He hugged her as pure euphoria made him feel drunk with joy, and he grinned. Stratton was no more, Erin was going to live forever, and Crispin could call any minute, so he could get rid of the final person who could jeopardize his happiness with Erin. *"Just don't wake up yet, Goldilocks."*

As soon as he had sent out that thought, he wanted to kick himself. He realized immediately that something had changed. He watched as Erin's eyes opened, and she stared straight into his. "Dane," Erin said huskily.

TWENTY-TWO

As Dane watched Erin, his piercing blue eyes burned when his gaze clashed with hers.

"Shh, Goldilocks," he whispered, and she cringed at how overly loud his reassurance was to her sensitive ears. *"Give yourself time,"* he added telepathically.

The bed cracked as he moved closer to her. Somewhere a clock ticked, and the sound echoed through her. Even the persistent buzz of a fly disturbed her overactive hearing.

A sob escaped her lips when hunger suddenly clawed at her belly. The deafening sounds were forgotten as satisfying her hunger became her only focus. Her stomach growled noisily, and when she spotted the bag of blood beside the bed, she reached out. Dane caught her wrist before she could grab it. She exploded in a flurry of movement, twisting and kicking, but his arms were immovable around her. She felt primitive and wild. She cried out in desperation.

"I know you're starving, and I'll feed you. But the blood bag was supposed to be for me after I fed you. Wouldn't you rather sink your teeth into me?"

His deep voice was smooth as black velvet while his eyes glittered with amusement. He exposed his throat, and her mouth watered. Her golden eyes were drawn to his neck, staring as if hypnotized. The ravenous appetite for blood beat through her veins. She clenched her bottom lip between her teeth in anticipation, but then winced in pain when her new elongated fangs cut her. She licked the wound, and it closed immediately.

"Go on," he murmured.

Her rational mind went blank, and she lunged at him with vampire speed. She slid her fangs into his neck, and his blood flowed onto her tongue. One sip, and she was addicted. His spicy taste burst through her, sending her senses spinning. She latched on as if she would starve without him.

He cupped the back of her head and pulled her closer, stroking her spine as she drank.

She shuddered against him as her hunger for blood turned into another hunger. He sensed her need because he slipped his left hand under her nightgown, cupping her breast. Goosebumps peppered her skin when he pinched her nipple, sending a jolt of fire straight to her damp core. She stopped drinking, and instinctively, she used her healing saliva to close the puncture wounds she had created with her fangs. She gripped his shoulders and dug her nails into his skin while his hand left her breast, caressing her stomach and moved downward.

She closed her eyes in bliss when he slipped his hand under her panties. Parting her folds, he probed where she ached. His thumb flicked teasingly over her clit, and she gasped. His fingers slid through her slit, entering her. Her inner muscles clamped down to keep him inside, and he chuckled.

She bit back her disappointment when he removed his fingers, but then he hooked his thumb in her panties before drawing them down, and she exhaled a sigh of relief.

She couldn't wait and dropped her hands to the waistband of his jeans. Her hands trembled as she unzipped him, tugging down the jeans together with his boxer briefs. He left the bed and stepped out of them, while she removed her nightgown. She had just thrown it on the ground when he returned to the bed. He moved fast, holding her down with the weight of his naked body and pinning her hands over her head.

Heat engulfed her when his eyes flared with need. He opened her legs and eased into her, stretching her with his rigid length until he was completely inside her. For a moment he didn't move. All he did was watch her face.

She moaned and arched her back. *Move!* she ordered telepathically.

He grinned before he withdrew partially from her, and then thrust forward. Buried deep, his lips brushed the supersensitive skin under her ear. She cried out in pleasure when his fangs sank into her neck. Her sheath tightened, and she wrapped her legs high around his waist.

He slid out until only the head of his cock remained inside her before slamming back into her again. Fire raced through her when he continued to ride her hard. His thrusts stilled, and then she exploded, screaming his name as waves of pleasure washed over her. His growl followed hers as he found his release.

Afterward, he shifted and pulled her limp body close to his chest.

"Go back to sleep," he said softly.

She closed her eyes, about to give in when the thought struck her that he could have tried to wear her out deliberately. She sat up and spun around before glaring at Dane. "Where's my father?"

He sighed. "We don't know. I'm waiting for Crispin to call me as soon as Merenda gets back to the church." He picked up the blood bag and sank his teeth into it before draining it.

"You need that blood to keep your strength up, so you can face my dad? Don't *I* need to keep my strength up?" she hissed. "You agreed not to exclude me."

"And I'm not," he said. "I would have let you know what happened after he had been dealt with."

Disappointment made her chest ache. She left the bed and put on the nightgown. "That is not what I meant when I let you turn me into a vampire, and you know it!"

"Fine!" he snapped. "Go ahead and get yourself killed then! You might as well kill me too." His eyes looked suspiciously wet, and her anger eased. She sat down on the bed and touched his face.

"I don't want to die, Dane, but I need to do this," she said gently. "I couldn't stand up to my dad before because I wanted to believe his lies. I know he killed your second-in-command, and you deserve retribution. But he almost killed me, and I need retribution more than anyone else."

"But he did kill you, Goldilocks," he said

261

hoarsely. He took her hand and kissed it. "You don't understand. This is not about getting even for what he did to Altman. It's for what he did to you and for what he could still do to you as long as he is alive. You're still a fledgling. You don't know how to use your vampiric powers, and your father stole the rest of yours."

"This isn't a suicide mission," she said. "I don't want to be in your way either, but I don't believe my dad took everything. I still have my blood, the blood of a witch and the blood of a voodoo priest. The power he stole from me was borrowed power."

He shook his head. "He took your werewolf too, and that was part of your blood. Who's to say that he didn't take it all?'

"I guess we don't know, but we'll find out. Come on, Dane. I need you to do this with me."

Dane left the bed and put on his jeans. "Okay. We're not alone anyway. Pauline wanted to help, and the werewolves will assist too because they're pissed off that your father took a werewolf away from them."

Her lips curved. "At least that's one positive outcome of my dad's ritual." She thought about her grandfather, wondering if he would become one since she had bitten him as she had shifted into the werewolf. Realization dawned. "Wait a minute. What happened to my grandfather?"

Dane shrugged. "We locked him up in the room next to Brock's. Why?"

"My grandfather should still possess my father's powers. My grandfather drained him, so my dad would be able to absorb more of mine as soon as he convinced me to give him my powers. I don't think my grandfather ever gave his powers back to him."

He narrowed his eyes. "Are you telling me that the only powers your father now has are yours?"

"Well, I suppose he still has his blood. In a way, he's a fledgling like me. He just got my powers and needs to learn how to use them too. Maybe my grandfather can help."

Dane rushed out of the room, and Erin followed him. They ran up the stairs, and Dane unlocked the door of her grandfather's room before throwing it open. For a moment, she thought her grandfather had used her father's powers to escape, because the room was empty, but then she saw him leave the bathroom, and she breathed more easily.

"You made it, pitit pitit fi mwen." The skinny Haitian smiled a little sadly at her. "I'm glad."

"You're still here," she said.

He arched his black eyebrows upwards. "The door was locked."

Dane put his hand on her shoulder. "I understand that you took your son's powers in some kind of ritual. You could have used them to get out."

"Oh, I wouldn't use Oliver's powers. Not anymore. He'd know. He always knows." Her grandfather cleared his throat nervously. "She didn't tell you? He made me take them."

"I don't understand," Dane said. "After you got his powers, why didn't you fight back?"

"Of course not! He was testing me, testing my loyalty. Sabas has powers too. If he thought for one second that I would betray my son, Sabas would have intervened."

"Instead, you betrayed your granddaughter," Dane pointed out.

Color crept up her grandfather's face. "I know. I'm sorry Erin. I guess that's what I do. I betray my family. When I went to Hope Acres twenty years ago, I betrayed Oliver. I tried to imprison him, so he wouldn't kill innocents anymore. I thought I was strong enough to subdue him. He went home with me, but he ended up imprisoning me instead." He snorted. "I was delusional for thinking I could control him."

"You can help us subdue him now," Erin said.

Dane tightened his grip on her shoulder. "No. You can't trust him."

"Your man is right," her grandfather agreed easily.

"But you could have gotten out. You stayed here," she insisted. She refused to believe that her grandfather really wanted to hurt her.

He shook his head. "I wasn't acting noble. I just thought I'd be safer here. I didn't want my son to find me and drain me again. He'll come for me. As you know, I have something of his." She couldn't detect any bitterness in her grandfather's voice. Just resignation.

"So you just accept it?" she asked.

He sighed. "I had a brush with death a couple of years ago. I met my loa then, and Kalfu wasn't happy with me. He showed me what awaits me after I die. Sorry Erin, but your granpè is a coward. I wouldn't dare use Oliver's powers against him."

"Let it go, Goldilocks. He's an old man who has been controlled by his son for too long to stand up to him," Dane said. "He can stay here. At least that way, Oliver won't be able to get his powers back. I don't suppose you want to stay here to keep an eye on him?"

She frowned at him. "Just because he doesn't want to use my father's powers against him, doesn't mean that we shouldn't use them."

Dane's head swung around as his eyes widened with shock. He immediately understood what she meant. "You can forget about that! I'm not letting you get anywhere near that altar again!"

She laid her hand on his chest, trying to calm him down. "It's only an idea. It's not that I want to get his powers, but my grandfather won't use them, and people have tried to fight my father before and failed. He killed some pretty powerful people."

Dane studied her, his face a mask of total resolve. "Your father and Sabas are outnumbered. We have the werewolves, my clan and even a witch on our side. We don't need you to risk yourself further."

"Well, uh, technically I would be the one risking myself," her grandfather said softly. "Not Erin. It's not just my son and Sabas you would need to fight. Oliver has black magic on his side. As a bokor, he controls the dead, you know. He should still be able to do that. I never drained him completely." He took a step back when Dane studied him like a predator would watch its prey. But then her grandfather surprised her when he defiantly raised his chin and warned them, "Maybe he would control you too… You're both vampires. He did manage to get your second-in-command to kill himself, didn't he?"

The hair on her neck stood up when she recalled

Altman stabbing himself through his heart.

"I think you need Oliver's powers to succeed. I'll do it. I can always say that you forced me to give them. I think this is what my loa would want me to do."

"Your loa would want you to shut the hell up!" Dane snapped. "Or fight your son instead of letting a girl do the fighting for you."

Erin scowled. If only she could shift into her leopard form and teach him not to underestimate her. She felt the rub of fangs against her tongue and realized she wasn't completely powerless. *But I could use some help.*

She saw the eager expression on her grandfather's face. "Thanks, granpè, I accept. Don't worry Dane. As soon as we have defeated my father I will give the powers back to him. He's right though. He might be able to control us because we're now both considered undead. What if he uses us against the werewolves? Do you want to risk that?"

Worry filled Dane's face. "No. But I don't want to risk you either. Let me have them."

"No." Her voice was resolute. "This is my battle. Don't make me fight you too."

He inhaled sharply. "If this goes wrong, I will track you down in the afterlife!"

She gave him a cautious smile and leaned in to brush a kiss against his lips. "If this goes wrong, I will come back to haunt you."

He cupped her face in his hands and gently returned her kiss. "Promise?" His warm breath stirred the curls against her cheeks.

"I promise," she said.

TWENTY-THREE

"**A**re you sure we shouldn't put manacles on *him?*" Dane asked Erin telepathically as they walked toward the Devereaux Church with her grandfather in tow. Dane had parked his SUV several blocks from the church to avoid alerting her father of their presence, but she wondered if anything could be hidden from her father. It worried her that he hadn't returned to the church, almost as if he had known she would survive, and he was lying in wait for her to come back so he could try out his new powers on the one he had stolen them from.

It seemed like such a peaceful night to be out on a stroll. The warm evening breeze made the Spanish moss sway softly on the live oaks. Erin listened closely for any sounds that would indicate the return of her father and Sabas, but instead all she heard were the werewolves and vampires mumbling. There had to be at least twenty people surrounding the gothic building, but except for the alpha, they were hidden well.

Crispin gave her a faint smile as he approached them, a smile that she assumed was meant as reassurance. If so, it didn't work. His burr cut hairdo combined with his intense brown eyes and military style clothes made her feel as if they were about to start a war. She inhaled a deep breath of the warm evening air. Her hands tightened into fists. *I can do this.*

She missed the voices encouraging her. Dane must have sensed her anxiety because he reached out, took her hand and gave it a little squeeze. "You've got this," he said before turning to Crispin. "Has he shown himself yet?"

The alpha shook his head. "Are you sure she's ready?"

"*She* can talk," she snapped. "And if *she* isn't ready, *she* will be soon. Shall we?" she asked her grandfather.

With a quick, nervous glance toward the werewolf, her grandfather nodded and followed her into the church.

As soon as she entered the basement, she froze. Her heart dropped. Her breath caught in her throat when she saw the altar in front of her. An image of herself trapped on that thing instantly flashed through her mind. She could almost feel her father's iron grip on her wrists as he refused let go while he painfully drained the life out of her. She felt a cold sweat cover her body, chilling her to the bone. Her stomach churned with such bile that she pressed her hand to her mouth.

"Take a breath, pitit pitit fi mwen," her grandfather murmured. He put his hand on her shoulder in support.

She turned around. "I can't do this. I could kill you. What if I completely drain you?"

He smiled at her, and his golden eyes glinted. "I trust you, and I'm not just saying that. You know how much I don't want to die."

She swallowed hard. "I may have killed you already when I bit you."

"What do you mean?"

"Don't you sense the werewolf?" she whispered.

His eyes widened in dismay. "What werewolf? Are you telling me that I'm going to turn into a werewolf during the next full moon?"

She cleared her throat. "Well, maybe not. I mean, if you haven't sensed him, maybe my bite didn't break the skin." *But I tasted blood...*

"Yes, it did!" he said.

"Well, maybe you'll get lucky, and I'll drain the werewolf out of you now too." She hoped she was wrong. *Maybe I can't take the werewolf if he hasn't shown himself yet. Please let that be the case.* "See, there are benefits for you too as long as he doesn't find out you gave his powers to me voluntarily."

She witnessed the horrific realization slam into her grandfather's brain the moment the words were out of her mouth. "Oh no! I forgot about the cameras!" he said.

"What cameras?" she asked. "There are cameras here? No wonder he hasn't arrived!"

He sighed in frustration. "Oh, don't worry. He'd never leave the country without the altar and the other equipment."

Footsteps approached, and Erin looked up to see Dane join them. "I heard you talking about cameras?"

"Yes, Sabas kept an eye on what was happening in here, so he'd know what actions to take. Oliver had instructed Sabas beforehand that as soon as he told you the story about me teaching him how to drain people that you'd be ready for the next step. Then Sabas could bring the gun with blanks."

Erin suppressed the embarrassment she felt when confronted with how gullible she had been. She tried to keep her tone casual when she turned to Dane. "Should we abort now we know that he's watching us?"

She knew she hadn't fooled Dane when he said, "Don't blame yourself, Goldilocks. Your father is a master at tricking people. He's so cunning that he's managed to convince even the most cynical people. You're his daughter, so of course you'd want to believe the best of him."

Dane then turned to her grandfather. "Show us where the cameras are. We can at least stop him from seeing what we're doing next." Her grandfather didn't move. "Why are you hesitating? The cat is out of the bag! He knows you're helping us already. If Sabas was listening in on the conversations between Oliver and Erin, then there had to be sound. He was going to come after you anyway. Help us, and the chances are that he won't succeed this time!"

Her grandfather entered the prison and moved one of the bricks in the wall to reveal a small camera. He pulled it out and walked up to a wooden mask that he lifted. It had also been hiding a camera. He handed them over to Dane who threw them on the ground before stepping on them several times until they were completely destroyed.

Her grandfather didn't stand still to watch the destruction. Instead, he climbed on the altar and lay down. "Erin," he said.

Seeing her grandfather lie on the altar created another flashback. Her mouth felt dry.

Dane kicked the pieces of broken camera away. "Go on, Goldilocks. I will watch over you. Crispin and the others will keep an eye on the perimeter."

Erin sat down on the throne and took hold of her grandfather's wrists.

"Don't kill me, okay?" her grandfather said, and she immediately released him. "Just kidding," he added. "Really. I trust you."

Reluctantly, Erin grabbed him again, and seconds later, her grandfather recited the French spell on the wall.

When he was done, they waited, but they didn't have to wait long. Seconds passed before she heard a gasp, and then the thrashing and struggling began.

"Don't let go!" Dane ordered.

She tightened her grip on her grandfather while his ragged breathing echoed in her ears. A flash of bright light blinded her, and she closed her eyes in protection. A combination of heat and power filled her when the sparks from his aura touched her hands, rushing through her entire body. The sensation was addictive, and soon all she could think of was the need to feed that energy her body was suddenly craving. The hunger roared inside her.

"Erin stop. Let him go. It's enough." Dane's order reached her telepathically, and it had the same effect as if a light switch had been flipped. Erin opened her hands and eyes. Vivid spots appeared at the edge of her vision, and she blinked several times.

"How are you feeling?" Dane asked softly,

leaning over her.

"Granpè?" she murmured.

She heard a small whimpering sound and Dane said, "He's fine."

She got up from the throne and stumbled, mind reeling. Dane caught her and held her up. The energy she had absorbed raced through her body. She took several steps, and the whirling in her head disappeared. "Thanks. I'm okay now."

He eyed her with suspicion as he released her. She studied her arms, surprised that they looked so normal. Based on how she felt, she would have expected them to glow.

Her grandfather stood up too before sitting down on the altar. "It's quite a rush, right?"

She focused on her new power and sensed the bodies that were buried around the Devereaux Church. Somehow, she knew there were forty-eight of them. Thirty-two of them were men, fifteen were women and one was a baby girl. Excitement and power swirled together into a heady cocktail, drugging her. Drunk with the power flowing through her veins, she smiled at Dane. *"It's amazing. Can you feel it?"*

Dane frowned. "I experience some of it through our bond. You sense the dead?" he asked.

She nodded.

"Can you sense where all the vampires are too?" His voice was filled with concern.

She thought about Dane's clan, picturing Brock, and then she instantly knew he was standing beside Victor. She even knew how the vampire felt about the werewolf.

Dane raised his hands. "You don't need to say it. I felt it too. I just hope it's because of our bond that you sensed my second-in-command and that it's not related to your father's power."

"We're about to find out," Crispin said behind them. Startled, Erin spun around. She had been so concentrated on her newfound power, that she hadn't even heard him enter the room. *A bad sign.*

"What?" Dane asked.

Coldness swept through her. Everyone knew what Crispin's message was.

"They're here," she said.

She was about to leave the basement when Dane put his hand on her shoulder, turning her around. His fingers tangled in her hair as his head swooped down. His lips covered hers, claiming her. A hard, desperate growl escaped his chest, and she melted into him, completely forgetting that Crispin and her grandfather were there.

Dane lifted his head to stare down at her as if he was memorizing her face. There was something possessive in his expression. "My instincts are screaming at me to lock you away while I get rid of your father, but I know how much you want this. However, if I sense that you're losing the fight, I'll step in. I won't lose you tonight," he vowed. "We're in this together."

Erin took his hand from her hair and gave it a small kiss. "Thank you."

Her grandfather cleared his throat. "Great. Is it okay if I don't join you? I have no more powers left, so I would only be in the way."

Dane glared at him, but Erin understood. "That's

fine," she said. "We can even lock you up in here if you like? If you're locked in here, then my father won't think you helped us, so it might save your life if we don't make it."

"He would have seen the video, but okay," her grandfather said. She locked the door. Then she moved to the stairs where Dane stopped her once more. "We *will* make it."

Erin nodded. "Of course, they are outnumbered." She led the way, but while her mind told her that the odds were in their favor, she couldn't suppress the feeling that they were kidding themselves.

TWENTY-FOUR

Silently, Erin, Crispin and Dane walked upstairs to the chapel. Erin was grateful that the men trusted her enough to let her walk in front of them, but she still had to fight down the waves of nausea as she thought about the battle ahead.

She didn't have a gun anymore, but that was probably for the best. She didn't want to risk her father controlling her mind and making her shoot Pauline. She told herself that as a vampire she had fangs, the power to mesmerize, super speed, super hearing and immortality. Unfortunately, except for speed and immortality, her father had the same abilities as well as all the other powers he had stolen from her. She hoped that the magic she inherited from her mother was still part of her blood. If it wasn't, she would have to find a way to use her father's voodoo magic, which was now coursing through her veins.

The dark magic sang to her. As they left the church, she had to suppress the part of her that desperately wanted to reach out to the buried bodies surrounding them. She imagined making them do her bidding. She thought of Michael Jackson's Thriller video and suppressed a nervous giggle. Another part of her was terrified that she would enjoy the power too much. There was something appealing about having power over the dead—controlling death itself.

Pauline and Billy ran up to them. Her old roommate touched her arm. "Are you okay?"

Erin opened her mouth to respond when she heard the beating of drums. Her head snapped up, and she caught sight of her father and Sabas approaching them. Pauline saw them too, so she and Billy quickly joined the team behind Erin. Erin's lips curved into a smile. *They literally have my back,* she thought. The smile faded when she saw the diabolical grin on her father's face. *I hope I can protect them.*

She frowned while she studied her foes. The sound of drums followed them. She could hear their thundering beat pulling at her, but she couldn't see anyone hitting the drums.

"It has to be a recording," Dane told her telepathically. *"Ignore it."*

They were both dressed in red. Her father had a red scarf on his head, whereas Sabas' scarf was gold. Sabas was holding a torch blazing with bright red flames. Her father's shadow loomed over one of the gravestones, and she shivered when she sensed the body in that grave. *Do you feel her too?*

The color of the albino's eyes had changed to black, and he was weeping while chanting in a foreign language. Despite the warm temperature, Erin broke out in a cold sweat.

She took a long, deep breath and then swallowed heavily. Her mouth felt dry. Her father wasn't hiding his evilness from her anymore. The darkness radiated from inside him.

"Erin, come to me," he ordered softly. His voice induced a deep trance, and without thought, she obeyed.

"No Erin," Dane said in her mind. *"You don't want this. Fight it or I will fight him for you."*

She froze. Her jaw tightened as she fought to shatter the compulsion. She blinked several times, and then saw realization in her father's face that something had interrupted his thrall. His wicked eyes narrowed as they settled on Dane.

"Dane Lynch, bring my daughter to me," her father murmured.

Before Erin could say anything to counter his command, Dane grabbed her arm, and he took a step forward as he pulled her along with him.

"Dane, stop it right now," she reached out using their vampiric bond. *"You're supposed to fight him too."*

Their connection worked. Dane immediately moved backward, dragging her away from her father before releasing her. She heard him swear.

Two can play this game, she thought as she decided to use her vampiric thrall on him in the same way he'd tried to use his control over the dead on her. "Father, you want to come to me," she said. She kept her voice low and steady as she locked her gaze with his, enthralling him to get lost in the fathomless depths of her eyes.

Mesmerized, her father took a step in her direction, but Sabas interrupted his chanting to wave the torch in front of his master. The flames touched her father's arm, and he cried out a scream of pain. He glared at his arm and was about to snap at Sabas when he recognized the rescue. Intrigued, he turned to study Erin, and he startled her when his laughter echoed in the darkness of the graveyard.

"Finally, a real challenge! Oh Erin, we're well matched! You really are my daughter," he said, with a certain amount of pride. "Amazing. How many lives do you have? It'd be such a waste to kill you."

He looked at the people behind her and sighed. "Listen, you can keep your undead life and your new friends. All I want is to pick up my father and my altar. Don't interfere, and you'll never see me again. Unless you'd like to…"

She wouldn't allow his friendly demeanor to trick her again. It dawned on her that her father didn't know that her grandfather had transferred his powers to her. *Maybe I can use them against him.* She noticed Sabas watching her suspiciously. He hadn't continued chanting, so she focused on his twitchy eyes. "Sabas, you want to set my father on fire," she said, using her hypnotic voice to ensnare him.

Sabas lowered the torch, and it was about to touch her father when her father cried out, "Sabas stop!" Sabas stood still and stared at the torch in horror. Sweat ran down his pale face, and he glowered.

"You disappoint me, ma petite," her father said. She drew in her breath in shock when he pulled a knife out of his belt and slashed open his hand. Blood gushed from the wound, and as it splattered over the grave beside him, Sabas began to chant again, his voice matching the beat of the drums. The melody pounded through her.

Erin sensed movement beneath the earth. Her

father wasn't just reaching out to the woman in the grave he had covered with his own blood, he was calling out to all the bodies in the graveyard.

"Sabas, set him on fire!" she repeated.

"No Sabas!" her father said, but he didn't have to worry about Sabas. Her panic had resonated in her voice, hurting her powers of persuasion. "Everyone will shut up and watch Sabas chant with me instead."

She opened her mouth, but no sound came out. Her father had joined Sabas in his chanting and while she didn't understand what they were saying, she felt what was happening. She saw the earth move in several places. *"We're about to have company,"* she told Dane telepathically.

At first, it was as if branches were growing out of the ground at an accelerated speed. But then she recognized the first skeleton hand, followed by a skeleton arm. The sight chilled Erin to her core. About ten feet from where she stood, a hand that was still covered in flesh poked through the earth. A second hand materialized. When the corpse managed to push itself out of the ground, Erin had to cover her mouth to stop herself from gagging. There had to be over a hundred maggots crawling on the back of its head.

A hand touched her arm, and Erin jumped. She turned to her old roommate who backed away. "Sorry," Pauline mouthed. She pointed at the other dead climbing out of their graves. Erin had been so transfixed by that one body, that she was missing the other corpses joining them. They were now facing her father as they stood on wobbly legs. *"Waiting for his command."* The foul stench of rotten flesh made her eyes water, and she swallowed down the bile rising in her throat.

"Well Erin, you put up a good fight," Dane answered. *"It's time for me to signal the werewolves and vampires, so we can shut them up!"*

She clenched her fists as she saw several zombies turn around to face her. Some had glazed-over eyes rolling in their exposed sockets. They stank of rotting flesh. Some had cracked skin with mold growing on it while others looked like skeletons. Their clothes had a greenish color. She flinched when she felt the baby's struggle. The child couldn't claw her way out of the grave, but that didn't stop her from trying. *"This is horrific. If he dies, will they then stop acting like zombies?"*

"I suppose. Now, are you ready to let us take over?" Dane's voice echoed impatiently in her mind.

"Wait! I have his power! Some are already looking at me. Let me take over!"

"They're looking at you because they want to eat your brains," Dane replied. *"But fine. Speak! But this is your last attempt!"*

Erin opened her mouth and sliced her fangs across her wrists. She now had the attention of all the zombies. Unfortunately, the smell of her blood combined with the scent of her father's blood was also affecting the vampires and werewolves if the growls behind her were any indication. The violent sounds of hunger behind her were making her skin crawl. *Oh shit, do I have to control the werewolves too?* Suddenly, another thought struck her. *What if the werewolf was already part of my grandfather when I took his powers? Will I shift now too? As if I don't have enough to worry about already!*

She couldn't sense any creatures pushing against her flesh from the inside, so she decided to filter out the sounds of the shifting werewolves behind her and focused on the zombies in front of her instead.

Mesmerized, they watched her drip her blood on the gravestone closest to her. The zombies didn't move. They merely stood watching her.

Her father had stopped chanting, and his silence caught her attention. She saw him blink several times, and then their eyes met. He looked at her with a stunned, confused expression. His nostrils flared, and he snarled in protest as his knees gave way, and he dropped to all fours.

"No!" he bellowed. "Attack them!"

Dane moved, ready to shield her from the zombies, but she shook her head. She knew they wouldn't touch her. With sudden insight, Erin realized that her father's ritual was also calling out the werewolf he had taken from her, and it was interfering with his ability to control the zombies. This was the first time that Erin was grateful that Billy had bitten her. Her mouth spread into a triumphant grin.

She watched her father's jaw crack as his body twisted in transformation before he arched up and howled at the moon. His face stretched into a muzzle with razor-sharp teeth. "Attack her!" The words were barely intelligible, as his voice had become more animal than human. The zombies stood still. She sensed they were waiting for her command.

All around, Erin heard menacing growls. Several werewolves had moved in front of her, ready to attack the new wolf, but they appeared to be weary of the zombies.

"It's okay," she said. She stared at the zombies, but she wasn't sure if she was trying to reassure them, the werewolves or herself. She was furious at her father for forcing these bodies to act as his puppets. She wondered if they were aware of what was happening.

She faced the zombie closest to her. The woman was one of the few who were well preserved. She wore a greenish wedding dress. "It's okay," she repeated. "What would you like?"

"Erin?" Dane whispered. "What are you doing?"

"Giving them a choice," she said without taking her gaze from the woman. "Would you like to leave this body now, or would you like revenge on your maker first?" She pointed at the large black werewolf, whose muscles were still contorting.

"Erin, I don't think she can understand you," Pauline said. "And I think you need to hurry."

"Yes," Erin agreed. From the corner of her eye, she watched her father rise up. She still felt the hopelessness of the baby who could not join them. The zombies' gazes were vacant, but their emotions were still there. They hated the man who had created them, and Erin could not help but think it was poetic justice if the voodoo priest was brought to an end by the beings he had sought to dominate.

"Have your revenge!" she commanded. "Kill them so nobody will be forced to crawl out of their graves ever again."

All forty-seven zombies turned to her werewolf father and his albino helper. They surrounded them and shambled toward them. Her father let out a roar of outrage. His wolf body lowered into a crouching position, and then he jumped on one of the zombies. He bit into the corpse's arm, tearing it off easily, but the other arm was still there to push at the wolf's eyes, and the zombie still had teeth to sink into the wolf's neck. Her father let out a long-drawn out whine. He managed to tear off the zombie's other arm and shake him off, but then three other zombies replaced the one he had incapacitated.

Erin turned to see some of the other zombies attack Sabas and pull him down to the ground. She watched them chew on his arms, legs and neck. Sabas screamed, and it was clear that he couldn't fight them off. There were just too many. Slurping noises came from the zombies as they feasted on his body. Blood and bits of flesh sprayed the ground. Sabas made wheezing gurgles as he lay dying.

"Wow, I'd better not get you mad," Pauline whispered, touching her left arm.

Crispin had shifted back to his human form. "Usually, my wolf would want to join in on a kill, but this is too gory even for me."

There was an odd calm about Erin as she observed her father and Sabas being devoured. To her, it was as if what she was seeing wasn't real. Time slowly ticked by.

"Are you okay?" Dane asked.

She nodded. "Is it bad that I don't feel sorry?"

Dane's mouth twitched, and humor lit his blue eyes. "No, they would have done the same to us if they could have. I'm lucky that my mate is such a badass."

Erin opened her mouth, but she forgot what she was about to say when she saw that the zombies were done munching on their prey. Her father and Sabas were no more.

The zombies rose and turned to her again. *Waiting for my next command,* she thought.

"Thank you," she said to them. "I set you free now."

They didn't do anything, other than stare at her. *Shit. Why won't they go?*

"Maybe I can help," a familiar voice said behind them. They spun around to see Ramin Sceledorse walk up to them. He was still in the body of the taxi driver, showing his rotten teeth as he grinned at them.

"What the hell are you doing here?" she snapped.

"I can't believe we couldn't sense him before!" Crispin said.

"I can," Erin said, pointing at the zombies. Their stench was worse than that of Ramin, but not much worse.

"I knew something was about to happen, so I decided to stay in case anyone required my help. And you do!" He giggled.

Dane glared at him. "Get the hell out!"

The demon shrugged. "It's your funeral. But if you're clever, you'll let me help you gain control of them. For a price of course."

Erin still felt the baby clawing at its coffin lid, and she wanted them to be at peace as soon as possible. "What do you want?"

"Erin, no!" Dane said.

"Finally, some sensh!" Ramin lisped.

"Erin, wait, I think I got it. I just think you need

to spill more blood," Pauline said. "That's how you got them to listen to you the first time, right? Or maybe use a spell?"

"Or maybe combine the two?" Erin suggested. When she saw the disappointed look on Ramin's face, she knew she had to try. She glanced at her wrist, the one she had cut open earlier. The wound had healed completely. She raised her wrist to her mouth once more and used her fangs to slash it open. Blood sprayed from the open wound, and she covered several graves with it. Then closing her eyes, she said:

> "*Powers That Be,*
> *Please set these poor zombies free.*
> *As is my will, so mote it be."*

A surge of energy filled her, connecting her to the zombies. For a moment, she was afraid that she would sense their resentment of her using them to kill her father and Sabas, but the only emotion she got from them was peace. The power rose inside her, making her shiver until it erupted in a warm glow. She fell, but Dane was there to catch her.

When she opened her eyes, Erin found herself lying in Dane's arms. She gazed at the graveyard, and she was relieved to see that the zombies had disappeared.

Dane leaned in to brush a kiss on her temple.

"I guess I'm not such a badass after all," she muttered.

"Are you kidding me? You're the biggest badass

I know. You would have been a fantastic enforcer." Erin jerked her head in Crispin's direction. He was studying her with a twinkle sparkling in his brown eyes.

"Thanks," she said. Her legs shook when she pushed herself to her feet. "I fainted though."

Admiration flashed in the alpha's expression. Then he turned to Dane. "I'm sorry to let such a powerful addition to my pack go. She's lucky she's a vampire, otherwise I'd be tempted to bite her myself!"

Dane's teeth clenched. "I know you're only kidding, but really, it's too soon to joke about that."

"Who says I'm kidding?" Crispin chuckled. Then he waved at her. "Don't worry. I know when I'm not wanted. Okay guys. Let's go."

Erin watched the werewolves leave. Then she turned to face her old roommate. She threw her arms around her, hugging her goodbye. When Pauline whispered, "I'm so proud of you," Erin had to blink back her tears.

"Shall we release your grandfather now?" Dane asked.

Pauline let her go, and said with a wide smile, "And I know when *I*'m not wanted. Erin, I'll give you a call tomorrow evening."

Erin nodded, wishing her friend a fond farewell as she watched her leave with Billy by her side. Then she and Dane turned and returned to the basement. Seeing the relief that washed over her grandfather when he caught sight of them warmed her heart until she realized that if her father had been the one to enter the basement instead of them, her grandfather would have gotten locked up again. *Maybe he's just happy to see me because he knows I won't torture him. Or maybe he's eager to get his son's powers back.*

The idea of having to lie down on the altar again and let him drain her caused panicky feelings in the pit of her stomach, and she sucked in her breath.

"Erin, what is it?" Dane asked. He took her hand and gave it a little squeeze. She tried to smile reassuringly, but she wasn't very successful because her grandfather said, "I think she's afraid that I'm expecting to get my son's powers back."

Dane frowned at her grandfather, who held up his hands in a shrug. "Hey, I'm happy to let her keep them! I'll have enough to deal with when it's time for the next full moon!"

"W-what?" she stammered. "But you told me you hadn't sensed the werewolf yet. Has something changed?"

"Well uh..." He cleared his throat. "I heard all the growling outside, and then I think I smelled blood, and something inside me—something wild— was pushing against my skin, like it wanted to get out."

In horror, she studied her grandfather's frail physique. She couldn't imagine him surviving the painful shift into a werewolf. Most people didn't. With his gray hair and thin build, she expected the black man to be at least seventy years old.

She closed her eyes briefly. "The shift will kill you," she muttered. "My bite—"

"Don't blame yourself pitit pitit fi mwen," he grandfather interrupted. "I was keeping you prisoner, and you were only trying to escape. I don't think I would have lived much longer anyway. If my son had come for me now, I probably wouldn't have survived either. If I don't survive the transformation, at least I'll get to spend my last days in freedom. Or so I hope." Her grandfather wiggled his eyebrows at the locked door, and Erin quickly unlocked it.

"You'll need to stay with Crispin's pack, so they can help you with your werewolf. He was bummed that he lost me, but this way, he'll still have a part of me. As long as—"

"As long as the shift doesn't kill me," her grandfather said. He sighed. "It's probably what I deserve. Before your dad locked me up, I performed similar rituals on criminals. He was right that I was the one who taught him. I thought it was what they deserved. But after being on the receiving end for the past twenty years, the experience has really opened my eyes."

"What should we do with all this voodoo stuff?" Dane asked Erin.

"I think we should destroy it," her grandfather proposed as he left the prison. "Can we leave the altar and throne in the church and then blow it up? This is such a bad place."

Of course it's a bad place, she thought. *My mom and sister were murdered here!*

"Good idea. You might want to ask Margot for explosives," Dane said.

Puzzled, Erin shook her head. "Margot? You mean Stratton's secretary? What are you talking about?"

Dane grinned, "Of course! I forgot to tell you

with everything else going on, but while you were recovering from becoming a vampire, I got a call that Jonathan Stratton had died. He was blown up."

She rolled her eyes, but her lips curved. "I don't believe it. So he won't be threatening my friends anymore? And you think Margot did it?"

He shook his head. "Just kidding. Sandy told me they didn't know who was responsible. It would have been nice if she had fought back though, right?"

She remembered Stratton's words when he had ordered her to kill her father. *Nobody can survive an explosion, Erin.* And then she thought about Margot's amputated toe and the time Stratton had humiliated her to stop her from leaving him. Margot hadn't given her all the explosives when she had gone to Haiti. *I hope you really did blow him up!*

"If the police want to punish her, could you maybe arrange a lawyer?" she asked.

Dane put his arm around her. "Of course, but I'm sure that won't be necessary. Now, what do you think? Are you okay with keeping your father's powers and blowing up the church even if that means that you'll be stuck with these powers forever?"

She realized that when she had decided to get her father's powers, she hadn't really thought things through. The idea of having to lie back on the altar terrified her. She didn't ever want to feel so powerless again.

"I'll keep them," she said.

TWENTY-FIVE

Erin discovered that pruning roses in Dane's garden had a calming effect on her. As she threw the pile of broken and dead wood into a bin, she wondered if she should now consider it her garden too. She glanced up when the intercom beeped. She knew that Maura was responsible for deciding who to let in, but when her extraordinary hearing picked up Margot's voice, she dropped the pruning shears. She walked up to the gate and opened it.

Margot scanned Erin from head to toe while displaying a ghost of a smile. An uncomfortable silence settled over them as Stratton's ex-secretary examined Erin's mud stained jeans, disheveled hair and dirty gardening gloves.

Mortified, Erin removed the gloves. "Hi Margot. What a surprise!" She stuck out her bare hand and was relieved when Margot shook it. "I hope you're well?"

Margot smiled, and Erin thought she looked ten years younger. She was also dressed differently. She no longer kept her long, brown hair in a tight bun, and instead of her usual dress suit and high-heeled shoes, she wore jeans and sneakers. "Are you wondering if I'm on the run—trying to flee the cops?"

Color flamed Erin's cheeks, and she peered at the mansion to see if anyone was watching them. "I'm not wondering that at all! Would you like to come in?"

Margot shook her head. "No thanks. I'm good."

"We don't bite. Well, not usually." Erin chuckled.

"Ah yes, Stratton told me you had become a vampire now."

Erin laughed at the look of disgust on Margot's face. "They're not all like Stratton."

Margot snorted. "Right! Didn't your Dane Lynch enjoy setting vampires on fire? Oh, I'm sorry, that was rude."

Erin wasn't offended. "Not if it's true. But if you dislike us so much, why are you here? You could have called."

"No. Telephone conversations might be recorded." Margot winced. "Not that I think you would record it… Oh hell. I'm not sure. I felt bad about our last conversation, and I didn't want to leave the US without telling you."

Erin shot her an incredulous look. "You traveled all the way to Hope Acres from Las Vegas just to say you felt bad?"

"Okay, maybe not. I guess I wanted to share what happened with someone. The only person I have in my life is my brother, but he's not able to communicate anymore ever since he overdosed."

"I'm sorry," Erin said.

"It's been five years, but I'm still so angry at him

for throwing away his life like that. So now it's just me. I was angry with you too for making me think I could get away from Stratton. Then I blamed you when he found out and cut off my toe."

Erin sighed. "You were right to be angry. He caught me off guard. I'm glad he's not in our lives anymore." She leaned forward and whispered, "Do I have you to thank for that?"

Margot's lips curved again. "I used the extra explosives that he made me get for your trip to Haiti. I was a nervous wreck when I put the bomb on his desk, and he asked me some questions. I kept thinking I was going to die with him."

"Are you worried about the police? Is that why you decided to leave the country? We'd be happy to help you with a good defense lawyer. Dane's filthy rich."

Margot's eyes twinkled. "Thanks, but I'm not worried. The cops found Stratton's trophies and realized that he had a lot of enemies. I'm not even a blip on their radar. Edward said that they even found some compromising information on the head of the police department."

"Edward was his second-in-command, right? Is he going to become the new master vampire of Las Vegas?" Erin asked. *Dane would want to know.*

Margot shrugged. "Probably. I don't know. Now that I'm out, I don't really care about vampire politics anymore."

"Fair enough," Erin agreed. "So, where are you going to?"

"I thought I could travel to Europe. I always wanted to go. Jonathan Stratton was a monster, but he did pay well, so I can finally enjoy the money I saved."

"Well, I'm glad you're okay," Erin said. "If you need any help, please let me know."

"Thanks. You know, in a way I'm glad that it happened the way it did."

Of its own volition, her gaze slid toward Margot's foot.

"Well, not that part, but I'm glad that I had the chance to stand up to him. I suppose that if we hadn't had our conversation, I'd have stayed with Stratton until my retirement or until one of his twisted games finally killed me. I lost a toe, but I gained my self-respect. I feel victorious. You know what I mean?"

Erin nodded, and they said goodbye. She turned to her new home to find Dane watching her from the front entrance. "So she feels victorious?" he said as she walked up to him.

She dropped a kiss on his lips. "And so do I."

When Erin and Dane turned onto the road leading to the Hope Acres cemetery, Erin had a moment of nervous fright. Her hands tightened on the bouquet of lavender and mint. Her pulse raced, and her breath caught in her throat. *What if I can't do it?"*

Sitting on the driver's side, Dane glanced sideways at her before turning his attention back to the road. "You'll be fine. If you can't do it, you'll have Pauline to help you with the ritual."

She managed a weak smile. "I know. I'm just

afraid that I'm about to find out that I no longer have the witch in me. My mom always wanted me to do magic. At first, I fought it because I wanted to be normal so badly. I fought her. She was so proud when I finally learned to embrace that part of me."

"Even if your father took the magic you inherited from your mother, I'm sure she'd still be proud of you. Besides, except for the eyes, you look just like her."

She sighed. "I know. I'm just bummed that I wasted so much time resisting who I was." She spotted Pauline at the entrance and waved to her. "Unlike my previous roommate." While Pauline wore white, Erin had decided to wear a black dress.

Dane parked his SUV in the parking lot, and as soon as they got out of the car, Pauline walked up to them. She stood beaming before them, and her eyes glowed with excitement. "I already set everything up. Ah great, you got the flowers and mint. I put my stuff in front of your mother's urn. Your sister's urn was put beside hers."

"Thanks," Erin said. They walked through an ornamental iron gate and entered the cemetery. The driveway was draped with oak trees. Erin had thought it would be creepy walking in the cemetery after dark, but she found it surprisingly peaceful. Birds were singing in harmony, and some of her tension seeped out of her. Several graves were adorned with carved stone angels while others were surrounded by scalloped picket fences.

"It's pretty," she concluded.

Pauline raised her eyebrows. "You sound as if you've never been here before."

Erin felt a flush rising in her cheeks. "That's right. I've never visited this place, but I didn't have to. Until last week, my mom was always there, watching over me. Now it's been six days since I last heard her voice." *And I miss her.*

A quick look of understanding crossed Pauline's face, and they continued their walk in silence. Just like the Devereaux church, Erin could detect exactly where the bodies were located. She instinctively knew their gender, and she knew she could raise them. It was a great relief when she did not sense the ashes in the urns they passed.

Erin and Dane followed Pauline through a maze of tombs until they stopped in front of a row of gray granite cremation benches.

Pauline picked up her tote bag and took out two purple candles that she placed on top of the benches. She then gave Erin a box of matches, a water bottle that she had filled with holy water and some licorice root. Erin removed the purple ribbon from the bouquet and put the flowers into the empty vase beside the candle. The mint she held on to.

"Do you want to do it yourself?" Pauline whispered.

Erin glanced at Dane, who nodded at her, and then she turned to Pauline. "Yes, but thanks for being here."

Pauline and Dane took a step back to allow her to perform the ritual that would protect her mother and Leila in their journey to the afterlife for witches. She was blessing them on their journey to the Summerland. She refused to believe that Leila wasn't with her mother even though Leila wasn't a witch, and they technically weren't related by blood.

Erin had a picture of her mother embracing Leila in front of their old house. She placed it in the middle of the two candles. She lit the candles and blew out the match before putting it back in the matchbox. She then took the ribbon and put it around the mint and licorice root. She squeezed the herbs and opened the plastic bottle to sprinkle the mint and licorice root with the holy water. Next, she splashed some water on the cremation benches, close to the candles. She put each candle in her hand and licked her dry lips. She closed her eyes and deeply inhaled. *Okay mom and Leila, this is for you.* Aloud, Erin said:

"With licorice root, holy water and mint times three,
Please Goddess protect those that were once a part of me,
After their painful lives, they deserve peace,
I beg for their soul to find release,
In the wonderful, joyful place where they belong,
In the Summerland, where their spirits shine strong,
Cherish them, hear my plea,
As is my will so mote it be."

For at least ten seconds, there was silence. Even the birds seemed to stop singing. But then her eyes flashed open as a wave of energy hit her so hard that she fell to her knees. The energy swirled around her, stirring the hair on the back of her neck. She gasped when the landscape in front of her changed as colors became brighter, and she found herself kneeling in the middle of a field surrounded by summer flowers. *I know this place. I was here with Altman.*

She felt the goddess touch her, and her vision blurred briefly. But when she blinked, she saw her mother and Leila standing in front of her. They were glowing with inner lights, and they looked astonishingly beautiful. Tears burned Erin's eyes when she saw their joy at seeing her there with them. Her heart ached, but she knew she couldn't stay.

Goodbye.

The heat of the goddess burst through her, hitting her with wild power. Erin experienced a connection to nature that tied every living creature to her. She felt love flaring through her as she threw her head back, spread her arms and cried out in happiness before passing out.

When she opened her eyes, she found herself in Dane's arms. "You're always there to catch me," she said hoarsely.

"Always," he vowed. He stared at her in concern. "Are you okay?"

Pauline crouched down beside her. "That looked amazing. I can't believe you didn't drop the candles! Well, you can be sure that you still have the witch in you. It was like the goddess embraced you."

Erin glanced at the candles in her hands. Then she got up and put them back on the cremation benches. "Yes, I still have magic, so maybe my dad didn't take that part away from me. Unless…" A chill crept down her spine at her next thought.

"Unless what?" Pauline asked.

Dane answered for Erin. "Unless the magic came from another witch her father drained."

"That would be awful," Erin said with a shudder.

Pauline shook her head. "I don't think the goddess would have blessed you like that if the powers had been stolen. She knows that you'll use the powers for good. You were successful, right? Or do you want me to do a reading to see if they've really crossed over?"

Erin sent her a small smile. "No thanks. I saw them in the Summerland. It was the most beautiful sight I've ever seen." She cleared her throat, and her eyes stung. "I think you're right. I did feel blessed."

"Good. I'll leave you two to celebrate," Pauline said. "I'll be doing some celebrating too." She grinned. "I have a date with Billy."

"Really? Cool," Erin said. "Have fun, but be careful."

"Careful like you because vampires are so much safer than werewolves?" Shaking her head, Pauline chuckled. She picked up her bag and left the cemetery.

Erin stared into the light of the flickering flames of the candles on the cremation bench. Dane stood behind her and put his arms around her waist. "Well done," he murmured.

She enjoyed leaning against him. "They looked so happy. Do you think they know that I fought their killer and won?"

"They know. You were amazing, but now I need you to relax." She heard his low voice echo through her ear. "My heart can't take all the excitement. Let's just lock ourselves up in the bedroom for the next couple of years, and you'd better stop confronting powerful beings from now on."

She laughed quietly. "I remember a time when I confronted you. Or was it you who confronted me?"

He tightened his embrace before releasing her. "And look where it got you." He grinned. It made him look like a predator, all teeth and ready to pounce.

"Spending my immortality with Dane Lynch. It's rather ironic when you think about the time we first met as adults." Her tone became serious for a moment.

He sighed heavily. "I know. I was scared. I thought that you would make me weak."

"*You* were scared! I thought you were going to kill me."

He rubbed a hand over the back of his neck. "As a master vampire, I told myself not to feel, and you made me feel from the moment I first laid eyes on you, and it made me vulnerable. Enemies could use you against me. Stratton did."

"They still could," she warned.

He nodded. "Yes, they could. But what I didn't realize then is that being with you wouldn't make me weaker. It's made me stronger. Spending immortality terrifying people so I can keep my position as Hope Acres' master vampire is a sad way to live. I'd rather spend a few moments with you, than spend eternity alone. I'm glad that my terrorizing you didn't scare you away."

She could see the love in his eyes, and she brushed her lips against his in an enticing kiss. "I'm glad too."

He wrapped his strong arms around her, holding

her close. He made her feel safe and warm.

"Of course," he added, "Now that people know that you killed Oliver Merenda, they'll think twice before going after you. And if they dare to go after me, they know they'll have to face your wrath." He laughed. "It helps that you're a badass."

Her lips curved. "We both are."

"That you took your father's powers helped. I hope you won't regret having a part of him in you."

"No, he would always have been a part of me. I'm sad that he stole all these powers, but they helped me stop him from stealing more. I hope his victims will find peace in that."

Dane's hand gently caressed her hair. "I think they will. I'm glad you decided to keep them. I do have a lot of enemies. Although... With Stratton and your father gone, I actually don't have that many enemies left, but I'll probably attract new ones. I like the idea of you being able to defend yourself."

She embraced him. A profound sense of peace and rightness washed over her. "I tend to attract enemies too. From now on, we'll fight them together."

He pressed his lips to her temple. "Forever."

THE END

AUTHOR

As a child, Nicole always wanted to be an actress. However, her only shot at becoming the next Meryl Streep was during her one-second appearance in Paul Verhoeven's film 'Black Book' where her shirt got ripped off her body. After that, she decided to focus on her writing career instead.

When she's not writing, she spends her time as crazy cat lady, playing with her cats Buffy and Garfield. In addition, Nicole's hobbies include trying to chase tornadoes (although she still hasn't seen any), fantasizing about villains (isn't Lex Luthor far more interesting than Clark Kent?), and most of all reading stories somebody else wrote.